THE
CHRONOS
CHRONICLES

A TIME TRAVEL ANTHOLOGY

TITLES BY
INDIE AUTHORS PRESS

Issues of Tomorrow: a science fiction anthology
Altered States II: a cyberpunk anthology
Control Theory
Spooky Halloween Drabbles 2016
Raiders of the Seventh Planet
Blood of Nyx
Corpus Deluxe: Undead Tales of Terror
Spooky Halloween Drabbles 2015
Speculative Valentine Drabbles 2015
Altered States: a cyberpunk sci-fi anthology
Spooky Halloween Drabbles 2014
A Forest of Dreams, a fantasy anthology
British Process Servers Guide
Learning About Love

Forthcoming titles can be found on
www.salgado-reyes.com.

THE
CHRONOS
CHRONICLES

A TIME TRAVEL ANTHOLOGY

ABOUT OUR EDITORS

 ROY C. BOOTH is a published author, comedian, poet, journalist, essayist, optioned screenwriter, and an internationally awarded playwright with 57 plays published to date (Samuel French, Heuer, et al) with 850+ productions in 30 countries and in ten languages. A graduate of Pillager High School, Booth also has an AA degree from Central Lakes College (Brainerd, MN, and he is a hall of fame inductee in both schools), and a BA in English/Speech-Theatre and an MA in English with a Creative Writing Emphasis from Bemidji State University. Booth resides in Downtown Bemidji, Minnesota with his wife and three sons (writers all) where he has also owned/managed Roy's Comics & Games since 1992. An impartial list of his publications may be found at www.amazon.com/author/roycbooth.

 JORGE SALGADO-REYES is a Chilean and British sci-fi/cyberpunk author, private investigator, and photographer. Salgado-Reyes founded Indie Authors Press in June 2011 when he saw that the publishing industry continued to evolve away from the established gatekeepers. Born in Temuco, Chile, Salgado-Reyes left his country of birth at age seven in 1975 with his family, driven into exile by the Pinochet dictatorship. Salgado-Reyes is currently working towards his BA (Honours) in English Literature and Creative Writing and spends time in both the United Kingdom and Chile. A list of his publications may be found at www.amazon.com/Jorge-Salgado-Reyes/e/B009G0CTPO.

THE CHRONOS CHRONICLES
a time travel anthology

A catalog record for this book is available from the British Library.

ISBN: 978-1-910910-17-7
Paperback Edition

Indie Authors Press

London | Chile | USA

CONTENTS

INTRODUCTION

I THINK TIME TRAVEL is almost certainly impossible. I say "almost" only because I certainly don't know everything—certainly not everything about time travel—and I might well have overlooked or misunderstood something in my analysis. But I don't think so. It seems to me that time travel to the past with the intent of changing something is impossible, because if it changed that thing or event, how would I have known to travel to the past to change that in the first place? Only a multiple-reality scenario would allow it: PL1 from R1 travels to the past, causes the change, which brings into being R2 in which PL2 would have no motivation to change anything, because it never happened, due to PL1's intervention, but that's okay, because PL1 from R1 is the one who made the change, not PL2 from R2. But, come on, that multiple-realities hypothesis, with a new reality coming into play with very tip of the time-traveler's hat, is even more incredible than the time travel itself. And as for travel to the future—well, if I travel to tomorrow and see you are wearing a blue shirt, does that mean you will have no free will tomorrow regarding what color shirt to put on? Time travel to the future, in other words, is not compatible with free will, which I take to be an indisputable part of life.

So, time travel is very likely impossible. But that's what makes writing and reading about it so much fun—especially when the stories manage to make the unbelievable so appealingly believable. Which brings me to the stories in The Chronos Chronicles.

The anthology is a riotous feast of time travel stories, fresh and profound, touching the classic bases with a surprising originality and diversity of style. You'll find wormholes in space, cabins beneath the Florida Keys, starships on Mars, bad weather in the Midwest, and much more as portals to time travel in these pages. You'll meet JFK and Marilyn, ancient Roman enemies, the end of time, and all manner of memorable characters struggling to save the world and themselves, either via or against the ravages of time travel, when they're not worrying about what clothes to wear in their travels, worrying a butterscotch in their mouths, or bringing on the end of the universe by their very actions. Scars start negligibly and progress to gaping wounds, texting comes from the future, alternate timelines aren't shy about colliding on this brave new terrain.

I should point out that most of the stories in this anthology are by authors that most of you likely have not yet encountered—not by "big name" writers. So how did the editors—Roy C. Booth and Jorge Salgado-Reyes—get so lucky? Here's a wild hypothesis: maybe they traveled into the future, saw the great recognition these authors had achieved, and then came back and invited them to contribute a little tale to The Chronos Chronicles. Read the stories, stick around for a few years, and see if that proves out...

Paul Levinson
New York City
April 2018

ANOTHER SECOND CHANCE

Karl Lykken

THIS ENDLESS WAITING IS hell. Dr. Murdoch may not have the guts to go ahead with the test, but I do, and I'm through screwing around.

"Let's go through the wormhole today," I say, for what feels like the millionth time.

Murdoch shakes his ancient head with such vigor that I think his brittle neck might snap. "We need to do more tests. We still have no conception of what might happen to us if we go through."

"I'm awful tired of this song and dance, Murdoch." I say, clenching my fists in frustration. "I get it, you wish it were the twenty-first century, and we could still do animal testing. But it's not, and it's not going to be unless we go through the wormhole. So, let's just do it already."

"Perhaps we have," Murdoch chuckles. After eight years alone in this ship with him, three billion miles from the nearest reasonable person, I'm pretty far from being in the mood for his stupid jokes. It's high time I find out if I will be ten minutes ago.

"I signed up to fly through the hole. That's what I'm here for. And a ship is ruled by its captain, not its passenger. So, Murdoch, I'm no longer asking; I'm telling. We're going through the wormhole, now."

The look of horror on Murdoch's face brings a smile to mine as I turn toward the cockpit.

"You can't do that," he says. "You could kill us both. Or something worse, something we can't even conceive of."

"I'll take our chances," I reply without turning around. I stride toward the cockpit, feeling excited for the first time in years.

It's finally time. I'll finally fulfill my destiny, finally become the first person to travel back in—

The pain rattles about inside my skull as I fall forward onto my hands and knees. I touch the gash on the back of my head and look around. Murdoch is standing over me, his smashed tablet still clutched tightly in his hands.

"Are you out of your mind, Murdoch?"

"No, apparently I'm the only one of us who's sane." His voice is much calmer than his eyes, which are zooming back and forth from me to the tablet, searching for some evidence that he just imagined trying to knock me out and I actually cut my head by accident while bumping it against his tablet in a feeble effort to turn it on.

I climb to my feet, shaking slightly either with fury or due to the head trauma. "For a smart guy, that was a real stupid thing for you to do, Doc."

Murdoch collects himself and focuses his gaze solely on me. "We're not going through the wormhole. Not without further testing. There's no two ways about that. The only choice you have is whether you spend the duration of the testing period helping me out or locked in a storeroom with a cracked skull."

"I've never been a fan of false dichotomies, Doc. There's always a third choice. For instance, you don't only have the options of giving me that tablet or having me take it from you. You could also eject out of the airlock and clutch it tightly in your hands until your lungs explode." I take a step towards him as he steps back.

"I don't want to hurt you, but I will," he warns, but the distinct note of fear in his voice makes it hard to be intimidated.

"That's the difference between us, Murdoch. I do want to hurt you, but I'll refrain if you hand me that tablet right now." My threat seems more effective. His eyes go back to doing laps from my face to the tablet with surprising stamina before eventually coming to rest on his feet. "This offer is about to expire, Doc."

"All right," he says, slowly extending the tablet toward me.

"Good choice, though I must admit I was hoping you'd make me take it by force," I say, enjoying every moment of me finally exerting power over him for a change. I reach out for the tablet when he suddenly pulls it back and then swings it at my head. I catch his wrist before he can hit me, and I wrestle the tablet out of his hand. "Poor choice, Murdoch."

"My only poor choice was accepting you as my pilot." He tries to punch me, but I jerk to the side, out of the way. He just doesn't learn, but I'm gonna find a way to teach him. I raise up the tablet and bring it back down into his head, hard.

He crumples to the ground, and my anger turns to panic. "Murdoch? Dr. Murdoch?"

He lies still, apart from the pool of blood expanding around his head. I crouch down beside him and check for his pulse. Nothing. He's dead. I killed him. I killed Murdoch.

This isn't how it was supposed to happen. I was supposed to go home a hero, a legend. Not a murderer. And it isn't even really my fault. It's Murdoch's fault. He's the one who attacked me, who drove me to it. If he wasn't such a stubborn coward, if he had just listened to reason, then none of this would have had to happen. And I'll be damned if I have to pay for his sins.

I'll just tell people that he went mad and left me no choice. It's completely reasonable. I mean, it's the truth, more or less. People will understand, right? Or I could just say it was an accident. It's not like they would perform an autopsy, not if they had the word of the pioneer of time travel that there was nothing suspicious about it.

Unless some petty coward wanted to destroy me out of jealousy. People are always sinking to lower and lower depths, and they'd love to drag me down with them, just like Murdoch's trying to. Well, I'm not going to let you, Murdoch, or anyone else. I'll jettison the body. That's what I'll do. I'll just tell everyone he died of natural causes, that his heart gave out from the excitement of traveling through the fourth dimension. And then that I couldn't stand having the corpse of my friend rotting on the ship, so I gave him the best burial that I could under the circumstances.

No one could blame me for that. And if there isn't a body, how could anyone prove it isn't the truth? He's an old man, and old men die. It's the natural order. And I just responded like any reasonable person might. And that will be that. I'll go call in to report his death now.

No, no I won't. Not yet. I should make the trip first. I don't know what the response to his death will be, and I can't risk anyone interfering with this. I've come too far, and I want it too bad. I wouldn't let Murdoch stop me in life, and I'm sure not gonna let him stop me now that he's dead. I'll take the ship to the accelerated mouth, and then I'll make history. Or unmake it, as the case might be. God, I sound like Murdoch now. Maybe his spirit has possessed me.

I look down at his body. The paleness from being cooped up inside this ship for years is nothing compared to his current shade of white. I suddenly feel like vomiting, though I suppose that could be from the pain of the gash in my head. I should really take care of that wound, even before the trip through the wormhole.

I make my way to the small infirmary, trying hard not to think about Murdoch. I've got a bright future now, and I won't let him darken it. I won't. I arrive at the infirmary and get a NewSkin patch out from the cabinet. I gingerly apply it to the back of my head, wincing as it starts to disinfect the cut. Well, that's one less thing. Now, to the cockpit and my destiny.

I make my way to the front of the ship, taking care not to look down as I pass Murdoch's body. Murdoch's body... What will happen to Murdoch's body when I go back in time?

I stop in my tracks. I've never pretended to understand time travel. Honestly, it's the uncertainty of it that makes it so exciting. Well, that and the glory. But experimenting with the effects of time travel on a dead body is a little too exciting, even for me. I'll have to jettison him before I go.

I turn back and approach his body, then grab his limp ankles. I drag him toward the airlock, leaving a trail of blood behind. Oh, well, cleaning it will give me something to do on the long, lonely journey back home.

I reach the airlock and thank God, he was so light. I drag him inside, then step back into the hall and close the door. I look at him through the small window for a few moments. It's your own fault, Murdoch. You don't bite the big dog if you can't handle being bit back. And you don't deny a man his shot at eternal glory, not when he's devoted a quarter of his life to the mission. You brought this on yourself, Murdoch, so don't you dare blame me.

I pull the airlock evacuation switch, and his body is sucked out into space. I watch it float away until it's just another meaningless dot in the vast darkness. Good riddance.

Now, at long last, it's time. I walk back to the cockpit and set a course for the accelerated mouth. It's not too far from the stationary mouth where Murdoch has had us parked while he once again examined the diagnostic equipment that we'd sent through the wormhole for the hundredth time. But the time for tests is over.

I fire up the engine and start the short journey. It's hard to even imagine what this will be like, so I don't even try. Instead, I think about what it will be like when I'm back home. When I'm being hailed as a hero. When I, Blake Peabody, the boy who came from nothing, return with proof that I traveled through time.

But what proof? In all the excitement I never even thought about it. What proof will I have that I did it, that I didn't just come out here and wuss out? I mean, the ship's location records will show the jump, I think, but the fact is those could be faked. So why should anyone believe me?

Murdoch must have had a plan for this. He was so meticulous, he must have had a plan for everything. Except me turning on him, I guess. But he'd have had a plan for this. It would be in his files on his tablet... Which we broke against each other's skulls. Damn. I'll never know what his plan was.

Unless I go back and ask him. The time frame should work, right? It's set for a trip to the near past. If I can get there soon enough, I can go back to just before he died. Then I won't just be the first person to go back in time; I'll be the first to bring the dead back to life.

And this time I'll keep my head. I'll be calm, and I'll tell him that he had an accident, that he slipped and cracked his skull, so I went back in time to save him. He'll be so grateful, and if he knows I went through successfully, surely, he'll be willing to go through again? It'll be perfect.

Unless he doesn't come back. I mean, if I go through, will I go back to when he was alive, or will it be earlier but he'll still be dead? Screw it. I'm not going to puzzle this out. I'll learn by doing, as always.

And soon. The accelerating mouth of the wormhole is just ahead. I set a course directly into it. I close my eyes. Finally, the wait is over.

THIS ENDLESS WAITING IS hell. Dr. Murdoch may not have the guts to go ahead with the test, but I do, and I'm through screwing around.

"Let's go through the wormhole today," I say, for what feels like the millionth time.

THE END

KARL LYKKEN writes both stories and software in Texas. His science fiction has appeared in Theme of Absence, Fictional Pairings, and The Flash Fiction Press.

THE BABUSHKA LADY

C.R. Berry

CRAP. WE KILLED THEM. JFK *and* Marilyn. We killed them both.

All right, it's probably not as simple as that, given that I don't fully understand Rachel Evans' abilities. I don't really know what to think. But since I'm in charge of reporting back to Boone on Rachel-shaped progress, I have to be thorough.

I suppose I should explain who Rachel Evans is. She's one of our latest assets, brought to us because she is able to see the events of a parallel timeline. And when I say parallel, I guess I mean *original*. The timeline as it was before our Time Travel Department made certain interventions, certain changes to advance our work. Rachel can see how things were before.

Our doctors and scientists are still trying to get a handle on her abilities, to pinpoint how and why they occur. It's involved lots of non-invasive procedures, some rather nasty invasive ones, and a regime of hypnotherapy.

I'm listening to a recording of Rachel's most recent hypnotherapy session. She's just recounted, under hypnosis, the details of a world-famous speech delivered by President John F. Kennedy about ending the Vietnam War, which she says she remembered learning about in school.

"Er—sorry, Rachel," says hypnotherapist Dr Masood. "Can we backtrack? You said President *Kennedy* ended the Vietnam War? W-when was this?"

"Mid-'60s, I think," Rachel replies.

The tape is silent for a minute or so. This monumental development has obviously caught Dr Masood off guard.

"So, you don't recall anything happening to President Kennedy in November 1963?" asks Dr Masood.

"Er—no."

Wow. Rachel knows nothing of JFK's visit to Dallas, Texas when he had been shot in the throat and the head by Lee Harvey Oswald at Dealey Plaza. According to her, JFK completed a two-term presidency and left office when Hubert Humphrey was elected. In our timeline, Hubert Humphrey never made it higher than Vice President.

On another tape, Rachel talks about going to the cinema to see the movie *Titanic* in 1997. That famous blockbuster movie we're all familiar with, starring Leonardo DiCaprio as Jack Dawson, Claire Danes as a young Rose Dawson and... Marilyn Monroe as an elderly Rose Dawson.

Again, there's silence on the tape, as Dr Masood processes what she's hearing. "S-so Marilyn Monroe was in *Titanic?*"

"Yeah. Marked a bit of a career resurgence," says Rachel. "It's funny though. Marilyn Monroe was only seventy when they filmed it, but she was playing a 100-year-old. They say that because of Marilyn's smoking and drinking over the years, she hardly needed any make-up."

So, Marilyn didn't die aged thirty-six. She wasn't found dead in her home in Brentwood, Los Angeles, the result of acute barbiturate poisoning, in August 1962. Not in the *original* timeline.

I've decided I need to get a handle on what happened in *this* timeline before I compile my report for Boone.

CHRIST. I LOOK AT Marilyn first and see how riddled with inconsistencies the official records are. No wonder her murder is one of the most famous conspiracy theories of all time. Why has no one blown this wide open?

The first big question is the timings. Allegedly, it was after midnight that housekeeper Eunice Murray decided that something was wrong and called Marilyn's doctors. Both her psychiatrist and physician attended and indicated that her time of death was about 12.30 am.

Yet the undertaker argued that the state of rigor mortis in Marilyn's body suggested an earlier time of death, between 9.30 and 11.30pm.

And then both doctors went and changed their stories, claiming instead that Marilyn died just before 4 am—six hours later than the undertaker's estimate.

Even more bizarre is the fact that Marilyn's lawyer, Mickey Rudin, informed her agent, Arthur Jacobs, at *10.30 pm* that she had overdosed.

So how could her time of death be 4am? And how did Mickey Rudin know about the overdose before Eunice Murray and the doctors?

Why, also, did Eunice Murray travel to Europe so shortly after Marilyn's death, even though she was a key witness? Then go on to change her story numerous times over the next few decades?

Somebody's pants are on fire.

The next big question is the medical evidence. The cause of death was a self-induced drug overdose, but the autopsy results were destroyed and much of the rest of the medical evidence went missing. And wait... Pathologists said the overdose wasn't from swallowing the drugs or an injection. So how did they get in her system? The only other option would be an enema.

Suicide by enema?

This is more than a paranoid conspiracy theory. Even Sergeant Jack Clemmons, the first LAPD officer to arrive at the death scene, believes Marilyn was murdered, saying, "It was the most obviously staged death I have ever seen."

Alright, so if *we* did this, we did a really botch job.

Onto JFK...

THERE ARE TONS OF unanswered questions with this one. Officially, Lee Harvey Oswald fired the shots that killed the president from the sixth-floor window of the Texas School Book Depository building, as the presidential limousine, carrying Kennedy, his wife Jackie, Governor Connolly and his wife Nellie, passed through Dealey Plaza. It's undisputed that the bullet that hit Kennedy's throat came from the back—the direction of the Depository. But that bullet also had to have been the same one that hit Governor Connolly a split second later, because there wasn't enough time between the wounding of the two men for Oswald to have reloaded his gun and fired a second shot.

And yet, if it was the same bullet, there's the pertinent issue of the physics-defying trajectory the bullet would've had to have taken. It would've had to have changed direction several times to cause the injuries it did to Governor Connolly. Conspiracy theorists call it the 'magic bullet.' They use it to argue that there must've been a second bullet.

A second bullet that, because of the timing, couldn't have been fired by Oswald.

Added to this are numerous witnesses who testified to hearing shots coming from the grassy knoll, a small, sloping hill on completely the other side of Dealey Plaza to the Depository.

I watch the Zapruder film—Abraham Zapruder's amateur footage of the assassination. The fatal bullet—the one that blows half of Kennedy's brain across the back of the limo—hits him from the *front*. I mean, surely it does. It's right here for everyone to see! The Depository is behind him, but the bullet blows the *front* of his head off and knocks him *backward*. A bullet fired from the Depository wouldn't have done that, but a bullet fired from the grassy knoll...

I'm now convinced that Oswald didn't act alone when he shot JFK. There was a second shooter somewhere on the grassy knoll. I'm sure of it.

Shit.

One of the witnesses was an unidentified woman with a camera. She was right there as the motorcade went past, camera to her face, snapping away. In fact, she continued snapping photos after the first shots were fired, even though all the other witnesses took cover. Not remotely afraid.

She never came forward with her photos. Nobody knows who she is. They call her the "Babushka Lady" because of the pink headscarf she was wearing, similar to the headscarves worn by elderly Russian women. "Babushka" means "old lady" in Russian.

That's my headscarf.

No question. Most of the photos are blurry or distant, but there's one close-up photo of the headscarf, and it's got the same floral patterns like the one my Russian grandmother gave to me—the one she *made* for me. It's unique.

And since she's also wearing a trench coat that looks exactly like the one I own, it's certainly becoming clear why the Babushka Lady never came forward.

She's me.

Bloody hell.

I wasn't really expecting today to turn out quite like this. But I think I've got enough to go to Boone.

"WE DIDN'T DO IT," says Boone at the start of my meeting with her.

"I'm sorry, ma'am?" I say.

"I should clarify. We didn't do it—*yet.*"

"You mean, killed JFK and Marilyn Monroe?"

"None of our operations have involved orchestrating the murders of President Kennedy or Miss Monroe. But that's not to say we won't orchestrate their deaths at some point in the future."

I snigger. "You mean the past?"

Boone is straight-faced. "I mean *our* future."

I know what she means, but the paradoxical absurdity of time travel amuses me.

"Not that I can think of any reason why we would want to have them killed," Boone continues. "Do you have any theories, Draper?"

Shit. She has my full written report in front of her. I think it's probably the best piece of work I've ever done, but at no point in it have I proposed any theories as to why we might've wanted to kill JFK and Marilyn. I thought she wanted the facts, not conjecture. Talk about being put on the spot.

"I—er—" A couple of ideas dart through my head as I sit there in Boone's office. "Well, nowadays it's pretty much common knowledge that JFK and Marilyn Monroe were having an affair. UFO nuts say that the government assassinated them because JFK learned more than he was supposed to about aliens and Roswell and shared those secrets with Marilyn during their trysts. Thing is, perhaps it's not UFOs he learned about. Perhaps it's us."

"You think JFK knew about us?"

"It's just a theory, but it makes sense."

"Hopefully you can verify it when you go back."

I basically knew that was coming, but I was hardly going to volunteer. Yes, I work in the Time Travel Department, but we're not all time travellers. I've been quite happy reporting on Rachel Evans and her parallel memories. "Er—go back?"

"Yes. If I read your report correctly, you've identified yourself as the Babushka Lady."

"Er, well, I was just—that was purely—"

"Don't get cold feet now, Draper. You've got plenty of time to train and prepare yourself. The past isn't going anywhere."

"Are those your orders?"

"Well, yes, I suppose. Insofar as I can order you to do something you're already predestined to do."

"Er... yes." When the paradoxical absurdity of time travel isn't amusing me, it's giving me a fricking headache.

"Good luck, Draper. Keep me apprised regularly. I hope your investigation proves fruitful."

AFTER WEEKS OF TIME travel training, researching and psyching myself up, I go back to Los Angeles, 1962. Well, what I think is 1962. I actually end up in 1937, only realising I'm twenty-five years too early when I see a copy of the *Los Angeles Times*: celebrated pilot Amelia Earhart just disappeared over the Pacific Ocean. I thought I selected the correct date—maybe I didn't. I'm hardly a pro at this—I failed time travel training three times, and when I finally passed, my trainer warned Boone that she should avoid sending me on time travel missions wherever possible!

Anyway, my little accident means I have to make an extra jump, from 1937 to 1962. Not ideal, but my body's coping with the stresses. The time travel doesn't seem to be affecting me like I've seen it affect my colleagues.

I spend two months in 1962 not really getting anywhere. A week and a day before Marilyn's death, everything changes.

I've not been able to get near Marilyn's house—the grounds are always swarming with bodyguards. Then, late in the evening, I clock the housekeeper, Eunice Murray, leaving Marilyn's home. I follow her in my lovely 1961 Cadillac to a bar in Santa Monica called The Lucky Munchkin. She purchases a gin and tonic and looks upset, cheeks and eyes red.

"Are you alright?" I ask, joining her at the bar.

"I'm fine," the bespectacled lady replies sharply. "Please leave me be."

"Forgive me, but you look like you've got the weight of the world on your shoulders."

"Go away. You don't know the half of it."

Right. Time to change gear.

"I bet I know *all* of it."

Murray does a quick head-turn towards me. Her previously sullen features stiffen into angst—lips apart, eyes virtually out on stalks. Way to look guilty.

"What do you mean?" she asks, a slight quiver in her voice.

"I mean I know. About Marilyn."

"Did he send you?"

He?

I'll play along. "Yes, he did."

"Look, I'm sorry it's taking so long. But tell him it's all in hand. It *will* happen. It's just taking longer than I expected to arrange everything."

Wow.

"He understands this isn't easy," I say.

"Tell him I'll call him when I know exactly when it's going to happen. And please stop following me."

She downs the rest of her gin and tonic and hotfoots it out of the bar.

Christ almighty. After two months of nothing, I get *that*!

Looks like Eunice Murray is in on the whole thing, but there's someone else pulling the strings. Could this 'he' be one of us?

I DON'T SEE EUNICE Murray again. I pretend to be a reporter doing a piece about the medical profession in LA and try to arrange meetings with the two doctors who changed their stories. But they refuse to meet me. And I can't get anywhere near Marilyn's house on the night of her death because of her security.

So, Marilyn dies. And, while I know now that Eunice Murray was part of a conspiracy to murder her, I've hit a wall.

What does Boone expect me to do? I'm here on my own. No support, no special means of getting in and out of places undetected, no real plan, and I'm not supposed to interfere with the timeline. Even my brief meeting with Murray—and my attempted meetings with the doctors—were risky moves. But how else does Boone expect me to investigate?

I call her, tell her what's happened, explain the predicament. She's not mad. Not at all. She takes the pressure off, actually. Says she expects my best, nothing more. I can't interfere with the timeline, which naturally limits my ability to investigate. She says to do what I can, and if I come back with zilch, so be it.

So, I jump forwards to October 1963 and initiate the next stage of my mission. I fly to Dallas, Texas, base myself at a Downtown Dallas hotel and tail Lee Harvey Oswald in the weeks leading up to the JFK assassination. I figure that makes the most sense. Oswald works at the Texas School Book Depository as an order-filler, stays at a boarding house in Oak Cliff, Dallas during the week, and goes home to his wife in Irving on the weekends. He doesn't drive; he commutes between Irving and Dallas with a co-worker, and during the week, he walks.

I slip inside the Depository one afternoon and locate the beige jacket he always wears, hanging up in the staff room. I secure a listening device in the jacket lining—twenty-first-century tech that he wouldn't detect even if he was looking for it—and slink back out of the building.

Frustratingly, I record nothing but a couple of phone calls Oswald makes to his wife from the communal phone at the boarding house. Perhaps he's communicating with his co-conspirators by letter? I do see him making regular trips to the post office during his lunch hours.

Or maybe the lack of communication is because everything is already in place. Kennedy's trip to Dallas was publicly announced back in September—ample time for the architects of this conspiracy to prepare.

Conjecture is getting me nowhere.

Ironically, the day I most need Oswald to wear the jacket is the day he leaves it at the boarding house: November twenty-second. Assassination day.

Not that I'm planning to stay in my hotel room listening to Oswald's interactions anyway. I've somewhere to be, don't I? Must do as history says. Not sure what would happen if I didn't... *Would all of time unravel?* Probably best not to think about it.

Wearing my trench coat and my grandmother's 'babushka' headscarf, armed with the bulky Kodak camera I purchased last week, I leave the hotel and head to Dealey Plaza.

The morning rain has stopped, the clouds have dispersed, and a light breeze fans the trees. Shame. If the rain had persisted, they might've kept the top up on Kennedy's limousine, making the assassins' job a lot more difficult.

Arriving at Dealey Plaza, I go to stand on the grass between Elm Street and Main Street. It's just before 11am when I get there. The biggest crowds are on Main Street; this area is a bit quieter.

It's surreal and haunting to stand there, knowing full well what is coming. My chest is thudding. A film of sweat breaks out across my body. I want to take off the trench coat—it's hardly cold. But I know I can't—because I didn't.

I try to focus on the task at hand. Being the only one there with foresight, I observe the grassy knoll, which is in front of me on the other side of Elm Street. I keep a close eye on the steps that go up the knoll to the Bryan pergola and the wooden stockade fence, flanked by trees, that separates the knoll from a parking lot—where many people thought the second gunman fired from.

It isn't until 11.40am, fifty minutes before the assassination, that I notice something moving behind the fence, darkening the slim gaps between the fence posts. For a moment I can't tell if they are just shadows cast by the windblown trees.

Then a silhouetted head, donning a fedora hat, peeks over the fence. I raise my camera to snap a picture, but he ducks down again by the time my finger's over the shutter button. I snap a picture anyway.

Ladies and gentlemen, we have our second shooter.

I wait, watch and bite off all my fingernails. The next fifty minutes are literally an eternity.

The man behind the fence stays hidden, but I think he's positioned himself about two metres back from the corner. Previously, sunlight was squeezing through the slits in that part of the fence—now something's blocking it. He's still there, waiting for his moment.

When the first car in Kennedy's motorcade, a white sedan, makes the sharp left turn from Houston Street onto Elm Street and excitement billows through the crowds, flutters of panic rise from the pit of my belly and claw up my throat. I check my watch. 12.30pm.

Oh, God.

The president's limousine turns onto Elm Street. JFK is waving to the crowds. I raise my camera to my face, look through the viewfinder and hone in on the stockade fence. Trying to maintain my aim—not easy with trembling hands—I arc my gaze around the camera so I can see the fence with my own eyes. I thumb the wind-on lever and push the shutter button, snapping a picture. Wind-on lever, shutter button. Wide-on lever, shutter button.

And there he is. The fedora-wearing shooter rises from behind the fence, and I detect the shadowy contour of a rifle. He takes aim.

Wind-on lever, shutter button.

Shots ring out.

The president's limousine goes past. I glance fleetingly at it. JFK is hunched over in his seat, leaning towards his wife, Jackie—he's been hit. My eyes dart back to the fence.

Bang.

The shooter's rifle flashes. My eyes, quick as the bullet that's slicing through the air, are on Kennedy.

Wish they hadn't been.

Seeing the bullet blow open the president's head—flecks of blood, bone, and brain flying across the back of the limo—will be etched in my memory forever.

When my eyes are back on the fence, the shooter is already gone. My eyes pore over the entire length of the fence that is visible, searching for movement.

Wind-on lever, shutter button. It's now an automatic process. I'm not even aware I'm doing it.

The Kennedy limo hastens through the triple underpass, out of Dealey Plaza. There's a secret service agent on the trunk, trying to shield the president and his wife from further gunshots. Members of the crowd have dived for cover. I continue snapping pictures—though I'm not sure what of anymore.

The rest of the cars in the motorcade go by. After the second White House Press bus passes, some of the crowd—including several cops who've been accompanying the motorcade on motorcycles—scramble up the grassy knoll to search for the shooter. I join them, putting away my camera in my handbag and crossing Elm Street, climbing the steps to the stockade fence. Along with others, I look over the arrowhead-shaped fence posts. Police are checking the cars in the parking lot, but the shooter is nowhere in sight.

Now what?

It's as I go back down the grassy knoll onto Elm Street that I see a figure in a grey fedora walking behind the Bryan pergola, headed for the short Elm Street abutment that runs along the front of the Texas School Book Depository. There are loads of people around, plenty wearing fedoras so he could be anyone. But something in my gut is telling me otherwise.

Walking east along Elm Street, I'm parallel to the man for a moment, before he walks away from the pergola and out of my sight. I carry on along Elm Street, walking towards the Depository, hoping to regain sight of him.

Reaching the corner of Elm and Houston Street, near the front entrance of the Depository, there he is. He's wearing a grey suit to match the fedora, carrying a long briefcase, and though his face is only visible from the side, I see the contour of spectacles. He's conversing with a man in dark trousers and a white t-shirt, a man whose face I've gotten to know extremely well over the last month.

Oswald.

Gotcha.

After a brief exchange, the pair diverges, Oswald heading along Elm Street, the briefcase man up Houston Street.

Fired with adrenaline, I pursue Briefcase Man along Houston Street. He crosses another parking lot onto Ross Avenue, which has a wide spread of buildings, plenty of cars and pedestrians and nowhere for me to accost him. Fortunately for me, he turns up a street of tightly clustered apartment buildings and then down a narrow alley between them—exactly the kind of claustrophobic space I've been waiting for, with only walls as witnesses.

I reach into my handbag and take out my firearm, capped with a silencer. I shoot him in the right calf.

What?

Briefcase Man gives a distinctly *female* groan, staggers to his knees and drops the briefcase, which hits the pavement with a crack and springs open.

Red-handed and then some. A rifle tumbles out.

By the time the assassin has turned on the ground, I'm standing over... her. Jesus. Briefcase Man is a woman. And a woman I know.

"You!" she says breathlessly to me, lips quivering, propping herself up against the wall and clutching her bleeding leg.

"Eunice Murray?"

"I—p-please! I did what he asked!" she splutters.

"Is that the gun that killed President Kennedy?"

"Y-yes!"

"And did you pull the trigger?"

"I-I—!"

I press the muzzle of my gun against Murray's forehead. "Did you?"

"Yes!"

"Who are you working for?"

"What? You mean you're—you're not—?"

I press the gun harder against her head and say in a gritted voice, "I won't ask again."

"D-Delfino!" she screams. "Mack Delfino. He's a—he's a banker in LA."

No bells are ringing. Is Mr Delfino one of our employees?

"Delfino's the 'he' you referred to when I met you in that bar?"

"Y-yes."

"So, he instructed you to kill Marilyn Monroe as well?"

"M-me and a couple of others, yes." Her gasps for breath crack into sobs. "I—I needed the money."

"*Money?*"

"Yes. I had loans. So many loans, loans I couldn't pay. I was so stupid."

"But you were the housekeeper for the biggest star in Hollywood."

"Yeah. But Marilyn wasn't paying me enough to settle the loans. Not nearly enough. I had loan sharks chasing me. Threatening me. Threatening my children. Mack paid them off, but the condition was that I... that I be part of this. A plot to kill Marilyn and... and the president."

"So, you just shot President Kennedy to pay off a loan?"

"I tried to back out. After Mack paid the loans, I tried to reason with him, tried to convince him that surely there was another way. He got nasty too. Threatened my children just like the loan sharks did. I had nowhere to turn."

"The police?"

"Mack Delfino's a powerful man. Surely, you've heard of his father, Jon Delfino. Probably the richest lawyer in LA, and he's got half the LAPD on his payroll."

Maybe Jon Delfino is connected to us? Still, no bells are ringing. "Why did Mack Delfino want Monroe and Kennedy dead?"

"I don't know. That's the truth, I swear. He never said why."

"Is that all you know?" My gun'll perforate her skull if I press any harder. She winces into the pain.

"YES!"

I pull the gun away, her taut grimace loosening in relief.

"Get up," I say, stepping back. "Take the gun and do whatever you were about to do. When you go to the hospital, tell them you were mugged at gunpoint or something. And never tell a living soul of your encounters with me. Is that understood?"

"Y-yes. Understood." She labours to her feet, in between yelps of pain, picks up the gun and replaces it in the briefcase.

"Go. Get out of here."

She limps down the alley and disappears behind the buildings.

I head back to my hotel. By now the news of the Dealey Plaza tragedy has spread through Downtown, furore swelling. Everyone on the streets is talking about it, but I zone them out. Even the voices in earshot are nothing but a jangling blur of sound.

Once I'm back at the hotel, I take some Prozac and lie on the bed for five minutes, just so I can breathe.

Eunice Murray was always suspected of being involved in the death of Marilyn Monroe.

But no one ever accused her of killing the president.

Composing myself, I dig out my chronopad, which gives me access to the internet of the future. I Google 'Mack Delfino—banker—Los Angeles'.

Google brings up a news story about a young, staunchly Catholic banker who worked in Downtown LA and, despite being Catholic, committed suicide in 1968, five years from now.

It seems that Mack Delfino was known for having an obsession with Jackie Kennedy, and for persistently sending her letters professing his love for her. His obsession soon spilled into his professional life. In 1961, he was fired by City National Bank, after continually missing deadlines and taking time off so he could attend Mrs Kennedy's public engagements. Friends believed he had a shrine to her in his apartment, a fact confirmed when police investigated his suicide.

He was found hanged in his home in Westchester, Los Angeles, on October 20th, 1968—the day Jackie Kennedy remarried. A note by the body read: *Jackie, I'll always love you.*

I can't quite take it all in.

But even though a picture is coming together, there are pieces missing, and I want to find them.

I book my flight back to LA—I leave tonight. I'm going to try and locate this Mack Delfino. I check in with Boone, but I don't tell her what I've learned. Not yet. I mainly just want to make sure I've not done anything to bugger up the timeline. (In hindsight, I probably shouldn't have shot Eunice Murray. Guess I was getting impatient, after weeks of tailing Oswald to little gain.) Luckily the timeline is intact.

And I'm not going to confront Delfino. History knows nothing of his connection to Kennedy and Monroe, which means I have to keep it that way.

I have a plan...

"WELCOME BACK, DRAPER," BOONE says to me at the start of our review meeting, after I arrive back in the present. "Are you well?"

"I'm well, ma'am," I lie.

"What's the lowdown?"

I give it to her—*nearly*. I'm certainly not going to give her the whole story.

"I can guess what the motive might be," she says after I explain that Jackie Kennedy-obsessed nut Mack Delfino orchestrated JFK and Monroe's deaths.

"Yes, ma'am," I say. "I guessed the same, but I wanted some proof. So, I found out where he lived in LA and broke into his house while he was out. I found a scrapbook in a box under his bed. It couldn't have spelled out his motive clearer. Photos of Jackie Kennedy plastered across every page. Newspaper clippings about her, love poems he'd written to her, even drawings he'd done of her. And the last two pages had photos of President Kennedy and Marilyn Monroe with their faces scratched out. Bible passages about infidelity. And a headline, written in red, deliberately made to look like dripping blood, that read: *Jackie, I will avenge you.*"

"So Delfino was punishing Kennedy and Monroe for their affair. Because he was infatuated with Jackie."

"Sure looks like it."

"Did you find out what Defino's connection is to us?"

"No, ma'am, I didn't. That was the only piece of the puzzle I wasn't able to find." Okay, so that part *isn't* true.

"Then our little mystery shall remain unsolved."

"For now, yes. But perhaps JFK and Marilyn Monroe's deaths are actually nothing to do with us. There's still a lot we don't understand about Rachel Evans' abilities. Not every timeline abnormality she detects is necessarily our doing."

"Perhaps not."

I don't expect her to agree. I'm talking out of my arse.

See, what I deliberately leave out of my story is that I did some further research into Mack Delfino's background. I found out some more about his father, Jon Delfino—the "richest lawyer in LA"—as Eunice Murray described him. He has enough of a profile to have a Wikipedia page. The head section says: *Jon Delfino was an LA lawyer between the 1930s and the 1970s, most recognised for representing famous athletes and sports personalities.*

But it's the "Personal Life" section that drew my attention: *In 1937, Jon Delfino met his wife Gillian by accident. He bumped into someone on the streets of Downtown LA, dropping a folder of case papers on the sidewalk. By the time he had picked up his papers and was on his way, he had missed the bus he normally took to his office. He caught a later bus and on it met Gillian. They dated briefly, married six months later and had their first child, Mack, the following year.*

When I looked again at the black and white photo of him on his Wiki page, I was hit with a twist of dread that I suspect won't ever leave me.

I remembered him.

I'd only just arrived in 1937. I was disoriented from the time travel. I hadn't yet realised that I'd accidentally gone back to the wrong time.

The someone Jon Delfino bumped into—the one who made him drop his papers and miss his bus—was me.

THE END

C.R. BERRY is a British author with a penchant for mystery and conspiracy and a big hard-on for time travel. His forthcoming novel, *Million Eyes*, is Doctor

Who meets The Da Vinci Code meets 24. Berry has been published in *Phantaxis, Suspense Magazine, Storgy, Tigershark, Scribble* and *Metamorphose*. He won second prize in the *To Hull and Back Humorous Short Story Competition 2014*, was shortlisted in the *Aeon Award Contest 2015*, and was highly commended by *Writers' Forum* in 2016. You can follow C.R. Berry at crberryauthor.wordpress.com, or find him on Twitter and Facebook (@CRBerry1).

CLOSING SCHRODINGER'S BOX

Michael W. Lucht

WITH TWO STEPS, NATASHA closed the gap separating them. *Quite forward of her, given that they only knew each other professionally.* Not that Brad minded. As always, he was impressed by how young she looked despite pushing forty; probably thanks to all the time she had spent indoors, thinking, and not outdoors, wrinkling. However, she had dark rings around her eyes.

"They won't destroy New York City," she complained.

"Sorry?" He had only just invited her in, and besides exchanging greetings, this was the first thing she had said.

She raised an eyebrow; hers were shaped to extend the curves of her nose. Brad wondered whether her other curves were as carefully maintained.

"You haven't followed the news?" she asked, glancing in the direction of his 42-inch LED.

"Not lately," he smiled disarmingly. Should he explain?

But before he had the chance, she went on. "Well, basically I was trying to create an alternative explanation for what you saw."

What you saw—how horrifying those three innocent words were to Brad.

AFTER SIX MONTHS OF gruelling competition against hundreds of astronauts and fellow pilots, the honour of operating the time-viewer had gone to him. From the outside, it was a large charcoal-black cube, similar in size and appearance to the Kaaba in Mecca. In fact, some silly people had protested the construction of the time-viewer in New York's Central Park because they interpreted it as some sort of Muslim conspiracy.

In Brad's opinion, the concord between the scientific and the Holy was appropriate. After all, this machine would allow humanity to see the future. The ancient Greeks had built temples for their oracles; if anything in the modern age deserved such honour, then surely this was it.

Brad entered the cube through its only door, expecting—well, he wasn't sure exactly, but definitely more than the inside of a large black cube. The emptiness unsettled him; there should have been some equipment and not just six windowless surfaces, uniform and smooth. He asked the scientist giving him the tour about it.

"All recording equipment, every instrument, even a hundred bucks digital camera would affect the experiment," the scientist explained. "To minimise the variables, we are simplifying the initial human trial down to the single essential recording device—*you!* As for the machinery that drives this thing, like the nuclear batteries, it's under the floor where it's out of the way."

"Why's the cube so big?"

"Simple economics. Building it large costs nearly the same as small, and the extra space can be useful. It already came in pretty handy when we tested with the bottle-nosed dolphins."

They had also tested the time-viewer with chimpanzees, gorillas, and orangutans—over loud and very naked PETA protests—because an advanced consciousness was necessary, not just for being a passenger in the time-viewer, but to become part of it. As it turned out, the animal experiments were failures. On the evening news, the very cute Dr Natasha Meitner had explained that an advanced consciousness alone was not enough; it also had to be aware of what was happening to it.

On the day of the first human trial, Brad wore a crown of multicoloured wires that disappeared into the floor, and a pair of wrap-around sunglasses. The glasses were to protect his eyes against the sudden transition from total darkness, which engulfed him when they closed the door, to the bright lights of the future two years hence.

Brad waited patiently in the blackness. He had long since realised that the title of 'pilot,' was not nearly as glamorous as it sounded. On a conscious level, he did absolutely nothing to control the machine. He was a glorified cog, contributing his sentience to make the whole shebang work.

He nearly missed the historic moment, for the increase in brightness was marginal. This was unexpected because he was meant to 'arrive' at the same time of day as he had left, around midday. He removed his glasses and cast his eyes skywards. Just as the scientists had promised, the walls and ceiling of the cube had turned transparent, allowing him to see outside.

Overlapping black clouds blocked out every trace of blue, carpeting the heavens like a thick, stained rug. As for the ground, it was a desert of grey ash punctuated by charred tree stumps. Desperate for an explanation, Brad strained his eyes to the limits of their vision. Beyond the rubble of the once proud buildings surrounding Central Park, he saw semi-melted storey-high columns sticking from the ground like the fingers of the Grim Reaper.

THOSE WERE INTENSE MEMORIES. Brad blinked, hoping to absorb the beginnings of a tear before Natasha noticed.

"So, I've made a proposal to the government," she continued. "I advised them to evacuate and destroy New York City. By doing it on purpose, it becomes possible for what you observed to occur without the need for a nuclear war. Pity about the city, but no one will die, and it sure beats the alternative."

"But I also saw nuclear winter," Brad objected.

"Not quite. You reported darkness during the day."

"Yeeeah," he drawled.

"That doesn't necessarily make it a nuclear winter. In 1780 in New England, the day turned so dark that candles had to be lit and many thought that judgement was at hand. The cause remains a mystery, but it sure wasn't nuclear war."

"Straws," Brad muttered.

"Straws are all we have," she replied, coming yet another step closer. Why was she doing that? How to talk about the end of the world with her sweet, unobtainable body within touching range?

"I know that the most likely explanation remains war," she went on, "but it doesn't have to be the *only* explanation. Destroying New York City would at least give us a chance."

Brad made a noise halfway between a laugh and a grunt. "You are mistaken. There are no odds, only the future, and I've *seen* it. Before twenty-one months are up, there *will* be a nuclear war. All we can do is enjoy each day. That's why I've given up on the news—what would be the point? Speaking of enjoying the day, why don't we sit?"

Brad's first impulse was to steer her towards the plush sofa facing his television. However, his armchairs were more inviting, warmed as they were by the morning sun shining in through the French windows. The chairs were positioned for watching birds in his lavish garden; he rotated them to face one another before offering one to Natasha.

She placed her handbag by the side and dragged her armchair closer until their knees touched. Brad luxuriated in the physical contact.

"No, *you* are mistaken," she said, leaning forwards. "Besides destroying New York, there exists one other desperate option. It involved you and me. Between the two of us, we can return hope to the world!"

"Sorry, I can't see it." Brad wished that she would just let it go. If she fell into his arms, he would console her.

"Do you know about Schrödinger's Cat?"

"Huh?"

Natasha smiled, both sweet and sad. "Please humour me."

Puzzled as he was by the non sequitur, Brad was eager to demonstrate that he was more than just a handsome pilot. "As I recall, a cat is placed in a box with a radioactive atom that has an even chance of breaking apart within an hour. If it does, poison is released, and the cat dies. Some very smart people say there's a half-dead, half-alive cat in the box before it's opened."

"The cat exists in a superposition of states," Natasha agreed, "until the box is opened and a particular possibility becomes real. The box in which the cat is kept is called Schrödinger's Box. Are you aware that the time-viewer is a kind of Schrödinger's Box?"

"It is?"

"In the original Schrödinger's Cat experiment, *space* is divided between the inside of Schrödinger's Box and the rest of the universe. In time-viewing, *time* is divided between the inside of Schrödinger's Box and the rest of the universe. Instead of a cat, Schrödinger's Box contains the future. Opening it, we discovered a dead cat."

"Nuclear war?"

Natasha gave a tight-lipped nod.

Brad cleared his throat. "Well, that says it all, doesn't it?"

With the intensity of someone proclaiming herself Mary, mother of Jesus, she declared, "I know how to close Schrödinger's Box!"

To round off her impression of a mental case, she hid her face in the palms of her hands and gently rocked back and forth in the armchair.

"Go on," Brad said, his stomach feeling sick.

Slowly she drew down her hands, like a frightened child glancing over a fence. He saw no tears, but her eyes were glistening. "You'll have to die."

"Sorry?"

"I – I – I'm so sorry," her voice broke, "but you have to die."

"But why?"

"To eliminate the only observer in the universe who knows beyond a shadow of a doubt that a nuclear war will occur."

"But *you* know. Hell, *everybody* knows!"

"Yes, you've told us, but we don't know for sure. After all, you might have been lying." Her voice became steadier as she spoke.

"I wasn't lying!"

"That's fine. As far as you are concerned, you spoke the truth and war will happen. However, as far as everyone else is concerned, you lied and war doesn't take place."

"Both can't be true," Brad objected.

"Actually, according to temporal quantum mechanics, *both* realities can coexist, as long as they *never* meet head-to-head. You see, if you remain alive, then your truth and our truth will clash, and your reality takes precedence.

"Alternatively, if you are dead, then you obviously won't be able to perceive that the war which you saw didn't take place. Hence, your reality and ours can continue to coexist. The future that you saw vanishes back inside Schrödinger's Box, its contents restored to a superposition of possible futures, good and bad."

Brad rubbed his chin. "Are you sure?"

Natasha nodded, her face expressionless.

"Then – I guess..." He inserted a dramatic pause. "I guess I should be doing myself in?"

Natasha remained silent.

"How soon?"

She spoke mechanically. "Every second that you remain alive increases the risk."

"Then I better get on with it." Brad stood up, attempting to look valiant. He must have succeeded because she was in his arms, her head cradled against his chest.

"You are a great hero," she whispered. "A greater hero than I imagined."

He guided her face to his, their noses touching. "All part of my job."

That was a lie, of course, because he had no intention of killing himself. Admittedly, she had discovered temporal quantum mechanics and designed the time-viewer while he nearly flunked basic calculus but, judging from the deep circles around her eyes, she had stayed awake many nights agonising about little else, and he doubted her judgement.

Natasha's present gullibility only confirmed his opinion. As much as Brad regretted his deceit, without it, their conversation would have turned into a futile argument. Instead, thanks to the lie, she was in a mood to talk and perhaps—just perhaps—he could persuade her to make peace with the inevitable.

However, the tips of her breasts lightly grazing his chest gave Brad very different ideas. It seemed like a bastardly thing to do, but how terrible was it really? She was expecting him to commit suicide based on her say-so. By comparison, what he had in mind was only natural. Besides, she clearly found him attractive, constantly trespassing on his personal space. He would probably be doing her a favour, giving her an excuse to do what she wanted to do anyhow.

"Don't cry," he told her. "I had a great life." He brushed a lone tear from her cheek. "And the best is still to come if I can but work up the courage to ask."

"Ask!" Natasha implored.

"It might embarrass you."

"Given the circumstances, given what you are about to do, ask for anything you please. Forget all barriers, they're gone."

Up to that point, Brad might still have backed down. For one thing, his stomach was feeling queasy, as if urging him to abort. But who could resist the words, *forget all barriers?*

"I love you!" he confessed, speaking rapidly before he could change his mind. "From long before I ever met you. I know you are down-to-earth about the facts of life; you even did an interview for Playboy. So, do you think *it* might be possible?"

Her lovely cheeks turned purple. Lowering her gaze, she replied guardedly, "I'm not sure what to say."

As the uncomfortable silence dragged on, Brad increasingly felt like a douche. Taking advantage of the damsel in distress, a fine hero *he* was!

"Never mind," he exhaled, feeling relief and regret in equal measures.

"No!" She finally glanced up, a faraway look in her eyes. "You are the saviour of mankind, a hero the likes of which the world has never known."

"That hardly gives me the right to..."

She put her finger to his lips. "Hector had Andromache, Aragorn had Arwen, and Arjuna had Draupadi. A hero's life deserves a hero's end, and I am honoured. Let Brad have Natasha!"

The kiss that followed melted away the last of Brad's misgivings. His hands disappeared down the back of her trousers. He was squeezing Dr Natasha Meitner's buttocks! He could hardly believe it. They were firm and round.

She broke off from the kiss. "Wait. Let me fix myself up a little."

"Must you?" Brad withdrew one hand from her pants and reached up, intending to cup a breast. Without warning, Natasha jumped backward, trapping his other hand, which was still deep inside her jeans, toppling him forward. He twisted his wrist and fell on the floor, yelping in pain.

"I'm sorry," Natasha apologised immediately.

"What was that about?" Brad demanded. Had Natasha caught on to his deceit?

"You… you took me by surprise."

"Well, now you *really* owe me," he said as he scrambled back on his legs, nursing his wrist.

"Owe you?"

Brad tried undoing the damage of his careless words. "I mean, it's not every day that I offer to lay down my life."

"Were you serious?" Natasha asked softly.

"Off course." She just stared at him. "Off course!" Brad reiterated.

Natasha stomped her foot, the thick rug dulling the sound. "I believed you!" She took a deep breath. "Look, if I had to prostitute myself to save humanity, I would do it. However, it has become fairly obvious that you have no intention of doing the honourable thing."

It pained Brad to discover that Natasha thought of him as little better than a john. He spoke his next word with much regret. "Goodbye."

"Please! I need more time," she pleaded. She even approached him again. "I'll explain better."

"Sorry, but no."

She walked to the armchair, retrieving her handbag. However, instead of leaving with it, she zipped it open and rummaged through it blindly while keeping her eyes on him.

Brad felt physically sick. All he wanted was for her to leave, make a tea to calm his stomach and enjoy some mindless action flick.

"Goodbye!" he repeated.

It was then that she extracted a gun from her handbag. Brad stepped backward, holding out his palms in what he hoped was a calming gesture. Having over the course of three months come to accept that he had less than two years left to live, he nevertheless found the prospect of his existence ending in the ever-present *now*, perhaps in mid-thought, terrifying.

"Don't do anything rash."

"Like pull the trigger and save the world?" she asked.

Holy crap! Until that moment, there had been an unreality about Natasha's insistence that he must die.

"Sit," Natasha ordered, waving the barrel at the armchairs. Brad sighed with relief. Had she ordered him to kneel, he would have pissed himself.

His legs shaking, his stomach knotted and his head faint, he obeyed. After glancing at her watch, Natasha joined him on the chair across, again dragging it closer, as if subconsciously she'd still rather be his lover.

It also meant that the gun was close enough for Brad to grab. As much as trying to disarm her was risky, so was waiting for her to work up the courage to shoot.

He kicked his left knee into her gun, simultaneously throwing his body out of harm's way to the right. Getting hold of Natasha's hand, he attempted to twist the barrel towards the floor, which she struggled against with surprising tenacity. What had become of his strength?

Suddenly, an ear-shattering bang and an intense pain overwhelmed every one of Brad's senses. He slumped backward, his eyes grimaced shut, his breath heavy.

Only gradually did the fog of agony lift. When Brad felt well enough to open his eyes, Natasha was still in her chair. She held the gun loosely, and her face was pale.

Brad glanced at his left thigh. Blood oozed from a wound just above his knee; a flow, not a squirt, so she must have missed his major vessels. He pressed his palm against the injury, stemming the flow.

"This wasn't meant to happen," Natasha said in a trembling voice. I can't even kill fish. It's an emotional thing, not intellectual. I eat meat, but I'm not up to the act of killing. Not like this."

Brad felt like shit. "So, why the gun?"

"In case you tried to escape."

"Escape from what?"

"Radioactive isotopes from the nuclear battery of the time-viewer..." she said in a tiny voice.

Overcome with nausea, Brad managed to lean sideways just barely in time to spare his armchair. The involuntary motion of his wounded leg with each retching spasm magnified the agony of throwing up. Brad would have preferred Natasha not seeing him like this, fouling his nest, staining his rug.

Mercifully, it didn't last long, and at least the vomiting had cured the chill from deep inside, although as a whole he still felt pretty awful. At least things made a lot more sense now.

"So that's why you always came so close?"

"Yes. And also, why I couldn't let you touch my breasts. It's in my bra."

"Have we received a lethal dose yet?" Brad asked, dreading the answer.

She shook her head.

"But you'll die too," Brad pointed out.

"It couldn't be helped. The only way I'm capable of killing you is indirectly, using a method that doesn't feel so much like murder. Besides, killing someone for the greater good is a terrible thing, and it's proper that it comes at a terrible cost."

"There's no changing your mind?"

"Ten billion lives, Brad. Ten billion!"

And that was that. His only other option was to scream for help, but that would be pointless since his nearest neighbour lived miles away.

"What now?" Brad wished he didn't sound so frightened.

"We'll be losing consciousness soon. I don't expect us to wake up."

The weird part was that despite her murderous intent, Brad still loved her. Years of obsession could not be washed away in a single hour. Besides, her large brown eyes weren't the eyes of a killer. Her expression was one of grim determination. What a choice to have to make. Become a murderess or humanity dies. Ultimately, it didn't matter whether she was right or wrong, to her that choice was *her* reality.

"Natasha, remove the radioactive material from your body," he said, surprised by the firmness of his voice.

"Sorry, I have to do this."

"Yes, I know, but there is no need for you to die too. Put the material down and retreat to the other side of the room. Don't worry, there's no way I will escape with that busted leg. And, besides, you'll be watching."

She just sat there.

"Well?"

"Why are you telling me not to die? You ought to hate me."

"Perhaps you deserve punishment, but not death. Nothing bad will happen to the world if you live."

"Not to the world," she sniffled, "but to *me*. You see, I never expected to come out of this alive. All my thinking was up to this point only. Now you are offering me back my life, and I'm frightened. I'll be a murderer. But I'm not a murderer. But I *will* be a murderer..."

"Seems to me that I'm not the only one caught between two contradictory realities."

She nodded. "Which are clashing."

A spell of light-headedness came over Brad, an ominous sign. He had to hurry.

"Natasha, much of what I did today I'm not proud of, but please believe me when I tell you that I've been in love with you for a long time, long before we've ever met. You already offered to do anything for me, and I was going to waste it on an adolescent fantasy. If you really meant what you said, then please do that one last thing for me."

"Sex would have been easier," she breathed, attempting a smile through her tears.

"Please!"

She undid her blouse. Less than an hour ago, Brad would have given anything for this sight, but the most erotic body part on display was her navel. She had tinfoil wrapped around her ribs to her armpits, no doubt as a partial shielding against the radiation, so much closer to her body than his. Inside the cleavage of her black sports bra, worn over the foil, was a black pellet secured by masking tape. She tried standing up, swayed, and sat down again.

"Crawl," Brad suggested.

She toppled out of the chair onto the floor, ripped off the masking tape and placed the pallet on the vacated seat. That done, she crawled over the rug, around his sofa, towards the far corner next to his television. Brad closed his eyes for a while. When he opened them again, Natasha sat in the corner, her back against the wall.

She took a deep breath. "I'm so sorry."

"You had no choice," Brad said, trying to make it easier on her. Nevertheless, he still could not understand how his death would make any difference; he had seen the devastation. "If you hadn't acted, I would have died anyway to no purpose, together with everybody else."

As he spoke, Natasha, his television, indeed the entire room, started dissolving into bright white light. He heard Natasha say something, but his brain was unable to process the words as if she had spoken in a foreign tongue. The flame of his consciousness was diminishing rapidly, threatening to extinguish with each flickering thought. Damn. So soon. He wasn't ready!

When his eyes could no longer see his mind took over, filling his vision with clouds like a stained rug, stumps in the ash, and the Reaper's fingers. And as he vanished into unreality, so did they. Schrödinger's Box was closing.

THE END

MICHAEL W. LUCHT is a mostly Australian writer residing in Hobart, Tasmania. When not writing, he has been known to lecture in mathematics and computing. With twin ambitions of publishing a fantasy novel and creating artificial life, he is currently prioritizing the novel to be completed in 2018. His fiction has appeared in *Nature Futures, The Drabblecast, Alternate Hilarities 3 & 4, Bards & Sages Quarterly* and *Island Magazine*. With respect to non-fiction, he has heterogeneously contributed to: *Physical Review A, The Journal of Chemical Physics, Artificial Life, The Skeptic* and *Cracked.com*. To find out more, see: http://www.michaelwlucht.com.

DIVERSIONS

J.D. Kotzman

"IT'S DONE."

"GOOD."

"AGENT Flint, you're certain this was absolutely necessary?" I asked.

"The temporal directives require the preservation of the timeline," he said, surveying the monitor of the strange handheld device he carried. A quantum event tracer, he told me. The unit, about the size of an antique iPhone, cast a dull, crimson glow through its translucent, almost nebulous, shell. After he'd appeared satisfied with the readings, Flint clasped his hands behind his back and looked at me with serious eyes. "You should know, Dr. Greene. After all, you drafted them… or will, at least."

"I should have remembered."

"History recorded that you attempted to prevent the Atlantean flu outbreak and that a temporal agent named Flint corrected the diversion." As if on cue, the tracer interrupted with a series of dulcet tones and began radiating a brilliant green light. "Ah, everything appears in order."

"In *order*? That outbreak could wipe out more than a third of the world's population."

"Actually, if memory serves, it was closer to half."

"Four billion people dead," I said, my voice fading to a whisper.

"Nasty bug," he said, with a kind of detachment reserved for the historically distant. "But in the aftermath, the world experienced a new sense of unity and formed the first Global Congress, and scientists discovered that the diminished population averted devastating shortages of food, water, and…"

"Then Beth saved us," I said. "She saved us all."

HE KNEW EVERYTHING ABOUT me. Every detail—my name, my birthday, the names of my parents, their birthdays—he knew them all. He knew about the spare power converter I'd pilfered from the lab last week. And he even knew about the yellowing, unsent letter to Stephen Hawking I kept tucked in the back of my dresser drawer. He knew things I'd never told anyone.

I met him in the park, near my apartment in Georgetown. I often went there early on Sunday mornings, before the grounds came alive with joggers, small children on bikes, and young mothers pushing strollers. On that particular day, he found me on my favorite bench beside the giant oak, drinking coffee under the overcast, autumn sky. I'd finished my usual inner deliberation about whether to quit my research job and take a teaching position and begun the one about whether to ask Beth to marry me when he suddenly appeared. He joined me on the rickety wooden seat, saying nothing at first. And until he uttered my name, only the rustling of the turning leaves broke the silence.

"Do I know you?" I asked.

"Not exactly, but I know you, Dr. Greene."

For the next hour, I listened, warming myself with an occasional sip of coffee, while a complete stranger recounted my own life story. I tried to rationalize the situation because his explanation seemed too impossible to believe. A practical joke, perhaps, or maybe some kind of government intelligence operation. For a moment, thoughts of wireless bugs, phone taps, and keyhole satellite images flitted through my mind. Except, other than the mirrored sunglasses he never removed, he didn't look like a CIA agent, more like an aging professor plucked from some tiny college in New England. He wore a shabby wool overcoat, with a gray Fedora pulled down over his haggard face and silvery hair, and his unkempt goatee looked on the verge of overtaking his pursed lips.

"Matters have become grave," he said, his tone icy. "We might need your assistance." I nodded in disbelief. I asked for his name, but he refused. "For your own protection," he said.

"I'll call you Ben."

"Why?"

"Short for Benrus."

"Oh, the watch," he said, with the slightest hint of a smile. "Sharp eye." He slid up his left cuff, allowing me to better admire the timepiece. "American servicemen wore them in World War II. It's an original, with a few... modifications."

"I'm kind of a history buff myself. I love things like this."

"Adam... I know."

"Interested in selling?"

"No," he said flatly. His attention shifted toward the horizon, as if searching for something hidden in the fog, then back to me. "It was a gift... from someone very special."

"Sentimental value. I understand."

"No matter," he said, turning to face me for the first time. Something about him felt familiar, like a half-remembered image after waking from a dream. "You'll have your own soon enough."

With that, he rose to take his leave. I stood with him and extended my hand. I judged him about thirty years older, but we shared the same tall, lanky build. "A unique pleasure," he said, his hand enfolding neatly around mine. I asked whether I would see him again. "I hope not," he said, "for both our sakes." He lulled there a moment longer, eyeing a pack of in-line skaters scurrying past, before starting off toward the wooded area in the middle of the park. I watched him go, the train of his coat rising and falling like an ocean swell as he disappeared into the mist. *Beth will never believe this*. After all, it wasn't every day I met a man who claims he's from the future.

Beth didn't believe it. Hours removed from the park, I wasn't certain I believed it either. When I told her about Ben, the mysterious man from tomorrow, she shook her head the way she always did when I proposed one of my wild theories that stretched the boundaries of accepted science. Sometimes, after I'd gone on for a while, she would put a hand to my mouth, open her green eyes wide, and hit me with one of her infectious smiles. I once asked Beth why she never stopped me sooner, why a beautiful, intelligent geneticist bothered to listen to the mad rants of a theoretical physicist. "Because I love that life hasn't taken your dreams," she said. "We need more dreamers, even if you are bordering on certifiable." Lately, though, I'd begun to wonder whether her patience would last. And she had a point about my sanity. Without Beth, I'd probably lose the last threads of my tether to reality. She kept me grounded.

"I'm telling you, he knew everything," I said, making one final plea.

"What about the time in Tahiti, with the rose petals and the candle wax? Did he know about that?" she asked, stifling a laugh.

"We didn't get that far."

"So, are you going to open your gift?" In all of my excitement about Ben, I'd forgotten about the present awaiting me when I returned home.

"What's the occasion again?"

"Does there need to be an *occasion*? I saw it and thought of you." She flopped down beside me on the couch and pulled her auburn hair back into a ponytail. "Go on. Open it. Maybe it will keep you here with us…? in this dimension."

I rolled my eyes and started to unwrap my present. Beth often bought me unexpected gifts at the most unexpected times. Last year, one blustery evening a few weeks after Christmas, she surprised me with the complete series of *Stargate Atlantis* on DVD. I knew she hated the show, all science fiction really, but she insisted we curl up on the couch with a bottle of Cabernet and watch together. A few hours into our marathon, after she'd closed her eyes and laid her head on my shoulder, I asked her why.

"I knew it would make you happy," she said. "It's the little things, you know?"

I'd realized then I didn't deserve her. *You never will*, I told myself, tearing the last of the candy-striped paper from the small, oblong box underneath. When I lifted the lid, I gasped, unable to speak.

"Hello?" she asked, waving a hand in front of my face. "Ground control to Major Tom."

"Where did you get this?" I asked.

"On eBay. Why? Don't you like it?"

"No… I mean, yes, I love it. It's not that."

"Well, what is it then?"

"He had the same watch."

"…THE OUTBREAK APPEARS TO have spread into parts of Europe and Latin America, despite the recently implemented quarantine, raising concerns among health officials about a possible global pandemic. The president plans to speak at a press conference later today in response to the mounting…"

"Enough of that," I said, switching off the holo-monitor. I glanced at the black-and-white photo of Beth I kept at my workstation. I'd snapped the shot almost thirty years ago, on the day we moved into our place near the park. Back then, the future, our future, seemed to hold the promise of something wondrous. Her image haunted me now. Even after all of those years, she still looked at me with playful eyes. "Damn it, Beth, I wish you were here. I wish none of this had happened."

Maybe it doesn't have to happen. I contacted my assistant Simon and told him to prepare the device. As for me, I had a long night of calculations ahead.

ONE SUMMER, ABOUT A month after I turned ten, I went to stay with my Aunt Marie and Uncle Lucas in Lewisberry, a little town in rural Pennsylvania. My parents fought almost constantly in those days, and I often locked myself in my room for hours, reading the works of Isaac Asimov, Jules Verne, or my other literary heroes. After the school year had ended, my father decided I needed to spend more time outside and less time with my head buried in books. So, off I went. My aunt and uncle lived in a spacious, drafty house built around a converted barn, and their property included a few acres of woodland, a grove of fruit trees, and a large yard with a well-tended vegetable garden. Most days, I spent my afternoons in the orchard, dreaming of voyages to the stars in my imaginary cockpit atop the old apple tree. I hid up there for hours, plotting missions to Jupiter or the Andromeda galaxy, until my aunt called me to the house for dinner. I felt completely lost amid those gnarled branches as if time itself didn't exist.

And I felt the same way that evening, contemplating the possibility that somehow humanity had pierced the temporal veil. Beth and I spent most of dinner discussing our future plans, or she did, at least. She tried to tell me about a job offer she'd received from some start-up biotech company, but my thoughts kept returning to Ben. After we'd finished eating, I invented an excuse about needing some papers from the lab and slipped out of the apartment. I wandered the downtown streets for a few hours, my mind skipping through every theory I'd ever read about time travel until I found myself on the bridge near the outskirts of the city. About halfway across, I stopped and peered over the limestone railing. In the distance, I saw the outlines of boats against the lights from the pier. The incandescent glow illuminated the river like a midnight sun, and the small watercraft appeared caught in its gravitational field. Admittedly, the glare had captured me as well. Only the sound of approaching footfalls disrupted my gaze.

"Hello, Dr. Greene."

"Ben?"

"Yes."

"How did you find me?"

"Adam, I think you know."

"Is it really possible?"

"Yes."

"Tell me how it works then," I said, still unable, or unwilling, to believe him. "How does your time machine work?"

"You should know, Dr. Greene, you invented it."

Ben rested a hand on my shoulder and guided me back toward the city. As we walked through the sea of edifices, he told me everything began with a paper I wrote. The article, which I managed to get published in *Physical Review Letters*, posited a theory about using exotic matter to establish a stable wormhole, a development that opened the possibility of travel to the past by bending time itself. Though the scientific community didn't show much interest in my work, the government, or at least some shadowy part of it, did. Two months later, I joined Project Chronos, a top secret research initiative that sought to develop the first functional time machine. The calculations took years to complete, and even after we'd come up with a working model for the device, the power requirements seemed unachievable. Our director had threatened to abandon the project, but I made a major breakthrough, creating a process for channelling massive amounts of energy from Scalar Field waves.

"But the vacuum fluctuations," I said, "how did you…"

"With this," he said, raising his arm and turning the face of his watch toward me. "It generates a harmonic field to stabilize them."

"But how do you locate…"

"The glasses. They detect temporal disturbances."

"This is incredible!"

"Yes, it is."

"Wait," I said, coming to a stop in the middle of an empty intersection. A light rain had begun to fall. "If you're back…?"

"It's an outbreak, a global pandemic. Something called Atlantean flu."

"*Atlantean?*"

"One last love letter, I suppose. She named it after your favorite television show."

"Beth? What does Beth have to do with this?"

Ben told me a story about Vaxtech, the start-up company that sent the offer to Beth. A few years after she took the job, the company placed her in charge of a team of researchers working on a novel vaccine against avian flu. They attempted to manipulate the genome of the virus to prevent transmissibility among humans. At first, they seemed to make progress, but something went awry. One of their experiments led to the creation of a new strain of flu, the deadliest the world had ever seen. When Beth tried to suspend the research, Vaxtech threatened to fire her. Two days later, the Pentagon took over the project and forced everyone involved to sign confidentially agreements. The military wanted to develop the virus into a biological weapon.

"I'm surprised Beth didn't go to the press anyway," I said, knowing her independent streak. But she'd never had a chance. A fatal car accident, he told me, at least according to official reports. "You think they killed her?" I asked.

"I never knew for certain," he said, "but I suspected."

"Did you know her well?"

"I loved her… very much."

"Oh, my God," I said, all of the pieces coalescing in my head. Beth, the watch, the physical similarities, the uncanny knowledge of my personal history—everything fit. "You're… me."

"Dr. Adam Greene," he said, a wry smile creeping across his weathered face, "pleasure to meet me."

People often talk about meeting their future selves, what they would say, or what they would ask. But standing there, actually facing me, thirty years or so on, I found myself at a loss for words. When my shock subsided a bit, we continued our walk through the quiet, damp streets to a cozy hole-in-the-wall both of us knew well. The place resembled a bohemian cafe, filled with mismatched furniture, tables, and bookshelves, but the mahogany bar stretching along the wall indicated otherwise. Amid the rabble, it stood like a sentinel, sworn to guard the cache of bottles towering behind its polished surface. We ordered a pair of gin-and-tonics and waded through the assortment of neighborhood regulars, yuppies, and aging hipsters to a little table away from the crowd. The two of us sat alone, quiet, emptying our glasses in the shadows. After a time, I caught his eye over the rim of my tumbler. We shared a brief chuckle over the absurdity of our circumstances, but their gravity quickly swallowed any traces of mirth.

"I can't believe I'm going to lose her," I said.

"Adam, listen. You have to stop Beth from taking the position at Vaxtech," he said, a flicker of desperation in his eyes. "I've done the calculations, and it's the only way to prevent the outbreak... the only way to save her." I nodded. All of a sudden, though, I wondered why he'd come. We'd already failed to avert the outbreak. We'd always failed. "I had to try," he said. "In theory, we're only dealing with probabilities. No one has ever proven the immutability of the future."

"In theory."

When we finished another round, he looked at his watch and offered a rueful smile. "Time to go," he said. "Good luck, Adam." And then I watched, with a confusing mix of amazement and melancholy, as my older self ducked behind a bookcase and vanished into the ether.

"DR. GREENE, ARE YOU certain about this?"

"Simon, I... no, I'm not," I said, "but I don't have a choice."

"Very well," he said, making some final adjustments to the controls. "Coordinates laid in. All systems go."

"Activate the device."

"Godspeed, Adam."

THE SOUND OF THE door squeaking on its hinges snapped me to attention, and I caught a glimpse of him in the mirror. "What's happened?" I asked, rinsing the last of the soap from my hands.

"I'm sorry, Adam." His reflection lunged at me, delivering a short, sharp shock to the right side of my neck. Within seconds, I began to lose consciousness. I attempted to steady myself against the porcelain, but my legs gave way, leaving me in a heap on the damp tiles below. Lying there, paralyzed, I saw him open an armored briefcase and remove a device—something resembling a phaser from an old *Star Trek* episode—before everything went black. Nothing, and then… the feeling of cold metal pressing against my temple, the sound of labored breathing, and the faint odor of piss and bleach. "Forget," I heard him whisper. "Forget."

"HE'S AGREED TO HELP us," I said.

"*You've* agreed," Simon corrected.

"Yes, *I've* agreed."

"Excellent, Dr. Greene, but we have another problem."

"What's wrong?" Simon motioned toward a straight-backed, burly man standing behind him on the far side of the lab. He looked out of place, though at ease, and wore a uniform unlike any I'd ever seen.

"He came through a temporal portal after you left."

"Who are you?" I asked the stranger.

"The name is Flint, Agent Flint. Dr. Greene, we need to talk."

SUNLIGHT EXPLODED THROUGH THE Venetian blinds, engulfing everything but the remotest corners of my bedroom. I grabbed the pillow beside me and covered my face, hoping to find some shade, but the unrelenting brightness overwhelmed my defenses. No relief. I tried rolling on my side, but the maneuver served only to intensify the pain amassing behind my right temple. *What happened last night? Hangover?* I didn't remember drinking. I walked to the bridge, watched the boats, and then… an utter blank. I had a vague awareness of other things that happened—possibly significant—but the details remained somewhere beyond the reach of memory. After I'd lay there for a while, every toss and turn stirring a small lightning storm in my head, I mustered the strength to drag myself from bed. The voyage across the parquet floor, over the Chinese rug, and into the adjoining bathroom took more effort.

I'd started fishing for a bottle of painkillers in the medicine cabinet when I noticed an opened Fed Ex stuffed in the small trashcan beside the sink. I salvaged the envelope from the refuse and checked the contents. Empty. *To Beth, from Vaxtech*, according to the label. *Vaxtech*. The name echoed in my mind, unearthing a sense of unexplained dread. Something about that name… I tried to concentrate, remember. I recalled… instructions. I had to do something or… stop someone from doing something but what?

And who? *It will come to me,* I thought, tossing the envelope back into the trash. *It will come.*

THE END

J. D. KOTZMAN works in the health policy field and lives in the Washington, D.C., area with his girlfriend and two pugs, Grendel and Ginger. Previously, he has served as an editor and writer for several print and online news publications. His fiction has appeared or is forthcoming in *After the Pause, The Bookends Review, Crack the Spine, Drunk Monkeys, Foliate Oak, Ink Stains* (a project of Dark Alley Press), *Inscape, Kentucky Review, Pidgeonholes, Slink Chunk Press, The Speculative Edge, Straylight, An Unlikely Companion* (a project of E&GJ Little Press), and *Yellow Chair Review.* Find more of his writing at amazon.com/author/jdkotzman.

FASHION EMERGENCY

Brian Koukol

ISOBEL ROCKED FORWARD ON the divan, willing her autonomous car to go faster, but its trajectory had already been optimized for traffic patterns and fuel economy. All she could do was wait, and it was killing her.

She snatched a butterscotch candy from the car's larder and popped it into her mouth. According to the HUD, she'd be home in 5 minutes, 12 seconds. That would give her less than ten minutes to change into something more suitable for dinner with the bosses and parse the new route. She'd make it work. She needed that promotion.

The car reached her driveway precisely when promised and she ran into the house, inadvertently trampling the emerging daffodils on the way.

Robert was seated in front of the coffee table, in his pyjamas, fiddling with his SpaceTime Inserter.

"What are you doing?" she asked. "Get dressed."

"I *am* dressed."

"Not for dinner with my bosses, you aren't."

He furrowed his brow, not bothering to look up from his machine. "Was that tonight?"?

"Not was," she said, sloughing off her coat. "Is. We need to be in the car in ten minutes."

"Can't do it. I have to go to work."

Isobel glared at him. "You're a SpaceTime traveler. Do your thing and come back one second after you left. It's not that hard..."

Robert finally looked up. "It's company policy to leave a gap of time in the present equal to that which you spend in the future," he said.

"Sing me a new song for once. Break a rule. Do it for your wife."

He shrugged. "It's out of my hands. Company policy." His glance drifted back down to the device. "I should be back in five hours."

Isobel crossed her arms and sucked on her candy. "I have a better idea. Why don't you come back five years ago? You know, back when I didn't think you were a selfish prick."

"Sounds good to me," he said. "I liked you better when you put out anyway. But we can't travel into the past with these things."

"Of course, you can. How else would you return to the present after a sortie?"

He scratched his chin. "I hadn't thought about that."

"Any engineer worth their salt knows that the mechanics are there, but the company limits past travel to simple return trips as a matter of prudence. Otherwise you and your travelers would try to hunt a Tyrannosaurus or something equally stupid."

"No way," Robert said. "Although one of the boys in the lab did try to go back to revisit his high school girlfriend..."

"Hence the failsafe."

"And I suppose you know how to bypass it, oh great engineer?"

"Of course."

"How?"

"Not a chance," she said. "I'm not letting you loose on poor Marguerite. She probably wore bobby socks."

Robert flushed "Not *my* high school girlfriend. One of the boys in the lab's..."

"Fool me once," she said, shaking her head as she disappeared into the bedroom to find something to wear. She'd wasted enough time already.

"I'm headed to Falkirk," he shouted from the other room as she picked out a kilt with a high hem from the wardrobe. "21 July, 2098. Just in case you care."

"Good to know," she replied, slipping on her chosen outfit. "If you don't come home, I'll know where not to be in twelve years."

"Come on now. This is important."

"Tell me about it. I can totally see how a pyjama party in future Scotland is so much more important than my promotion."

She rolled through several hues of tartan on the control tag of the kilt, studying her reflection in the mirror behind the bathroom door for the perfect scheme among the myriad combinations. Robert may have been able to wear his pyjamas to work, but she needed to dress to impress.

"It's not a pyjama party," he said. "The order of the Silk Templars will be a big deal in a decade.

"So you say. But what's preventing someone from traveling to next week and executing their leader before they can come to power?"

"Contracts."

"You seem to have an answer for everything," she said. "So, tell me this: green and gold or red and blue?"

"Well, the Silk Templars wear green before the summer solstice. Hence my attire. We could match."

Isobel cocked her head. "But you're traveling to 21 July."

A series of curses issued from the other room. Robert appeared in the doorway in his green pyjamas. "I have to change my clothes," he said.

As he made his way to the wardrobe, Isobel turned her back to the mirror and tried to look at her outfit from behind. "Before you do that, come tell me if this kilt makes my calves look fat."

Robert dug through his work clothes. "I thought you were a bloody engineer," he said. "Why do you care if your calves look fat? Aren't they promoting your brain?"

"In a perfect world," she replied, snatching a hand mirror to triangulate a better look at herself.

"If my work pans out," Robert's muffled voice said from inside the wardrobe, "things will be a lot more perfect in twenty years."

"For shareholder dividends or for gender equality?" she asked.

Robert slammed the wardrobe shut. "Maybe it's in the garage," he mumbled, brushing past Isobel toward the door.

"Tell me how this looks, you beauf," she said.

But he kept walking, oblivious to her dilemma. If she didn't get her clothes right, she'd be passed over once again. And she wasn't getting any younger. Tonight was make or break and she needed Robert's cooperation.

"Let's have sex," she said.

He stopped at the door and spun toward her, a boyish grin plastered across his face. "Really?"

"No. But now that I have your attention, does this kilt read competent yet coquettish to you?"

He frowned. "It makes you look like a slut," he said, and then scurried from the room.

Isobel sighed and worried the shrinking butterscotch in her mouth as she tried to appraise her ensemble in the mirror again.

"This isn't going to work," she said at last. "I'd need two of myself."

As she listened to Robert banging around among the boxes of overflow clothing in the garage, a smile crossed her face. If she went a few minutes into the past, there *would* be two of her. She could look at her own calves.

Isobel tiptoed to the front room and sat down in front of the SpaceTime Inserter on the coffee table.

It was a metallic puck embedded with a small screen featuring two sets of numbers: one for Space and one for Time. The coordinates for Falkirk filled the former, while the date of July 21, 2098 registered on the latter.

She pressed and held the "set" buttons for the two values and a tiny click issued from the back of the puck. The maintenance hub had popped.

Among the labyrinth of circuits and wires inside was a mottled orange and blue cord. She found it and then searched the front room area for a tool to sever it. There was nothing, so she used her teeth.

She needed to hold the wires apart with one hand while she engaged the device with the other to bypass the failsafe—then it would let her travel into the past at will. As long as the wire was sundered, she would be able to manipulate the SpaceTime values without activation. The instant they contacted again, the device would engage and she would travel.

It may have been a nerve-racking task for someone like Robert, but she had plenty of experience with this sort of thing.

Keeping the severed wires separate, Isobel flipped the Inserter so she could see the display and engaged the device. As expected, she didn't travel, but the values for Space and Time dropped to zero. Robert's settings had become the new default values; any new programming would be in relation to them.

She rolled the Time value back eight minutes and zero seconds and began calculating the new Space coordinates in her mind. She knew the position of her bedroom by heart. She was that kind of engineer.

Before she could input the calculus, a troubling thought arose from the back of her mind. She hadn't seen herself walk into her bedroom eight minutes ago to check out her calves, so her plan hadn't worked. Something must've gone wrong.

"What are you doing?" Robert demanded from the hallway.

Isobel jerked in surprise and lost contact with the orange and blue wire. The room exploded in crackling zincous light as her proprioception folded in on itself and then diffused.

ISOBEL STAGGERED SIDEWAYS INTO a muddy rut, still blinded from the Insertion, when a crushing blow to the chest threw her to the wet ground.

Flat on her back, she spat out the remnants of her butterscotch candy, struggling for breath. She was in Falkirk. That much she knew. She hadn't had time to adjust the Space coordinates before the jump.

Her vision returned with her wind and she watched as a grumbling man in a woollen cloak picked himself up from the mud beside an indignant horse. She couldn't discern the man's words, but his tone indicated expletives.

Beyond the horseman, the soggy road widened into a plaza inhabited by a cluster of carts and merchants surrounding a thick wooden cross atop a stone dais. Over Isobel's shoulder in the opposite direction loomed an imposing building of mottled stone. The reaching tower at the center of its cruciform shape brandished a wooden icon that proclaimed it as church. A pungent scent of excrement rode on the wind.

This wasn't eight minutes ago.

When the hell was she?

As the horseman brushed the mud from his cloak, the thick wooden door of a rustic bistro abutting the road swung open and a trio of strong men in odd dress emerged.

They wore quilted tunics, belted at the waist and stretching to their knees, which were covered in tight jackets. The older man in the middle, obviously the leader, sported a yellow tunic and red jacket, while his companions were clad in drab grays.

"What hath happed heere?" the man asked. He spoke English of a sort. Isobel had taken classes on it in her youth on a lark. It was obscure and so much uglier than her native French, but it had looked good on her college applications. She suspected the man was drunk.

He rushed to her side. "Art thou hurte, boy?"

"I am not injured," Isobel replied.

He squinted at the pitch of her voice, confused. Then he looked beyond her outfit, noticing her hair, facial structure and general conformation.

"It be a womman," he announced to his companions.

Suddenly more interested, they came to his side and laughed at what they found.

"Why doth sche weareth the clothyng of a man?" one of them asked.

The man in red and yellow glared at her. "Explayne thy atyre."

Isobel sputtered, trying to form the rough words on her tongue.

He recoiled from her, disgusted.

"Bettre suche a thing be tramped by the hors," he said.

The men eyed the horseman—who had remounted by that point—and then returned to the bistro.

When he was sure they couldn't hear him, the horseman glanced at Isobel.

"Hast thou no thoughte who that be, whelp?"

She shook her head.

"Sir John de Graham. Kyng Edward shalt payeth wele for his espye."

The name was familiar. Sir John de Graham was one of the founding fathers of the Scottish Empire, along with William Wallace. She'd learned about it in her English classes. If she were now contemporary to him, something had gone terribly wrong with her Insertion.

"What is the date?" she asked the horseman as he trotted past with a gleeful smile.

"Twenty-one July," he replied.

"Of what year?"

"1298, verraily," came the response.

And then he was gone.

Isobel chastised herself. She hadn't set the device back eight minutes and zero seconds, but eight hundred years. She'd severed the wrong wire in the rush and paid the price.

A lump formed in her throat. Where was the Inserter?

She dropped to her knees in the mud, searching for the device, but found only endless handfuls of muck. She was stranded.

And then she heard it. The kind of rhythmic, electronic beeping completely alien to thirteenth century Scotland. Following the sound, she quickly located the device, in large part because nothing else in the damp, weather-beaten landscape could hold a shine.

She limped to the mouth of a cobbled road that intersected the dirt avenue and snatched up the puck. Crude buildings lined the paved road, leading up to the ruins of a stone compound co-opted by a series of makeshift wooden shanties at the terminal end. Traces of an earthen wall stretched to either side.

But she wasn't going that far. Instead, Isobel pressed beneath the negligible eave of an adjacent building to shield herself from the rain while she reprogrammed the Inserter.

She manipulated the values of Space and Time back to the moment of her departure from home and then held both "set" buttons. The values returned to zero and the maintenance hub popped open. She breathed a sigh of relief. Everything appeared to be in working order.

Isobel spliced the orange and blue wire back together and then bit a second wire, this one blue and orange, in two. Somebody in manufacturing had a sense of humor, she'd give them that much.

Now she could manipulate hours, minutes and seconds instead of years. Holding the wires apart with the fingers of one hand, she engaged the device with the other and then began rolling the Time back eight minutes.

As she went about manipulating the values, a firm hand grabbed her by the back of the neck and mashed her face against the turf and clay wall of the building in front of her. The force of the surprise attack twisted her wrist and threatened to wrench the device from her grip, but she was able to hold on with one hand.

"Thou may dresse of man, but thou smelle of womman," a gruff voice said too close to her ear.

She managed to turn her head enough to get one eye on her assailant. It was one of Sir John's drab gray companions.

The back of her kilt was lifted and she felt rough, callused hands tear at her underclothes.

"I wajour thou be softe ynough undernethe," he said, droplets of his hot, sour breath condensing on her neck.

Rape. Of course. Fucking men.

As the beast fiddled with his tunic behind her, she finished programming the Time value one-handed.

Before the man had a chance to fulfill his basest instincts, she released the severed wire.

The alleyway exploded in electric light and she spun out of her primitive reality.

AS CLIMATE CONTROLLED WARMTH enveloped her and she waited for her sight to return, Isobel pondered whether she had traveled back a bit too early. The butterscotch candy had made the earlier jump with her, ferried through time within the confines of her mouth; she wondered what would've happened had she traveled home mid-rape. The thought of that monster stumbling around the alley—penisless and nursing electrical burns over what remained of his body—would almost have made the violation worth it. At least until she really thought about it.

"You're here," a familiar voice squeaked in English. "I barely had the thought and then here you are."

Isobel's vision cleared and she spotted an analog of herself standing in front of a mirror in a room that looked quite different from the one she had left earlier. In place of the ornate, gilded frame was a floating, minimalist edge.

"You speak English?" Isobel asked her twin. Well, fraternal twin, at least.

"Of course. What else would I speak?"

"French."

The other Isobel laughed. "Why would I do that? The only thing worth saying in French is 'I surrender' and 'Thank you, America.'"

"What is America?" Isobel asked.

Her double narrowed her gaze. "You messed something up, didn't you?"?

Isobel flushed. "I believe so."

"When and where?"

"Falkirk. 21 July 1298."

Isobel's double consulted a device embedded in the palm of her hand. "That's the day before the battle of Falkirk. When the Scots were defeated by the English."

"Defeated by the English? No. The Scots won their war of independence a few years later. Sir John de Graham led the first government."

The double shook her head. "Not according to the web," she said. "It says your Graham guy died at Falkirk on July 22. Whatever you did back then must've created a whole new timeline."

"*Merde*. Robert will kill me. I must repair this mistake."

The double cocked her head. "Who's Robert?"

A lump formed in Isobel's throat. "Our husband..."

"Husband? No way. The only thing we're married to is our work."

Isobel's anxiety evaporated. The weight of a burden she hadn't known she'd been carrying lifted from her shoulders. "And what is our work?"

The double smiled. "Head engineer and majority shareholder of SpaceTime International. I'm going to be addressing the board in an hour."

Isobel couldn't hide her grin. "I've always wanted a sister," she said.

"I know," the double said with a wink. She tried to size herself up in the mirror and then frowned. "Now tell me, sis—do these jeans make my ass look fat?"

Isobel scrutinized her better self. She was wearing thick fabric leggings that clung to her body, accentuating every curve. "Stylé. They look like they are painted on."

"Perfect," the double said with a satisfied nod. "But I own the company. I think I'll wear Bermuda shorts instead."

Isobel didn't know what Bermuda shorts were, but she grinned anyway. "I think I'm going to like it here."

THE END

BRIAN KOUKOL, raised in the suburbs of Los Angeles, now makes his home among the salt breezes and open spaces of California's Central Coast. A lifelong battle with muscular dystrophy has informed the majority of his work, which is written with the aid of voice recognition software. Despite his challenges, Brian maintains an adventurous spirit, a wicked sense of humor, and a willingness to delve into the darker sides of the human experience with his work. There is no genre he won't explore, but science fiction remains a lifelong favorite. His words have appeared in Phantaxis Magazine, GigaNotoSaurus, and The Society of Misfit Stories, amongst other places. Visit his author website: www.briankoukol.com

The Man Who Brought Down
The New York Times
Paul Levinson

A slightly earlier version of this story was published in *Analog Magazine* in December 2000.

HE CAME DOWN THE stairs, brandishing a copy of *The New York Times.*

I don't think I'd ever seen my father so angry.

"Nothing!" He threw the paper on to the kitchen table. "Not a word about my work!"

"Charles..." Mama stuck her head in from the dining room. "You can't control what they print. There's nothing you can do—"

"Oh, there's something I can do all right," Papa said. "They promised me. They promised they'd run the story this time. Bastards—"

Mama blushed.

Papa looked at me, standing by the door. "I'm sorry, Rebecca. I didn't mean to curse like that."

"It's ok, Papa. I once heard a boy say that in the school yard." I smiled my little girl smile. I'd always be his little girl. "It's hard being an inventor of something. My friend Janey once wrote a great poem—and it was so good, no one believed she really wrote it."

Mama was next to him now, her arms around him, trying to soothe him. "No one believes in people who invent things in their garages any more. It's all big corporations now. No point beating your head against the wall."

"There's a point," Papa insisted. "What's the use of inventing anything if no one knows about it?"

"You can't really blame the newspapers," Mama said. "If you don't even have a patent, how can you expect the *Times* to—"

"Patent?" Papa yelped. "How am I supposed to go about getting a patent on this machine? Just file a blueprint of my design with the Patent Office? It's a *time machine*, for God's sake! If someone else built it, if it fell into the wrong hands, it could wreak havoc on our world!"

"Ok then," Mama said. "How about some good hot oatmeal for breakfast?" She gestured towards a simmering pot on the stove.

"Let's sit down and eat. Forget about the *Times*. There's nothing you can do about it."

"Yes, there is." Papa sat down, ready to eat, but not mollified, "They promised me they'd print the story this time. Now they're going to pay."

WHATEVER PAPA DID TO make the newspaper pay, it didn't take him away from home very much.

Or maybe it did, and I didn't understand.

I overheard snippets of conversation, coming out of their bedroom late at night.

"You see, Dear, I could be gone for months, even years at a time, and you wouldn't notice the difference, because if I returned just a second after I left, it would seem to you and the world like I'd never been gone."

"Wouldn't you look older?" Mama asked.

"Well, I guess I would at that," Papa replied. "But do I?"

"No," Mama said.

"I guess that's because in fact I have not been gone for years or even months. I'm getting everything done in just a few hours or maybe a day or two each time. It's not that hard to trip them up on little things."

"I still don't like it," Mama said. "It's dangerous."

I CAN'T RECALL THE first time I noticed there that was a change in the world, because I guess it came on too gradually, like winter, sometimes. One day I just realized that things had become different—people were just more irritable, more jumpy, than they used to be. As if they couldn't trust in things the way they used to.

It was harder to tell with Papa, because he was tired and irritable anyway from all of his travelling.

He'd get up very early some mornings, fetch the paper from the front porch, and take it upstairs to his den. And he'd come down a little while later, a look of determination on his face as he kissed Mama and me goodbye and walked out the door to the garage. And then the door would open again, just a minute or two after, and Papa would come back in the house. Sometimes with rain or even snow on his face, though the morning was bright and sunny. He'd look at Mama and me, and not say a word to us, though I once heard him mumble to himself as he walked back upstairs. "I'll see what the paper looks like tomorrow."

This went on for years and years. Papa was able to keep his job at the Post Office because the whole routine never took much of his time—he was never late. He gradually seemed to become more satisfied. He never spoke again of his time machine, or *The New York Times*. He just carried that newspaper with him, up and down those stairs....

Eventually I went away to college. Eventually Papa retired from the Post Office. Eventually he retired from his routine.

I HAVE A HUSBAND and family of my own now. We live across the country. I come back every year with my husband and kids to visit Mama and Papa on the holidays.

I got a few minutes alone with Papa last December as he sat in his rocking chair on the front porch.

"It looks the same," he said, and pointed out to the lawn and beyond, "but somehow different."

"Well, it's a different world today, Papa. Not like it was when I was first growing up. Everyone's in a hurry today, rushing, pushing, shoving."

"Like they're afraid if they don't move quickly enough they'll make some terrible mistake," Papa said.

I looked at him.

"I guess it's my fault," he said.

"You can't know that for sure," I said.

"But I was right to do it!" He picked up a copy of *The New York Times* from underneath his chair. "They promised me they'd run the story. They promised!"

"I know, Papa."

"So, if they were going to lie to me, and the world, the least I could do was expose them for what they were. Maybe it undermined people's confidence in things, I don't know. But I had no choice. All the news that's fit to print? Hardly. All the omissions and errors that's fit to print—that's more like it! No wonder it's been dropping in circulation like a stone. No wonder all everyone's talking about these days is fake news. They say it's because of the Internet. But it's me."

He pointed to a little box on the bottom of the front page.

"They didn't believe in my time machine? Well, I had the last laugh. I picked a story, a fact in a story, a quote in a story, each time I went out. And I went back just a little bit in time in my machine and changed it—so the *Times* wound up having it wrong. I did it with other newspapers too—they're all the same. And it embarrassed them, got them so jittery, that now they make mistakes all the time without my help. It's become the norm!" He laughed, with a mixture of joy and something much darker. "They don't need me and my machine any more to make them look foolish."

His finger jabbed the bottom of the page. "*Errata*. Oh, they listed mistakes on their own, once in a while, before I got started. But now those apologies are here on the front page almost every day. That's my lasting gift to the newspapers of the world. No one will really have confidence in them ever again."

THE END

PAUL LEVINSON, PhD, is Professor of Communication & Media Studies at Fordham University in NYC. His science fiction novels include *The Silk Code* (winner of Locus Award for Best First Science Fiction Novel of 1999), *Borrowed Tides* (2001), *The Consciousness Plague* (2002), *The Pixel Eye* (2003), *The Plot To Save Socrates* (2006), *Unburning Alexandria* (2013), and *Chronica* (2014). In addition to *The Plot to Save Socrates* trilogy, his best-known time travel stories include *The Loose Ends Saga* (1997-2016), *Ians, Ions, and Eons* (2011-2016), *Marilyn and Monet* (2017), and *The Chronology Protection Case* (1995), which was made into a short movie that plays at film festivals around the world and is always available on Amazon Prime.

His nonfiction books, including *The Soft Edge* (1997), Digital McLuhan (1999), *Realspace* (2003), *Cellphone* (2004), *New New Media* (2009; 2nd edition, 2012), *McLuhan in an Age of Social Media* (2015), *Fake News in Real Context* (2016), and *Cyber War and Peace* (2017), have been translated into twelve languages. He appears on CNN, MSNBC, Fox News, the Discovery Channel, National Geographic, the History Channel, NPR, the BBC, and numerous TV and radio programs. He was President of the Science Fiction and Fantasy Writers of America, 1998-2001. You can find him @PaulLev on Twitter, which was listed in *The Chronicle of Higher Education's* "Top 10 Academic Twitterers" in 2009.

LITTER PICKING ON THE MOON

Robert Bagnall

Originally appeared in *Don't Open 'Til Doomsday*, PunksWritePoems 2016.

JERSEY CHILD LAUGHINGLY CALLED it a portfolio career.

Two days a week she worked in a wholesalers trying to sort out a backlog of invoices and filing. This was in response to some unspecified future threat from the IRS which only the big boss, Michael, seemed to get. His take was, have the paperwork sorted and you make it look like you know what you're doing.

Immediate boss Eddie's take was, have the paperwork sorted and you make it easier for the IRS to find whatever it is that they'd be looking for.

Jersey's take was, have the paperwork sorted and you can make the things you need to disappear without trying to make them disappear at the same time as asking a man in a suit how he takes his coffee.

Eddie didn't like other people being right, particularly when the other people were females barely out of their teens. Jersey didn't think she'd be there much longer.

She also drove parcels for an internet delivery service. Sometimes she'd get a text to go pick up a parcel at another couriers' house, sometimes to collect at a customers' address. It all worked off barcodes printed off the internet, scanned with her smartphone. She never saw any of the people who ran the company, Crrs, and was paid directly to her bank by way of an opaque formula based on parcel mile divided by parcel minute.

When she wasn't couriering, or filing she was tutoring in French and Spanish via Virtual Rawlplug. Virtual Rawlplug 'plugged the gaps in the schedules of the busy'. It would monitor subscribers' schedules and GPS locations to identify gaps that it would fill. Never a dull moment, as the jingle went.

Jersey would call up subscribers who'd selected language practice with a 'Hola' or "*Je m'appelle Jersey, ca va?*" Mostly they treated her like she was trying to sell them insurance, but she got to flirt in a foreign language one in every ten or twenty. She gave Virtual Rawlplug about six months before it folded; she'd learnt that people valued their gaps.

Tuesdays and Wednesdays, she played guitar and sang in bars downtown. She didn't get paid except in beers and nachos, but maybe she'd get discovered one day. She tried out some original numbers amongst the covers, studying the drinkers and diners as she sang words written by her, to melodies written by her.

She expected all eyes to turn, expressions saying "this isn't Dylan," or "this isn't Springsteen." But drinkers continued to chug beer, diners to chat and chew. It was odd, slipping in her own compositions below the radar. She felt like she'd just impersonated somebody from the Rock and Roll Hall of Fame and gotten away with it.

She entered competitions, did surveys, and collected coupons. She wanted to work her way up to mystery shopper.

She also volunteered for medical trials but vowed that if she ever found herself actually taking any medicines, she'd pack her bags and go back to Minnesota. Then she knew that barrels were having their bottoms scraped. But she didn't mind being wired up and asked questions. Quite the reverse.

The advert was small and vague with, at the bottom, "School of Cognitive Psychology" which meant they probably weren't going to put anything in her bloodstream. She went through a basic psychometric and then, two days later, received an invite to a gymnasium hall in a local high school, not even in the university proper. No needles, no tablets, no medicines of any kind, no electrodes, nothing intrusive. Just thirty minutes at a computer terminal and then a structured questionnaire. Out in an hour. Fifty dollars. Not great, but easy enough. And the time she spent earning it meant she wasn't spending it.

She signed the waiver forms and the confidentiality agreement and found herself in a booth made out of grey, brown chipboard with the oldest computer she'd probably ever seen. Pity's sake, it had a CRT monitor. She'd seen pictures, but she wracked her brains as to whether she'd ever actually seen one before in the flesh.

She stared at the screen for a moment. Half an hour, or at least twenty exchanges. Sounded easy, but sitting there, in a booth...

As nothing had appeared on her screen yet, she assumed that she must be one of the fifty percent who had to start the conversation. She tried to think of a good opening gambit.

What's your name?

A moment later the reply came back, flashing across the screen.

tobias

Thirty minutes, fifty dollars. Easy.

How old are you?

hey is this some kinda grooming???

Jersey ran her tongue over her teeth. She hadn't expected the system to be programmed so... aggressively.

No, just asking. What are you up to?

The response came back like a bullet.

hanging out on pinboard thought thatd be obvious how else are we talking???

Jersey knew that she'd have to assess the conversation and hadn't been sure what that could mean. There was something slightly sarcastic about the system. She wondered whether everybody was getting this treatment.

What's 'Pinboard'?

whaaa??????

She sensed she needed another tack.

My name's Jersey Child. I'm 26 and I live in Baltimore but I'm from Minnesota. My last holiday I went to Atlantic City and won a hundred dollars on the slots.

A pause.

my names tobias garrard i'm 14 and i live in london my last holiday was litter picking on the moon

Litter picking on the Moon?

it was dads idea it sucked

Jersey was beginning to enjoy her absurdist exchange.

You don't sound so into it?

not my fault my dads gene garrard

Jersey replied with a single question mark, as much querying where the punctuation should be as its meaning.

as in garrardwear

"As in Garrardwear." Jersey stared at the words. She felt she was being caught out.

What's garrardwear?

what planet are you from??????

No, really, what is it?

my dad invented it

But what is it?

hey are you typing this or are you thinking so slow????

Tobias, I'd really like to know what Garrardwear is. Please tell me.

come on you must have heard of it nanoengineered fabric reacts to temperature and humidity the fibers expand when its cold to keep you warm when it'?s hot they narrow to let your skin breathe

That's clever

i thought everybodys heard my dads sales pitch about how we were all walking the cornish coast when I was a baby and I kept throwing my jumper off when the sun came out and clinging to it when it went in and dad thought he had something already in development that could make a jumper warm when it was cold and cold when it was warm jesus don'?t you have technology in baltimore????

Jersey smiled. Either the person typing or the person programming had a sour streak to them.

So, tell me about litter picking on the moon?

youre typing arent you??? you must be real backward in baltimore who types any more?????

This was getting weirder by the exchange.

Everybody types

do not

Tell me about your holiday

i wanted to go skiing in the arctic but dads really into the environment and since the moon was opened up for tourism hes been campaigning how its mans last desert and all the crap thats been dropped and left up there should be cleaned up so we had to spend a month clearing it up

A pause, and then another burst of text

whole family but his publicity

Save the whale, huh?

Jersey wondered where chatty may get her, but all it got was:
save the whale where are you from the twenty-first century????

And then a buzzer rang and they had to leave their screens.

She spent half an hour on her questionnaire filling it out diligently and methodically. Her conclusions were ambiguous. She didn't think that her conversation could have been with a computer program as what she was told was way too absurd, but absurdity with some internal logic, a consistency to it. And, for a computer program it seemed to cope when she referred it back to its baffling claims about holidays on the Moon, and she'd read enough about artificial intelligence to know that was a problem. But, also, she thought the responses were far too fast for a human to type. So, she didn't know what to think.

On balance, she ticked the "human" box and went on her way, fifty dollars up, which was barely breaking even, but hey, better than Minnesota. Perhaps she could turn it into a song....

NOT ONLY WAS CARTER Tearne clever, he knew he was clever which doesn't always add up to the same thing.

If Carter Tearne hadn't known he was clever, or at least not kept it at the front of his mind so much, perhaps he wouldn't have been so annoying and would have had more friends. But if he had had more friends maybe he wouldn't have come up with the Metababel.

What was the Metababel?

A computer?

No, although it was realized physically and had shape and size it was nearer to a computer program than an actual computer.

No, scrub that: it was more like an entire programming language, but actual, real. In the sense that you could touch it, although Carter wouldn't have let you.

On second thoughts, that didn't really describe it either. It wasn't really a new language: it was more fluid, more flexible than that. A language that allowed the computer to develop its own idiolect, its own idioms, its own meaning.

It was a language beyond languages. If it hadn't already been taken as a term, he would have called it a metalanguage. But whereas ML's evaluation strategies, parametric polymorphism, and pattern matching, were encapsulated within its deep code, Carter Tearne couldn't point to particular lines of symbols and say, "that does this." His creation was more like a seed, self-replicating, growing as it saw fit.

Even Carter Tearne didn't really know what his Metababel was capable of. It didn't have a defined purpose or end point. In point of fact, it probably counted as much as a discovery as an invention. So, for all he knew, maybe it would map out the future. Or the secret of eternal youth. Or God's phone number.

He'd been working on it for eight years. Carter Tearne was twenty-three.

It was late when he got the call from Bangalore. Bangalore processed the data, wrote it up into charts and graphs, bulked up bullet points and text messages into pages and paragraphs. Bangalore got a cut of the research funding, but none of the credit for the papers it produced. Carter Tearne had the Metababel engaged on research projects funded by the U.S. Department of Energy, the U.S. Fish and Childlife Service, the Bureau of Educational and Cultural Exchanges, the U.S. Institute of Peace, the U.S. Air Force Office of Scientific Research, the European Research Council, and a dozen other funding bodies around the globe. Bangalore was cheap, so cheap that Carter had forgotten Bangalore's name.

"Where are you calling from?" Carter asked, having failed to catch the name. He rubbed the sleep from his eyes and focused on the brown face on the screen in front of him. He could have put his glasses on but didn't want people to know that he wore lenses during the day.

"I am calling from Bangalore. It's the Turing Test research project. Baltimore. We have a glitch."

Carter struggled to separate the words out into separate sentences; they came at him as a blur.

"Glitch? What kind of glitch?"

"Glitch with the results."

"What kind of glitch?" Was he repeating himself? And what time was it?

"We have one too many results."

One too many results? That didn't sound too much of a problem.

"No, no. You are not understanding," the brown face implored. "We have had one more experimental result than the program has had."

Words were being chosen here that Carter felt had been selected to obscure rather than illuminate what was going on.

"You mean a conversation was logged for which there is no file?"

"Exactly."

Carter shrugged. "System trying to save two conversations at exactly the same moment, one gets overwritten? A caching issue?" He knew he hadn't convinced himself and so wouldn't have come anywhere near convincing Bangalore.

"No, no. You are not understanding. A conversation happened, exchanges were made, but exchanges were not with the Metababel."

"How can there have been a conversation if not with the program? That's what the conversations are with. No program, no conversation. I don't understand. You're going to need to check this."

Carter had his finger near the button to kill the conversation and Bangalore knew it.

"I have. I have been checking for six hours. Poring through the log files. I only call you when I am absolutely sure."

Carter's fingers went back to drumming, around but no longer on the off button.

"Send them over."

He breakfasted on black coffee and grapefruit, went for a run, shot hoops for half an hour then returned to his apartment. He spent the rest of the day trying to solve the riddle thrown at him by Bangalore, which, after poring through the logs and deciding that, as what he was looking for was an absence of record, so by definition wouldn't be there to be found, took him to a lock-up in Hoboken.

To the Metababel.

To look at the Metababel was at once a unique experience and nothing special, a grey translucent mass that filled a metal-sided tub the size of a small car to a depth of about three feet. At one end the Metababel was pure homogeneous jelly, but along the length of the tub, the jelly started to become crystalline, veins and lines forming in it like contour lines on a map or cracks in ice. These merged and solidified so, in the course of five feet or so, what had been a single fluid amorphous mass was now a web of hair-like strands, the color of graphite. These were then attached to more traditional circuit boards and thence to conventional processing units that sat alongside the tub. Traditional wiring looms then joined up with screens and keyboards.

Carter Tearne stared into the mass. The mass through which, but not with which, Jersey Child had had her conversation. Thirty-five exchanges; four hundred and thirteen words. His eyes slid from the dark grey hairs to the blue-grey synaptic jelly. If he'd been trying to work out the logic of the system's responses then possibly, just possibly, he could map the system states back and try to figure out how and why one system state followed on from the last. Putting aside the difficulty of dealing with a near infinity of data for each system state lasting a fraction of a moment.

But these were responses generated without system states. Generated via the Metababel, not by it, Bangalore had said. He wasn't even sure that made any sense as a description of the problem. There was nothing to find. So he went back to his theory of a caching error; the system had simply failed or forgotten to record what happened. Like when you go downstairs and forget what you're there for. If it can happen to a human, supposedly so many orders of magnitude more intelligent than any of humankind's creations, why shouldn't it happen to the Metababel? Carter Tearne wondered whether there was a research project in it and how he could get funding. What about The National Institute of Mental Health?

If Carter Tearne was as clever as he thought he was then this was the moment to prove it. But he had made the first and most catastrophic error of his life. He approached the problem from the point of view of solving an error, identifying the root cause of a problem. Instead of which he should have been identifying the greatest discovery of Mankind.

Carter Tearne never solved his glitch.

TOBIAS GARRARD PULLED OFF the 'phones, carefully clipping the cranial pads closed. It was a fifth generation device, costly and bleeding edge, with blink technology that allowed you to form your response on screen from thought alone and then, with another blink, verify and send. He could sit there, compose and send, while all around him were still muttering text into throat mikes. Fourth generation. To be honest, it was distracting.

Not that Tobias Garrard ever needed to be distracted by other people, even though his in-eye news ticker had announced the previous week that the population of the Earth had just reached twelve billion people. The Garrards had everything they needed on their island community, a floating man-made atoll, near silent but still less than ten minutes from London Estuary Airport.

They were lucky, and he knew it. Not just lucky that his father had invented Garrardwear, but that Garrardwear couldn't simply be produced on the ubiquitous 3-D printers. They'd flown to Sydney last winter, six hours, longest he'd ever spent on a plane. It felt longer when his father told them that the plane's engines had been produced on a 3-D printer; silica-plastic hybrids now meant you could. Quite why they'd hadn't taken the hypersonic escaped him; couldn't have been the price.

Except he knew the real reason and it would have something to do with carbon or plastic or sustainability. Like their trip to help clear the Moon. His father had done something similar on Everest as a student and wanted his entire family to share in the earnestness.

"But if you can't print out Garrardwear, who's going to buy it?"

The day before their trip, Elizabeth, his sixteen-year-old sister had scanned herself and had the printer give her a whole new wardrobe, some off the shelf designs, some that she'd drawn herself. Soft pseudocottons; smooth pseudosilks. Quite literally seamless.

"It does its job and it's the only thing that does its job, so there's a demand for it," his father had explained. "Plus it keeps people in work. You don't know what it was like. Two hundred and fifty years ago, the north of England was full of cotton mills and people working them. We made cloth for the world. Now, we're one of the last weavers left. We're twenty-second century Silas Marners."

Tobias Garrard looked out towards London, the city that had lifted itself above the rising waters. The outline of skyscrapers, joined together at the shoulder, could be seen on the western horizon. Traditionally the area to the east of London had been poor, caught in the city's effluent and pollution. By rights, this should be far from prime real estate. But ionization engines deflected the airstream, buffering them against the aircraft noise to boot. A flick of a switch could also bring up holographic birdlife over the Thames estuary. Swans, cormorants, gulls. Flocks of small birds, individual larger ones. Tobias toggled between a vee of ducks and a hunting bird hovering solo.

Save the whale, huh.

The dialogue he had had with—what did she call herself? Jersey Child, twenty-six, from Baltimore—preyed on his mind. There was no way on Earth that he's been talking to somebody from the past. From the Twenty-first Century. Was there?

He Ultragoogled the name. A plethora of near-simultaneous images, tens of thousands across a fraction of a second, blurred together on his eye-screen, the replacement lens that also corrected a slight astigmatism. His physiological reactions honed Ultragoogle's selection to a workable, visible shortlist.

Lots of current and recent web traffic didn't seem to fit. Many other pages had been pulled out of the Worldwide Internet Archive begun in 2028. Many just seemed random and arbitrary, restaurant reviews, company listings, social chatter long since gone stale. Twitter? He'd vaguely heard of that.

It would cost him fifty Europas, but he went on to FindMe. A face appeared, devoid of body. *Jersey Child, Baltimore, Twenty-six*, he thought, enunciating the words in his mind. The face nodded, turned and fled.

A moment later his field of vision was filled with four bleary faces of young women, apart from one who looked wired. He hadn't considered the time difference. *Anybody been to Atlantic City recently?* he thought and blinked.

The burble that came back seemed to extend from "huh" to "what the...?" "Atlantic City got washed away fifty years ago,"? he heard one of the Jersey Childs say.

The eye-screen went blank, apart from the message that another seven possible Jersey Childs were offline in the Baltimore area. He'd asked for Baltimore, not the Baltimore area.

He went back to Ultragoogle. Way down the list he found a reference to a singer-songwriter Jersey Child. A minor album track on a minor album from a minor artist: "Talking to Toby from 2121."

He listened through to it; there was only audio available. Plenty of stuff they hadn't talked about, and the date was a few years out, but, there in the chorus: *Soon, We'll be litter picking on the Moon...*

Jersey Child had been dead for going on seventy years; a lost voice.

"What would you do if you were talking to somebody from the past?" he asked his father that evening.

"Boil the water before you drink it," he said after a moment's thought.

"No, what about from a hundred years ago. Twenty-first century."

"Early or late?"

Tobias Garrard shrugged. "Early. She still typed."

His father frowned, not understanding. "Have they abandoned New York? Has Tokyo fallen?"

"I don't think so."

"Tell them the tipping point has not been reached, but they won't see it until its too late unless there's a paradigm shift. Is this a college thing?"

"Paradigm shift?"

"Everything they think is important isn't. They have to change how they think, how they see the world."

His eyes had gone glassy; Tobias could tell he was going to speechify. His father, of course, thought this was some kind of thought experiment. "Not everything about the modern world is great. We haven't got everything right and they didn't get everything wrong. There were jobs making things, transporting things, selling things. Now we have almost everything we need printed, on printers that have been made by other printers. High days and holidays are now the everyday."

"Nobody types anymore."

His father's expression showed that he at once agreed while simultaneously thinking that his son had entirely missed the point.

"President Kennedy, a hundred and fifty years ago, said they were doing something because it was hard, not because it was easy. Hard work is its own reward; we've kind of forgotten that. Learning by neural implant rather than putting the hours in."

Tobias sat and watched his own reflection in the glass of their living space, the waves on the water a ghostly overlay. He wondered whether it would be better to be Jersey Child back then or Tobias Garrard now. One of the seven, eight billion, or one of the twelve. Save the whale, he thought. You can't get everything off a 3D-printer.

"What was the thing they were doing?" he asked. "The thing that was hard?"

"Going to the Moon."

"Yeah," he agreed after a moment's reflection. "That was hard."

THE END

ROBERT BAGNALL's short fiction has been accepted by a variety of magazines and anthologies. Hailing from Torquay, Devon, England, you can find Robert's sci-fi blog at meschera.blogspot.co.uk.

PUTTING IT RIGHT

Gustavo Bondoni

"I'M NOT IMPRESSED. TWO and a half millennia and all they have to show for it is *this*? Even those upstarts should have done better. Did they learn nothing from us?"

A thin, greasy rain fell from an inky sky, illuminated both by the distant glow of the city and the much nearer lights that lit a large painting of some sort, with disturbingly familiar symbols on it. The buildings around them seemed to be made of brick and wood—not all that different from the ones that dotted their own cities—but were barely standing. The surface on which they stood was composed of gravel and mud.

"Don't judge us just yet. This is just an old steel mill, abandoned for sixty years, since the last big war. I think you'll like the city a little better." Tullis was a short man, pale and with nearly no hair, but he was tolerated because he professed to have the knowledge that could bring back the Rasna into this strange world where steel mills were abandoned. The claim he made of being a descendant of long-dead Tarchna itself was more difficult to verify, but in the end, it made no difference. Tullis would never be allowed to take part in the new council.

Cutu Camna gave the man a hard look. "Then show us these wonders," he said. He'd been convinced to come here at a time when his people needed him the most and had talked his two most trusted lieutenants, his sister Thana and his house general Marce Apucu, into accompanying him on his fantastic quest. If he were wrong, they would kill him themselves—a worthy fate for one who abandons his people.

"My car is just around the corner."

The man—could this one truly be the latest scion of the great Tarchnas—led them through the drizzle to a small metal carriage with four hinged doors. He stood beside one entrance and ushered the three Rasna into the vehicle's bowels. They'd hardly had time to adjust to the unusual odor of the interior when the chariot growled—presumably under their host's guidance—and shot away at an impossible speed to join a group of similar contrivances on a wide paved road. The bag full of tiny vials of blood clinked on Thana's lap.

Tullis seemed unconcerned by the enormous velocity. He nearly turned in his seat as he spoke to them. "This is a day I've worked for all my life. My grandmother was a Tarquini, you know. I always thought that Etruscans were truly responsible for the great age of Italian ascendancy. Romans were nothing but an Etruscan city, after all—and not even a pure-blooded one!"

Etruscans, Cutu thought. He gritted his teeth at the knowledge that nothing was sacred. The very name of the Rasna has been desecrated by Roman influence.

But even in his own day, it had been obvious to Cutu that the Romans would not be stopped. That had been the only reason he hadn't killed this weak, foolish man when he'd first appeared with his strange story and stranger proposal.

Whether or not he'd been wise to spare him would be for history to decide.

ROME.

THE WORD ITSELF was enough to send any military man who loved the Twelve Cities of the Rasna into spasms. The general public might hate the Romans as conquerors and a threat to the normal process of life, but military men had a special loathing for the southern invaders.

Their motives were simple: there was no way to explain to the council why, with fewer men and similar technology and tactics, the Roman armies were driving the Rasna back towards the mountains in the north. No reasonable explanation could be given for the fact that, of the Twelve Cities, only four were still under the council's control.

The truth was simple enough, of course, the Roman armies, though essentially Etrurian in nature, were better prepared, better drilled and better led.

Any general who admitted that, though, would soon find himself staring out at the world from the top of a spear, without the benefit of having his open-eyed head attached to the rest of his body.

Cutu and Marce Apucu felt the loathing as they watched the inexorable advance of the cloud of dust. That morning, it had been a slight discoloration on the southern horizon. By midday, it had grown, and the grey cloud ahead seemed to be as high as the sun.

Three hours after noon, Cutu could taste the dust on the wind. The Romans were nearly upon them, and the city at their backs, fair Pupluna, the port celebrated in song and verse, would be theirs within days.

Cutu ground his teeth, but his ragged men, exhausted from battle and running retreat, would be of little use against that implacable foe.

"I can help you."

The voice came from the tree line beside the road and spoke in strangely accented Greek. Cutu made no move, except to lift one finger, signal to Marce that his men should surround the trees. The house general, likewise, didn't even shift in his saddle as he signed for the troop movement. Moments later, a single sputtering man emerged from concealment at the point of a spear.

His strange form of dress made it clear that he wasn't Rasna, but there was no question of him being Roman. His skin was white as the moon, and his hair was pale yellow. "Don't kill him yet," Cutu said, noticing at the same time that the man showed no signs of being able to comprehend Rasna. Just another barbarian, *the noble thought,* I shouldn't even waste my time speaking to him.

But the man intrigued him. What was he doing out here? Where did he come from with his strange attire, close-fitting leg-wear, and strangely closed tunic? There was a mystery here, and Cutu could not afford mysteries, not with a Roman army bearing down on him.

He spoke to the man in Greek, but, he knew, with a much better accent. Rasna nobility prided themselves on knowing the great tongue. "Who are you?"

The man swallowed and tried to move away from the spears, but the guards simply pressed forward. "My name is Doctor Tullis. I need to talk to the council of the Twelve Cities."

His atrocious Greek was not the reason Cutu laughed. "The council, you say? They're a bit busy with the Roman invasion. Most of them have taken their families north—some have even gone to sea. You will not be visiting with the council, even if I decide not to kill you."

"You wouldn't kill me. You're Etruscan."

The two men with spears nearly ran him through. Only a signal from Marce saved the interloper. Cutu regarded the man coldly. "Never call us that. That word is used by our enemies only. We are the Rasna."

"I'm sorry," the man said. He was breathing hard, sweating profusely. "If you are Rasna, then you will not harm me. My grandmother was a Tarquini."

Cutu studied him. He claimed to descend from the Tarchna family— the oldest and most noble of Rasna clans—and yet he had none of their features. No sharp nose, no dark brown hair. "You lie. And your dishonesty will bring you death."

"Wait! I'm telling the truth, but you must listen. My story may be a little difficult to believe, but it is true. I come from a time more than two thousand years from now." He paused as if convinced that he would die then. When nothing happened, he breathed deeply and continued. "I was part of a research team, and we were using gravitational density to try to bend space in order to travel faster than light. It didn't work, but space-time got bent in a different direction, and we realized that we were actually moving along the temporal axis. So, you understand what that means?"

"Not a word of it. And if you value your life, I would advise you to correct that situation as quickly as you can." Cutu was intrigued, but if the man were unable to explain within the next hour or so, Roman outriders would be on them, making the whole thing moot.

"WELCOME TO THE LAB," Tullis said. He touched a wall and illumination flooded the room, white light like the middle of spring, but Cutu could see no flames, and there was certainly no flickering.

The three Rasna looked around. The room was stark. Sheets of brushed metal lined the walls and the furniture to waist height. Above that, gleaming tile reflected the light back at them. Even Thana's dark beauty seemed to pale in the bright illumination. "What is it you do here?" she whispered.

"It's closed, actually. Demonstrators shut us down. No one knows I'm back yet." The voice came from a woman who must have been seventy years old, with deep lines on her skin and strangely flattened features framed by her silver hair. Despite her strange appearance, Cutu immediately bowed his head to the venerable woman: she must be the head of a truly great family to have been cared for this long. He couldn't recall having seen anyone as old as this, ever. Not even among the greatest of the Rasna.

He was surprised that her Greek was almost as bad as Tullis'.

But Thana ignored her. As head of the Camna clan following the strange disappearance of her cousin, she would never acknowledge an equal without a proper introduction. Instead, she turned to Tullis. "Is this where you bend time?"

The woman laughed. "No, my child. This is where we copy people. My name is Doctor Han, by the way."

"Thana of the Camna, great family of Pupluna," Cutu's sister replied formally. "The Camna are happy to accept your hospitality." The two women clasped hands and Thana seemed to relax. "How is it, this copying of people?"

Tullis and the woman exchanged a few words in a guttural language. Cutu tensed and thought that if that was the language of this place and time, then there could be little of beauty or worth in it. They needed Rasna leadership even more than he'd originally guessed from seeing their rudimentary buildings and dirty city. Two thousand years should have brought them closer to the gods, and their cities should have been spires of ethereal beauty, not the solid, grimy thing he'd seen so far. Of course, what could one expect from a world in which the practical, short-sighted Romans could push aside an enlightened people like the Rasna?

He studied their hosts. Once again, the word that had been a constant since the moment they'd been whisked out of the city of Pupluna by some unknown force under Tullis control emerged, the only word that could explain how Cutu felt: unimpressive. Shouldn't people with two thousand years to grow closer to the knowledge of the gods look the part. These two were just— people. They seemed to come to a decision on something as he watched and the woman turned to him.

"We copy people by rebuilding them from tiny pieces of their bodies. We have enough within the vials of blood you took to recreate a hundred and fifty of the great men and women of the Etruscan nobility. They will live again, two thousand years after the Romans wiped them off the face of the world."

"They are alive today. This blood was taken from them this afternoon."

"The blood was taken from people thousands of years dead. Only Doctor Tullis' little machine could get them here—and we can't bring them all back. The power use would be noticed."

Tullis, beside her, nodded. Cutu assumed that that meant he agreed.

Thana spoke up. Her face had been turning deeper and deeper red as the conversation progressed. Cutu suppressed a smile; the two Doctors—and how curious it was that men and women could have the same first name in this time. Another Roman atrocity, surely—were about to feel his sister's wrath, something universally feared since the girl was five summers old. "This is monstrous," she said. "Abomination. How can you insult the gods this way? Manus and Mania will never stand for it, even if Uni does. Every educated person knows that, to create even a weak semblance of life in any but the natural way, one must pay for it with a strong life force. Mortals cannot win when dealing with the lords of the land of the dead!"

Silence followed this pronunciation, and it stretched for an uncomfortable period as the echoes of her words died down on the hard surfaces of the room. Finally, when Cutu's nerves could hardly stand it, the silence was broken.

Doctor Han chuckled, a dry, soft sound. "Child, since the time of your birth, many things have been discovered, and many things have been disproved. The existence of gods is not among those that have been disproved to everyone's satisfaction, but I can assure you than no reliable record of a god acting in the real world exists. Not one, not ever."

"I have seen, with my own eyes—"

"Yes, yes, of course, but still, I can assure you there is no risk."

"I will not be a part of this."

Doctor Han looked sad. "Before you take such a momentous decision, can I at least explain what we plan to do?" The venerable woman seemed to take Thana's silence for assent. "We will create exact copies of the individuals from cells within their bodies. We will not use donor cells from other people to germinate them with, but make functioning stem-cell copies of their beings."

The other Doctor, Tullis, interrupted in the guttural tongue again. Han looked irked but continued. "What I mean is that the copies will be perfect in all regards. We won't have to ask permission of any gods other than the laws of nature itself."

"When you delve into the gods' domain, they are involved, whether you summon them deliberately or not." Thana looked peeved but deflated. It wasn't often that someone laughed her off when she was angry.

"Where are your gods then? Where were they when the Romans overran Etruria?"

Silence met the question.

"I thought so," the wrinkled old woman continued. "Now, do you want to know how we're going to do this?"

Cutu spoke. "I probably wouldn't understand how, but I'd like to know why."

The female doctor chuckled again. "Oh, that's easy. It's because we hate the world."

"Now…"

"Oh, shut up Tullis." She turned to face the gathered Rasna. "Tullis has obsessed with the Etruscans for years, but would never have gone ahead with this if the university hadn't pulled his funding after the little time and space mix up. The people who controlled the resources thought it sounded a little too good to be true."

"I proved them wrong."

"Yes, but it took you six years to get any meaningful result— and if you hadn't been a spoiled inheritor, you'd still be teaching." When she was satisfied that the man would let her continue, she did. "And I am angry because this country put me in prison for performing perfectly legitimate research on stem cells, in which no human or animal was ever harmed. Ridiculous. And worthy of the most severe form of retaliation. I don't really care whether the Etruscans rule us or some Zulu war leader—I just need access to Tullis' little time machine to delete a few politicians when no one knew who they were, and no bodyguards guarded them. If your little-cloned descendants inherit the world thanks to the way we manipulate things, I don't really care."

Cutu had no idea what she was talking about but liked the tone. It was obvious that this woman fully expected to succeed, nothing more and nothing less. She spoke as if all that was left to sort out were unimportant little details. "I will take part," he said.

Thana glowered at him but did not command him to stand down. She also, he noted, refrained from volunteering.

"We actually want you to teach the children what it means to be Etruscan."

"Never. I will teach them what it means to be Rasna."

"All right, Rasna then."

"Agreed, but I also want a piece of me to be a part of the ruling class when it is grown."

Han nodded. It was obvious that it made no difference to her at all.

"YOUR CLONE SHOULD BE viable in about an hour," the female Doctor told him.

Cutu waited; he paced. They'd finally shown him some wonders worthy of the name, worthy of the two thousand years that had passed. A box with moving pictures, inside which the entire world seemed to fit. A machine that produced ghostly voices, despite no one being behind it.

And most of all, a double eyepiece into which one could look. The Doctors had assured him that what he was seeing were actually things that lived inside his body, tiny parts of his own makeup. He was enthralled as he watched them float around for hours.

They'd explained that, at first, the clone would be a few cells only. And then they showed him a cell in the "microscope." They'd explained that he would not be able to recognize himself in the cells, but he felt certain that he'd know when his new incarnation began.

He waited impatiently. Surely, an hour or more had passed. Surely it was ready. Yes, it must have been closer to two hours.

Suddenly the world spun around him, and he collapsed. Through closing eyes and weakening of the body, he saw Thana kneel beside him. "You fool," she said in Rasna, "you should have known that there is no cheating of Manus and Mania. You've thrown your life away." A single tear ran down her cheek, reflecting blindingly in the stark light.

He tried to tell her to take care of his new incarnation, but couldn't summon the strength to do so. Behind Thana, he saw Marce fall heavily to the ground, and then darkness took him.

***

THRESU KARKANA WATCHED THE dust cloud approach. With the disappearance of Cutu and Marce Apucu, he was the last of the house generals that remained to the Ransa.

But luck was with the people of the Twelve Cities today. The removal of the old guard, so ineffective against the Roman advance, had cleared the way for him. And he knew how to defeat the Romans. He would use their own tactics against them, and rout them by sowing confusion in their ranks. The very ordered, structured nature of the Roman military would prove their undoing on the battlefield today, and on many battlefields to come. He would not need to stop until the Romans had paid for every drop of Etruscan blood—including the ones he'd given that deserter Cutu and his pet warlock—many times over.

He'd cracked the enigma of how to defeat Rome, how to keep them from overrunning the Italian peninsula. And not only would he use it to crush them, but he also vowed to share it with their allies to the South, and any other enemies of Rome, or people threatened by the upstart city.

The name of Thresu Karkana would go down in history.

He turned to give the order to redeploy his troops into the formations that would crush the oncoming legions…

And suddenly, the world spun around him, and he collapsed. He felt a part of his essence being torn painfully away for some unknown purpose, and darkness closed in.

But he was a good Rasna and, as he died, his thoughts were not on his own agony, but on the fact that he'd failed his people. The Romans would proceed unchecked.

And then there were no more thoughts.

THE END

GUSTAVE BONDONI is an Argentine writer with over a hundred stories published in fourteen countries, in seven languages, and a winner in the National Space Society's "Return to Luna" contest as well as the SF Reader short fiction contest (2014) and the Marooned Award for Flash Fiction (2008). His short fiction has appeared in the *Texas STAAR English Test* cycle, *The Rose & Thorn*, *Albedo One*, *The Best of Every Day Fiction*, and many others.

THE ROAD TO UTOPIA PLAIN

Rick Kennett

Previously published in *EIDOLON* #15, 1994.

SOMETIMES IT'S CAUSED BY solar flares and sometimes by the passing echoes of distant novae. And sometimes it happens for no reason at all.

Five seconds before *Utopia Plain* kicked back into real space just beyond the orbit of Saturn, a subspace distortion wave shocked through the solar system at many times the speed of light. In that instant, time and space flexed and altered. The starship's exit hole stretched along her trajectory so that she bulleted back into reality, not in safe, empty space but on an imminent collision course with Mars.

Gravity rings back-rippled down her hull in frantic deceleration. Inwardly rotating, tilted to their maximum, they pushed simultaneously against every atom passing through them, causing no g-forces within. Her course began to alter, slowly. But Mars, in less than thirty seconds, had swelled on the ship's screens from a distant star, to a rushing disc, to a very solid planet.

Thirty seconds later she clipped the western edge of the atmosphere. Settlements at Cassius and Neith to the west, and on the Isidis and Elysium Plains in the east, saw her as a flash of white and silver racing an arc across their skies as she ricocheted off the atmosphere and belted back into space.

UTOPIA PLAIN DROPPED OUT of the pink noonday sky of Mars and belly-cradled in Styx City, thirteen hundred kilometers southeast of the rocky desert from which the starship took her name.

Medical personnel boarded and removed five injured crew members. Shortly afterward, the rest of the crew left for a suddenly well-deserved shore leave. Lieutenant Cy De Gerch, the ship's second-in-command and the second last to leave before repair technicians took charge, stepped through the forward hatch and walked down the pressure tunnel with her bag slung over her shoulder. Captain Brown ambled down after her, joining his young lieutenant at the spaceport windows where they looked ruefully back at the scorched, buckled metal of their ship.

"A close one," said Brown.

De Gerch said nothing to this. There was nothing to say. She was the navigator and knew intimately how close it'd been. It wasn't just atmospheric burning and damage, though there was enough of that in evidence. The ring-drive had had the guts pulled out of it—had, in fact, begun to discharge energy through the hull, as the damage showed. The results of a full burn-out would've been catastrophic.

"Funny how these things happen, Cy," said Brown. "Something that's commonplace, routine, done a thousand times, one day nearly kills you."

De Gerch nodded thoughtfully. "A minute either way on our emergence and we would never have known how close we'd come to dying." She shivered. "All the 'nearlys' that happen every day we're never aware of." Abruptly formal she said, "Permission to leave, sir."

"Permission granted. Going home?"

"To Phobos? Probably. Haven't seen Dad in months. He'd probably like to know his only daughter is still alive. Then again, I might just go back to my place at South Mie and hermit. We've got twenty days. I'll see." De Gerch snapped a salute, hefted her bag and hurried off.

As her footsteps receded others approached. Doctor Norsk, gray and smiling, said, "Five out of five, Ralph. Styx Hospital should be releasing the last of our injured in an hour."

"We were lucky today, Ben."

"Depends how you look at it. I'd rather it'd been one of those 'could've beens' we never know about."

"That's what Cy just said."

"Then young De Gerch must be a philosopher as well as everything else the Gartino geneticists made her."

One of Norsk's paramedics popped her head through the doorway leading to the next landing cradle. "Shuttle to Earth's boosting in fifteen minutes, Doctor."

"Thank you, Helen," Norsk replied, then to the Captain, "It's been a long time since I was home. I've had a fifth generation added to my family since we left." He produced a data wafer from his pocket. "I picked this up from the Comm Office on the way back from the hospital. Seems my great granddaughter in Montreal had a baby boy a month ago."

"Congratulations, Ben," said Brown, knowing that when Norsk, the only Earther in his crew, spoke of months it was certain he meant Earth's 30-day version, not the local 57 variety. "Everyone seems to be going back to family."

"Except you?"

"Well, I thought Evelyn would meet me here. Or I would've got some message from her. I suppose there was nothing for me at the Comm Office?"

"Sorry. No."

"Not to worry. For the moment I've got *her* to babysit." He glanced meaningfully through the window at his ship.

As Norsk left, he gave the captain a salute that was more an airy wave.

Brown watched his friend depart with a tolerant smile, knowing Norsk would never be Navy if he lived a second, 100 solar years.

CY DE GERCH, WHO hadn't quite lived eighteen solar years and genetically couldn't help but be Navy, had picked up two wafers at the spaceport, and as the monorail slid out of Styx City for South Mie, she fished in her tunic pocket for them. The one she brought out had been sent from Phobos. She thumbed it on. Its surface glistened, swirled and formed into the thin face of a middle-aged man. He smiled and said: "Welcome home, Cy." A simple message from a straightforward man, her father. The face dissolved into a color swirl, ready to start again.

On impulse, Cy glanced upward through the window in the vain hope of catching a glimpse of the little moon she still called home. There was nothing to be seen in the daytime sky but wisps of white cloud.

The cityscape passed at a growing pace: the above-ground portions of buildings and dwellings, the marching line of windmill power plants and their wide swinging blades, the red sand roads, the balloon-wheel vehicles.

Faster and faster...the exit from the city's artificial gravity...the last buildings whizzing by, windmills flicking past like fence posts.

The outside blurred green and yellow with the glassed in farm lands of sugar beet, soybean, corn, and wheat. Then constant red, rushing red like gushing blood—the unadulterated surface of Mars.

The monorail swept out across the red wilderness, and in less than a minute was over the horizon and gone.

THE DOOR LOCK OF her subsurface flat identified her palm print with a cheery chime and opened.

She stopped and looked into the flat, looked carefully at everything in it.

It was all wrong. Not that anything had been disturbed, everything was in order. But it was the wrong order.

Two chairs faced each another where there should've been one, in the corner. Between these was a table; she had a table, yes, but this was a different color, a different shape. There was a large hologram hanging on the wall: Jos Manxman and herself two years ago, togged up in full vacuum suits, standing on the cone edge of Mount Olympus, the mighty volcano far to the east. Its crater stretched away in white clouds, lost over the horizon. "We're standing on the shores of space," Jos had said. They'd been twenty-five kilometers above the mean datum of Mars and in a virtual vacuum.

That holo was the one taken during a long hike during a long leave, the first of many such adventures they'd planned together for the discovery of their planet and each other, a first adventure which proved to be their only. That holo was the one which used to hang there, the one she'd taken down nearly a year ago and re-hung in her cabin aboard *Utopia Plain*.

Cy moved slowly into the room, running her hands over the furnishings. She glanced up the spiral stairs leading to the observation or sun room which protruded through the surface. Were there chairs up there? She didn't have chairs up there.

85

In the bedroom, she found the twin set she'd got rid of after Jos died. There were articles of clothing lying on the quilt: bright red blouse, yellow-slashed metallic skirt, bathrobe of chaotic color and pattern. Not her clothes. Too bright. More the thing untidy Jos with her liking for flashy—

Cy caught herself. These things had not been worn by Jos, had not been left there by Jos. Josephine Manxman was dead, had been dead a solar year.

In her clothes closet, she found her civilian wear stored more or less the way she'd left them sixty days ago. She hesitated with her hand on the door of the other closet, the one which should be empty.

Don't be silly, she told herself. She dived into her own closet and picked out some house clothes. It was while changing out of operational fatigues that Cy discovered the second data wafer she'd picked up at the spaceport. Puzzling. It'd been sent from the Zephyria Terraforming base down on the equator. She was sure she knew no one there. But there was no mistake. It had her name on it. Thumbing it, she watched with growing disbelief as the familiar head and shoulders of a young woman with auburn hair appeared and said, "My darling, I need to be with you soon. Especially after what nearly happened to you today. Your way of life frightens me sometimes. Cy, I have seven days leave, and I'll be on the evening northbound mono. If we have the strength later, as promised, we'll hike to Viking. Love you."

CY PACED THE MONORAIL platform, listening to her own loud breathing in her oxygen helmet. South Mie was a small settlement on the eastern edge of the Utopia Plain, huddling on the southern slopes of the massive Mie Crater. It sported no fancy pressurized station like the big towns, such as Styx City. South Mie was lucky to have artificial gravity.

At first, she'd been shocked, thinking the message a cruel hoax. Then replaying the wafer, again and again, she didn't know what to think. She'd called South Mie's administration and, using voice ID, accessed tenant information on her own flat. Who lived there? The computer had answered in deceptively human tones: "De Gerch, Cyleen J., Manxman, Josephine S." What are their occupations? The computer replied: "Lieutenant, Defence Force,

Interstellar Fleet. Geologist in Training, Department of the Environment, Zephyria."

She'd looked at the data wafer message for a long time, watched the face, heard the voice, looked at the holo on the wall, at the bright, flashy clothes scattered about the bedroom. As evening drew in, she'd donned her vacuum suit and gone outside.

Every now and again Cy stared down the monorail platform into the south which was now fading into deep black.

It has to be a hoax. In which case I'm acting like a fool coming here. But who could be so cruel? On the other hand, if it's true—No, it can't be. It's impossible. The dead don't come back in corporeal form. The dead don't make wafers. The dead don't travel about on the mono. And yet here I am, waiting.

It was curiosity, she told herself. *I'm just curious to see what might happen. But what if Jos does come? Maybe she hadn't been killed in that accident. I never saw the body. Of course not. No one had seen the body. There'd been nothing to see after that meteor had hit her scout ship.*

She was clutching at irrational straws and knew it.

Way down in the south was a faraway dot of light, coming nearer, growing larger, almost here, growing to a headlamp, slowing to a stop.

A figure alighted and moved down the platform towards her with that peculiar half shuffle denoting those recently returned to artificial gravity after a long period in the natural .38 g of Mars— such as might be experienced at the Zephyria Terraforming base.

Cy told herself not to be silly, that it couldn't be Jos, that it couldn't be, couldn't be, *couldn't,* and tried to ignore the fluttering in her stomach, the way her breathing grew faster in her mask.

Then the figure raised a hand and waved.

Dream-like, Cy began to move. Dream-like, rational thought was firmly suppressed. And Cy, still thinking *couldn't be, couldn't be, couldn't,* ran down the platform to hug Jos Manxman, returned who-cares-how from the dead.

CY DE GERCH AWOKE and for several seconds stared vacantly into the darkness.

Had it all been just an erotic dream? The joy of return, sharp and overpowering logic. Few words, their passion speaking all that was needed. Sex had them eventually tired and happy asleep in one another's arms.

She wavered between disappointment and fear: disappointment that she had dreamt it all, fear that she had not.

She reached out a hand, then pulled it back before it touched anything. *What if there's a skeleton lying beside me? What if it's something else entirely, pretending?* She was being irrational again. Yet to expect Jos to be there was equally so. Last night, physical sensation had been everything. Now, with the shock of surprise over and the lust in her blood gone, she had time to think.

Sliding quietly from beneath the covers, she made her way into the living room where she collided noisily with the table.

"Damn!" She fell back into a chair, holding a stubbed toe. She'd forgotten the altered layout of her flat. She listened for a full minute, but there was no reaction from Jos—

No! She got to her feet. That was not Jos. Jos Manxman was dead and spread thin in the asteroid belt, and that was not her in there. She had not spent half the night fucking her dead lover. She would march in there. She would turn on the light. She would say—

She had no idea what she would say. She sat down again.

"Code lights, wall, soft," she murmured, and the walls emitted a gentle glow. At least environmental verbal controls were still the same, she thought, regarding the room. It was like someone else's room with someone else's furniture, someone else's taste and someone else's way of arranging things. It was as if she were in the wrong place. It was as if she were the one—

She stopped, considered the thought a moment and laughed with the shock of so simple an understanding. Yes. That was it. Nothing was wrong. Nothing was out of place. Everything was as it should be, including Jos Manxman. She, Cy De Gerch, was the one out of place. She was the one who shouldn't be there. But how? The subspace distortion wave? Was she clutching again or was this the only thing that made halfway sense? Had that wave pushed time sideways?

Yes. She believed it. Yes. It had to be. Yes. This wasn't *what is*. This was *what could've been*.

Smiling, weeping unawares, Cy verballed off the lights and climbed back into bed with Jos, cuddling her warmth, burying her face in her auburn hair. "Don't ever go away from me again," she whispered into her ear.

***

THE UTOPIA PLAIN, AN immensity of rocky desert, stretched rust red before them in the freezing midday sun of the following day. Their destination, two hundred kilometers due west, was the historic landing site of Viking II, one of the first probes to reach Mars.

Jos had woken that morning with the sunrise and got ready for the hike, very matter of fact, not at all like someone returned from oblivion. Cy helped ready their vacuum suits and backpacks in a mechanical way, lost in a mixed sensation of joy and unreality, smiling like an idiot.

Before they left they touched base with South Mie admin for weather information. As Jos, awkward in her suit under artificial gravity, went through the airlock to the surface, Cy made a call to her captain's private number on her suit's radio. Neutrino beam communication needed no satellite relays but simply passed through solid matter, including whole planets, as if it wasn't there.

Unfortunately, Captain Brown wasn't there either. Just his receive-and-record signal. He was probably in a conference with the spaceport's repair people. She left a message: "I think that distortion wave has put us a whole other place than where we think we are. Check with Mr. Womac of the 5D Room."

There was a road of sorts, bulldozed west: packed sand and buried rock. They traveled with the long, easy lope appropriate to the Martian gravity, a cross between a step and a jump. The Utopia Plain was a sometimes undulating, more often flat expanse scattered with a monotony of rocks ranging from fist size to boulders. Very occasionally a hummock or knob would mark the remains of a long-dead volcano. "The Utopia Plain's main feature is that it's virtually featureless," said Jos, ever the new geologist. "Wind erosion's wiped off all the early craters. It's so old... Cy, you can almost feel the weight of time on the Utopia Plain."

Once in a long while one of the more recent impact sites—"Later craters," Jos called them—loomed over the horizon and became an occasion for comment. But as the day progressed they saved their breath for the hike and played popular and classical music through their helmet phones.

It was this isolation that gave Cy time to eventually come to terms with her situation and then to think a few questions through to their inevitable dead ends. One was: Why had Jos left fleet training to become a geologist? Washed out? Thrown out?

Dropped out? Another was: What had happened in this world when the Jos of her own world had died in the scouter accident? Had it been just a matter of timing? Had someone said or done something differently? Or had they simply not gone? And the nagging one—where was the Cy De Gerch who properly inhabited this world? Was she "over there," trying to come to terms with Jos suddenly dead a year? Or had she been displaced and no longer existed in either world?

As night purpled in from the east, they stopped and made camp. Though traffic was infrequent, fogs and dust squalls had caused drivers to lose the road in the past, so they expanded their tent a couple of hundred meters away. Pressurized and brought up to temperature, it was a comfortable plastic igloo.

JOS SMILED SELF-CONSCIOUSLY OVER the two containers of self-heating soya she was tending. "What?"

"What?" said Cy, still watching her.

"You've never seen me before?"

"Not for a long time." Cy smiled.

A minute passed. The soya containers began to whistle and peel. Jos said, "Have you thought about what we discussed before you left on your last trip?"

"What did we discuss?" said Cy carefully. The year-long gap opened up before her.

"There's no need to be obtuse," Jos said with a touch of irritation. She pushed the readied container across the tent floor. "You know what I mean. Yesterday morning when I saw on the news what was happening to your ship... I ran outside and tried to see it go overhead because I thought it might be the last time I'd ever see you."

Cy thought of saying something like "It looked worse than it was." But she'd been at navigation and saw her carefully calculated subspace hole stretch and twist into chaos. She knew how close they'd come to crashing into Mars. And yet she knew she'd do it again and again and again if the result were to be the same. She said, "It looked worse than it was."

"That's not the point. The point is it could've happened. Tell me, have you considered what I asked you?"

Unsure what she meant, Cy thought quickly, putting together what Jos had said in her message, *your way of life frightens me sometimes*, and the fact that she'd left the fleet sometime in the last year. Cy took a punt. "You mean resign?"

"I mean just that."

What a change!

Three years ago, Jos had started in the same training program and had been just as eager to get a position aboard one of the new *Plain* class frigates. But of course, Jos hadn't been part of the Gartino genetics program and hadn't been genetically engineered for the job, hadn't been ingrained with a touch of the mad militarist, hadn't had her life mapped out before birth to this single end. And three years ago, was before the Battle of Bellatrix and the Battle of Rigel and the Battle of Capella and Deneb and The Orion Rift and Procyon and...

"What's more, you have people shooting at you," Jos continued as if reading Cy's thoughts.

"That's why we shoot at them," Cy answered defensively. "Anyway, I wouldn't call the enemy 'people,' Jos, you know I was mixed and cooked in a test tube specifically to do what I do. I can't just quit, especially not in the middle of a war."

"Hardly the middle. The war's almost finished. I don't want to lose you in some stupid tail-end 'mopping up' operation. And you don't have to do what you do. You could always get a position as an astrogator—"

"I am an astrogator."

"Yes, in a warship where you're also the fire control officer."

"Yes, and a damned good one, too."

"My point exactly, Cy. When you're out there, people and ships become targets, and targets are fast numbers in your head. You're a trained killer for the state. They made you as a weapon, not as a person. The day you wake up to that is the day you'll resign."

Cy didn't need to wake up to this fact. She knew it already and knew there was no escaping it.

The meal was eaten in a silence broken only by remarks on the falling temperature outside and estimates of the remaining distance to Viking. The stars were brilliant through the transparency of the tent. Shortly afterward, Jos said, "Good night," and pulled her sleeping bag up over herself.

"Did you see us?" said Cy.

"What?" said Jos, snuggling down.

"Did you see us go over when you heard the news?"

"No. You were too far north."

How our love must have grown, Cy thought, *to survive so long so diametrically opposed.*

When Jos was asleep Cy called her father on her suit radio, told him she was all right, not to worry, that she was hiking across the Utopia Plain with Josephine. She asked about her four brothers—she made a point of the number—to make sure they were all alive and had not become sisters in this reality. Yes, they were four, they were alive, they were not sisters, though two of them now had different names. As for her father, he sounded the same, whether in this reality or any other; an old man, long since a widower, never perturbed at anything, never moving from that little Martian moon.

Afterward, Cy stayed up a while to watch Phobos, penny small in the sky, rise in the west and flit backwards into the east, rushing through its phases, crescent, half moon, full, until it disappeared into the shadow of Mars.

She opaqued the tent and turned in.

THE GROUND WAS VIBRATING. Steady trembling.

Cy cleared a patch of the tent wall and peered out. It was pitch black with night fog. "Jos, you awake?"

"Yes," said Jos in the dark. "Who could sleep through this?"

"A quake?"

"Not likely. Mars is geologically D.O.A. in that regard."

They sat up, pressing their palms to the tent floor, feeling. Cy cleared bigger patches and saw the lights, frosty and blurred, tearing along the road one after the other.

"Looks like a convoy of heavy vehicles," said Jos.

"Into the Utopia Plain? What for?"

Jos shrugged sleepily. "Maybe they're making for one of the deep water-bore stations. They're in a damn hurry, whatever it's about."

The silent lights streamed past, disappearing into the west.

Next morning, they found not the slightest trace of tracks.

"DUST!"

CY HAD BEEN leading the way and so saw it first—a swirl of red dust looking for all the world like a smudge of blood pushing over the horizon to the north. She stopped with a little kangaroo hop. Jos almost ran into her from behind, despite the warning shout over the radio.

Jos took one look at what was coming and started breaking out the tent from her backpack. As Cy contacted South Mie admin, she mentally went through their rations and survival gear. Dust storms, she knew, could blow for days, planetary ones for months. They were much more prevalent in the southern hemisphere, while the big ones only occurred during the southern spring; and right now, it was winter down there. But there was no telling what terraforming was doing to the climate, and unlikely storms had to be prepared against. Within thirty seconds Jos had their tent pressurizing.

Their check with weather information before leaving had found no warnings posted for the whole northeast of the planet. Fair weather, they'd said. Light winds from the west and noonday temperatures reaching -10°. It was, after all, the northern summer.

Which was exactly what South Mie was telling Cy now: light winds from the west, no dust storms in sight over the whole northeast of Mars. She was inclined to believe them. The dust rising in the north hadn't risen very much. It seemed very concentrated, very local. The smallest dust storm she'd ever seen—if storm it was.

She cranked up magnification on her face glass and zeroed in on the cloud. "Belay the tent, Jos," she said. "I think it's a vehicle."

Jos moved to her side. "Coming this way?"

"No. Heading south or southwest." The movement of the dust was evident now, as was the metallic framework nosing briefly in and out at the boiling leading edge. Cy took a few shots of it from her helmet camera then imaged a map of the Utopia Plain on her glass. On its present heading, the vehicle would cross the road far ahead of them and plunge southwest into the plain's dead heart.

"Maybe it's the Rover." There was a hint of humor in Jos's voice, but not much.

"The what?"

"Haven't you ever heard the legend of the Rover?" Jos paused to set her helmet video tracking the distant, dusting thing. "It was Earth's eighth expedition to Mars. The mother ship landed on Phobos and sent a crew of ten down to the surface in a shuttle to set up a base camp. One day a fuel tank ruptured, and the shuttle exploded. The ten were marooned. The mother ship wasn't designed for a Martian landing, you see."

"Wait on! That was *way* back! What's it got to do with *that?*" Cy pointed to the dust cloud, elongated now and sprawling rapidly away.

"They all died, you know, Cy. Except one. As the CO_2 built up, they took pills or just walked outside unprotected."

"Except one?"

"He was the last one alive and drove off in the surface rover they used for long-range exploring. Just drove off to nowhere. Five years later the tenth expedition recovered the bodies in the base camp, but the last man and the surface rover were never found. Some say it's still out there, still driving on computer control over the plains and in and out of the canyons with a dead man at the wheel."

"It would've broken down long ago, Jos. It's lost. It's... it's at the bottom of Mariner Valley."

Jos shrugged, a gesture nearly lost inside her suit. "Others have seen it down the years. Now maybe we have too."

The dust cloud disappeared into the southwest leaving a rosy plume hanging in the air, but taking its mystery with it.

"YOU'RE RIGHT," HE SAID. "Which explains why Evelyn's been dead six months."

Cy and Jos were resting in the center of a patch of sand cleared of the ubiquitous red rocks. Jos was making a routine call-in to South Mie while Cy was checking their position by neutrino line fixes on her face glass map. "Viking by noon tomorrow," she said confidently as an outside call chimed in.

It was, as she expected, Captain Brown answering her earlier message about what she believed the distortion wave had done. He said, "You're right. Which explains why Evelyn's been dead six months."

Cy, hesitating, asked, "Your wife is dead?"

"I've just spent the last twenty-four hours trying to find out what happened. Apparently, she died in a silver fever epidemic last year here in Styx which, in our reality, happened over in South Arcadia."

As she listened it struck her that he didn't sound as sad or as shocked as she would've expected him to be at such news. In fact, in some ways he sounded... relieved? She said, "You are taking this very well, Ralph."

"Don't get me wrong, Cy. If I sound callous, I'm not. I'm sad that my wife in this reality isn't here, but it's because she died in this reality and not our own that I'm..." He trailed off vaguely, a second later his voice coming up strong again on the beam. "Have you lost someone in this reality? Your father perhaps, or one of your brothers?"

"Actually, Ralph, I've gained someone. Jos Manxman is alive."

There was a long silence. Then Brown said, "I see."

"So, what did our subspace expert have to say?" she asked.

"Yes," said the captain with a curious edge of caution. "I checked with Mr. Womac, which is how I know you're right about the distortion wave knocking us sidewise. Look... no, never mind. Enjoy yourself."

The beam broke off abruptly before she could make any reply or even ask "Never mind what?" It left her wondering uneasily.

CY STEPPED OUT OF the wraparound of their recycle shower. "Eleven point four," she said, glancing at the outside barometer.

"Pretty good, eh?" Jos said. "Not so long ago our highest pressure reading was only nine point one, and that was at the bottom of the Hellus Basin in summer. One day we won't need those." She pointed to their vacuum suits stored in the corner of the tent. "One day we'll have all the subsurface water up and the oxygen unlocked from the soil and the atmosphere."

"Still a long way away," said Cy, toweling.

"Yes. I wouldn't hold my breath."

They laughed. Cy said, "Do you find your work at Zephyria more rewarding than defense training?"

Jos, suddenly serious, said, "I thought we'd discussed that, Cy."

Cy bit her lip. She said, "Sorry," without really knowing what for. She had to be careful what she asked Jos, not knowing what had passed between her and that other Cy De Gerch over the previous year. She fell to thinking about what that other Cy had been like. *Not much different, surely,* she thought. *Jos seems to have seen no difference in me, though I can see such a change in her.* But Cy knew she was thinking of Jos as she used to be, when their love had been new and had died still new.

As she thought this she was surprised by a spasm of jealousy directed at that other self, the other Cy who had known Jos, in both senses of the word, for longer than fate had allowed her ever to do.

She shrugged it off as a meaningless emotion. There was no other. There had only been a gap, an absence, and now she'd returned.

Cy stretched out on top of her sleeping bag and began drying her legs slowly, having noticed Jos staring at her. She half rolled toward her, knowing Jos would lean over and begin to caress and kiss her. But Jos didn't lean over, and with a little shock, Cy realized it was not her nakedness Jos was staring at but the white, jagged scar on her left arm. The scar from the meteor that had holed her scouter a year ago in the asteroid belt. The asteroid belt where Jos had died.

Expectations of sex were instantly replaced by expectations of Jos making some comment, asking some question she had no idea how to answer. It was too evidently an old scar from a major injury. There was no way she could—

Jos got up and climbed into the recycle shower without removing her shorts and skivvy first. She did this inside the wraparound and flung them hard over the top rail.

"Something wrong?" Cy asked.

"No, nothing," said Jos in the tone that said, "Yes, everything." The shower splashed. The recycle motor hummed. Standing on tip-toes, Jos put her head over the rail and whispered, "I only wish you'd stop wearing it like a tattoo."

Cy regarded the scar on her arm. Wearing it like a tattoo? What the hell did she mean by that? It was just a scar... No, perhaps it was more than that. Yes, perhaps she did think of it as a memento won in her rite of passage. *Look at this, look, I've been through the wars, too. I know pain. I deserve my place.* Not that it mattered to the people she worked with, who would probably never see it. But it meant something to her. Yes.

But hardly a badge of bravery. More a souvenir of a stupid and wholly avoidable accident. No wonder it upset Jos.

So, what happened when the Jos of my world died, and the Jos of this did not?

The shower stopped. Jos stepped out wrapped about in a towel.

Tucking her left arm under her knee. Cy said. "I'm sorry."

"Yes, me too," said Jos, conciliatory. She paused at the end of Cy's sleeping bag. "It's not your fault, heaven knows it's not. But you have to admit it's a constant reminder."

Cy lay back on her sleeping bag as Jos returned to hers. *So, it seems the accident happened in this reality as well. But to me only and not to Jos? Was it that close call that scared her out of fleet training? Questions, questions, questions, none I can properly ask because I'm supposed to know the answers already.*

She would call the captain, she decided. See if he could access operational records, see what happened to Trainees Manxman and De Gerch on that day last year. Doctor Norsk would have the authority to check her medical—

She looked up in surprise to see Jos kneeling beside her, smiling. She said, "I think you had something in mind a moment ago, didn't you?" and let the towel slip from her shoulders.

"VIKING!"

THE JOYOUS SHOUT roared through Cy's phones, interrupting Beethoven's fifth in its second movement.

"Viking!"

Three or four jump steps brought her to Jos's side, where she stopped and stared out to the north.

"Viking!" they shouted together, and the horizon three kilometers away glittered with metal in the morning sun; a tiny spot three kilometers ahead at the end of a side road, glittering in the high angle light of the late morning sun.

As they bounded towards the ancient machine, three-legged squatting in the sand, they made out that it was not alone. Something as big as Viking itself stood or lay beside it. They stopped about a kilometre away and took in the view on high magnification.

"The Rover! Holy shit, Cy, *it's the Rover!*"

As irrational as it seemed, as illogical as it was, the vehicle parked beside Viking did look old, was grubby with clinging Martian dust, had a figure at its wheel which was thin and skull-white through the transparency of its helmet. Then a second later she wasn't sure what it was because it was no longer there.

They approached, taking small, cautious steps a couple of meters at a time.

Viking stood where it had landed 342 years before, though now domed over with thick plastic to protect it from the driving sand winds. The pads of its three feet were buried deep in the red sand.

"This is made of pure history, "Jos said, awed.

Cy nodded in mute agreement. History. The dish antenna angled up as if still listening for instructions from faraway Earth, the long robot arm touching the ground as if with a gesture of ownership, the American flag on one panel of its hexagonal body still bright in its red, white and blue—probably a result of some restoration project.

They looked for vehicle tracks, finding a few. But they were old, nearly filled in by the wind.

"This is not the most popular tour stop, for sure," said Jos, setting up the holo-camera. "Too remote for most trippers. But it does have its fans, especially among the history buffs and especially now, in summer. Maybe that's what we saw: a tour buggy of Earthies."

"Did you see it leave?" asked Cy.

"OK, then. It was the Rover. Which way do you want it?"

"Take the holo."

The holograph was taken: Jos and Cy togged up in full vacuum suits, standing, smiling beside Viking II, Canberra region, northeast Utopia Plain.

THEY TOOK PICTURES OF Viking from various angles, of Viking and themselves, of Viking and its red vista background.

They set up their tent to have a proper lunch, eaten and tasted and felt with the teeth and the tongue, not squeezed from a capsule into a plastic nipple, sucked from a tube. They called South Mie, told them they'd arrived but said nothing of what they saw or thought they saw. Then the dust began to rise in the south: a small hurrying cloud, distant but coming near.

When it was two kilometers away a balloon-tyred vehicle veered left out of the cloud and slowed, leaving the high, boiling dust to stretch out along its old course under momentum.

The vehicle stopped beside Viking in the exact same place, in the exact same attitude they'd seen that other vehicle standing. It was dusty and not the most recent vintage, but NORTHWEST REGION RANGER was stenciled down its side, and the lanky, blonde haired man in the pressure bubble waved to them, friendly, and Jos said. "It's Hil Cortonhorz."

"Who?"

"Hil Cortonhorz. One of the rangers responsible for the northwest. He sometimes does the supply run to Zephyria."

They ushered him in through their little airlock. Hil Cortonhorz removed his helmet and said, "As I live and breathe recycled air! It's Jos Manxman! By the living Harry, you're a long way from home."

"We're a long way from anywhere," said Jos, regarding the endless nowhere outside the tent. "This is Cy De Gerch, my soldier girl from the interstellar fleet. We've just hiked it from South Mie."

"Well!" said the ranger. He made an odd gesture with his head to Cy, something between a nod and a courtly bow. "Say, then maybe you can help me. An hour ago, I got a garbled message on the beam about a starship coming down around here. My equipment's playing up something chronic, you see, and I've got no idea what's happening. Either of you seen anything like a ship coming down?"

"Which ship?" asked Cy. Most of the people she knew worked in space.

"No saying, Cy. Not even sure it happened. Message was pretty much broken up."

"We saw some sort of vehicle racing along to the west about 100 klicks south of here yesterday morning," said Jos.

"No idea who that could be," said Hil, "unless it's someone else out looking." His mouth curved in a grim little smile. "Maybe you saw the Rover."

"The Rover's in Mariner Valley," said Cy.

Jos showed him the stills they'd taken.

Hil shrugged, no idea.

"Were you parked here by Viking an hour ago?" asked Jos.

He shook his head. "I just arrived from Arcadia."

"Then there's another ranger..." Cy began.

"No other in this area. Least, I don't think so. Mind if I use your beam?"

"Go ahead," Jos said. "But we've just been talking to South Mie, and no one said anything to us about a ship down."

South Mie still knew nothing about a ship down when Hil contacted them, nor did his base at Arcadia far to the east where he thought the original alarm had come from.

"I must be going mad, hearing about the desert after crashed ships that never were," said Hil.

"Poor dear," said Jos. "Never mind. Stop for lunch. We were about to have some solid food for the sheer spite of it."

"*And* to celebrate," said Cy, breaking out what she called "The good stuff": algae steak and rice. But there was more to Cy's selection than a sense of occasion and accomplishment. Algae steaks take the longest to self-heat and eat, and Cy needed time; time for the conversation to be steered so that Hil could ask questions she couldn't.

IT'S JUST AS WELL I used the algae steak and rice, Cy thought.

Hil had much to say about being a ranger on the Utopia Plain, its aches and pains and fortunes, its idiosyncrasies, the people he encountered and the day he saw the Rover. It wasn't until their algae dishes were all but licked clean that Cy's conversational opening finally came along.

"Yep, from West Utopia to Mount Olympus," Hil was saying, hardly pausing for a breath of recycled air. "That's my beat. And, of course, south to Zephyria. I'd take you for a bit of a grand tour next time I'm down at your station, Jos, but your lady might not like me whizzing you off like that." He gave Cy a quick wink. "I know what Navy girls are like."

Jos laughed. Cy smiled demurely.

"So," he went on, "how long you two been together as a couple?"

"Almost three years," said Jos. "Solar years, I mean."

"We met during training," said Cy, jumping in.

"Training?" said Hil.

"Jos never told you?" said Cy, sounding as innocent as possible. "We were a couple of fifteen-year-old trainees at the Styx City defense base, both specializing in astral and interdimensional navigation." She glanced across at Jos, whose mouth had set into a tight, puckered-in slit. The phrase 'staring daggers' came to mind.

"So how does a navigator in the defense force become a civilian geologist in the terraforming project, Jos?" Hil asked.

A moment of desperation flickered across Jos's face.

"There ... um, there was an accident," she said in a quiet voice. "I decided to get out while I was still alive."

"We were hit by meteors during scouter exercises in the asteroid belt," Cy said—and surprised herself because for the first time since the accident she felt no pain in speaking about it. Quite apart from getting an answer out of Jos, this was actually becoming therapeutic.

"You were lucky to come out in one piece," said Hil.

Cy said nothing; that might be pushing Jos too far. But then Jos said, "I was lucky, yes, but Cy got hit in the arm, didn't you, Cy?" For a moment Cy thought she was going to add, "Show the nice man your scar." But she didn't and there followed an awkward silence. Then Hil said, "And you stayed in and finished your training, did you, Cy?"

Cy shrugged. "I'm a Gartino." She admitted her genetic origins as if saying, "I'm very brave," or, "I have no brains," or "I have no choice."

Later, as Hil Cortonhorz was backing into the airlock on all fours, he said, "I'm off down south to Water Bore Four now, then tracking it across to Styx City. If you want to get your stuff packed, I'll give you a lift. You can catch the mono there for South Mie. Beats loping back, eh?"

Left to themselves, Jos said, "Did you really have to bring up the scouter accident?"

"And do you have to keep avoiding it all your life?" Cy replied. "So, you made a mistake. Do you wear your guilt the way you say I carry my scar?" She guessed here, riding the momentum of Hil's questions. She waited and watched for Jos's reaction.

"You were always better, weren't you?"

The unexpected bitterness hit Cy like a slap. "What?"

"Better. In navigation and ordinance and officer training and flight instruction and... hell, even in bed."

"I see," said Cy quietly. "And why do you think I was better, Jos? Hmmm? Because my mother's egg and my father's sperm were meddled with in a lab before they were allowed to come together. Because I never really was a little girl like you were once upon a time. You wouldn't want to be like me, Jos. Okay, so you took the lead with that scouter flight when you may not have been really qualified, and made a mess of it. You failed, you quit." She almost made a question out of 'quit,' but there was no reaction from Jos. Cy went on, feeling she had something now. "So, my arm was smashed. You took us into the meteors, sure, something anyone could've done. But I could've maneuvered out if I hadn't been so shit scared and only half qualified myself. My injury was my fault."

"No. That's not the lot of it. Cy, I panicked and left you."

"Panicked?" Unbidden, the events as she had lived them ran again through Cy's memory: the *thwack* of the meteor holing the egg-shell hull of the scouter; skin and bone flying like shrapnel; a sudden fog of blood; her suit closing down instantly over the injury. No pain, not yet; the flashing damage lights on thrust and lateral control; the view screen showing Jos's ship grazed by small rocks as she turned toward, trying to nudge Cy's scouter out; someone yelling in her helmet, maybe Jos, maybe herself—

Then the big rock hit and Jos and Jos's scouter were a million scattering pieces which were scattering still in that other universe.

Cy reached out and cuddled Jos. "Nothing happened you could've prevented."

"I should've turned toward and nudged you out."

"No, you did the right thing. One day I'll tell you how I know, but right now isn't the time. OK, so maybe you're not cut out to be a trained killer for the state, but look at it this way: in some other universe you *did* turn towards to nudge me out of the meteors, and in that universe, you died. Mars lost a budding geologist, and I lost you. Now, what's the point of that, eh?"

They donned their helmets, preparatory to depressurizing the tent and rebottling its air. The hike out to Viking had been a challenge to reach a goal. With that achieved, hitching a ride with Hil Cortonhorz back to Styx City didn't seem like cheating. Home couldn't be reached quick enough.

They crawled outside where Hil and his vehicle were nowhere in sight.

"SOUTH MIE AND ARCADIA say we're crazy," said Cy.

"Maybe we are," said Jos, gazing round and round. There was not so much as a receding dust cloud on the horizon.

They'd signaled South Mie who said Hil Cortonhorz, far from being anywhere near Viking II, was cruising the sand out to the east, and no, they still knew nothing about a ship coming down in the Utopia Plain.

"Cortonhorz called that in as well a half hour ago," South Mie said. "Have you all gone crazy out there?"

Arcadia also admitted to receiving a query a half hour before from Hil Cortonhorz about a crash, about which they had no knowledge. Arcadia then called Hil Cortonhorz and confirmed he was far to the east. He denied having been near Viking II and having met Jos Manxman and Cy De Gerch there. His radio was working perfectly and had been since the beginning of his patrol five days before. He denied having received a call about a down ship or making a query about one, even though Arcadia told him they had plainly heard him do so. Arcadia, exasperated, then asked if they'd all gone crazy out there.

Later that afternoon Jos saw something glittering far ahead.

They'd struck out for Water Bore Four to the south where they hoped to catch a supply run back to South Mie. Viking lays twenty-five kilometers behind them, and too much desert sprawled ahead. They loped steadily on with loud music playing on their phones in an effort to obliterate thought. The appearance and disappearance of Hil Cortonhorz, and then his denial of everything from too great a distance, had upset Jos with its inexplicability. Cy too was distressed, but with her it was because there *were* reasons. Time had fractured and let her slip sideways. Now maybe it was sliding back and forth, one reality to another. Was that how it was? Like a pendulum, like water finding its own level, was time—her time—coming back? Was that what Mr. Womac had told the Captain and the Captain refrained from telling her? Because it would've been too cruel? Yes, too cruel then, too unfair now... And then Jos called in something glittering in the afternoon sun far ahead.

Cy bounded up to her. "Where?"

Jos pointed. But even on full magnification, Cy could see only red rocks and red sand and nothing else.

"Cy...the desert up ahead's swarming with people and vehicles... there are sub-orbitals landing...that glittering—it's scattered metal!"

Jos started off in great leaps, leaving Cy standing scared and alone, staring at empty desert.

"Jos," she whispered.

But Jos was now well into the debris field, passing the people setting up temporary shacks and working amid the twisted shards of starship hull strewn around the edges of a brand new crater. Then there was Hil Cortonhorz sitting by the hole as if he'd been there for hours.

They looked at each other in bewilderment.

"Where did you go?" Jos asked.

"Where did you?" said Hil. "I turned around, and you'd packed your tent and disappeared. Along with this," he gestured to the activity around them, "we've also had parties out searching for you and your lady the last three days."

"Three days? What are you talking about, Hil? It's barely been three hours."

Hil shook his head and peered down into the crater, almost a kilometre wide. "She came down three days ago. Hit hard. Popped out of subspace too close, they say."

Jos, cold as time, spun around. "Cy!"

There was no one behind her in the desert and nothing to be heard, but the ghost of a whisper called her name and said something that might've been "I love you." And then silence.

For a long time only silence, and then a young woman's sudden hysterical crying.

UTOPIA PLAIN DROPPED OUT of the pink, noonday sky of Mars and belly-cradled in Styx City, thirteen hundred kilometers southeast of the rocky desert from which the starship took her name.

Medical personnel boarded and removed five injured crew members. Shortly afterward the rest of the crew left for a suddenly well-deserved shore leave. Lieutenant Cy De Gerch stepped through the forward hatch and walked down the pressure tunnel with her bag slung over her shoulder. Captain Brown ambled down after her, joining his young lieutenant at the spaceport windows where they looked ruefully back at the scorched, buckled metal of their ship.

"A close one," said Brown.

De Gerch said nothing to this. There was nothing to say. She was the navigator and knew intimately how close it'd been. Abruptly formal, she said, "Permission to leave, sir."

"Permission granted. Going home?"

"To Phobos? Probably. Haven't seen Dad in..."

She trailed off, overcome by a growing sensation of *deja-vu* which, by his sudden odd expression, she knew her captain was sharing.

At the Comm Office Captain Brown found a message from his wife saying she'd been delayed, that she'd be there presently. Doctor Norsk had news of the birth of a baby girl to his great-granddaughter on Earth.

For Lieutenant De Gerch there was a data wafer of a middle-aged man saying, "Welcome home, Cy." A simple message from a straightforward man, her father. She turned to go, then hesitated with a feeling that there should be something else, a vague expectancy of there being another message, something from somewhere she'd never been, from someone she hadn't seen in a long, long time. She looked again.

There was nothing.

THE END

RICK KENNETT is an Australian writer of science fiction, horror, and ghost stories with several published books and many stories in a wide variety of magazines, anthologies, and podcasts. The novella *The Devil and the Deep Blue Sea* and the novella *In Quinn's Paddock* feature his reoccurring character Ernie Pine, the "reluctant ghost hunter." Another reoccurring character is genetically engineered Martian space girl Cy De Gerch, who appears in the novel *Presumed Dead* and the collection *Thirty Minutes for New Hell*. Some of Kennett's work is science fiction, but some of his science fiction stories feature ghosts, thus his work crosses genre boundaries that are often kept separate. For more about Rick and his work, please visit his website at www.rickkennett.wordpress.com.

THE SCAR
Frank Roger

1

I DISCOVERED SOMETHING STRANGE this morning as I was taking a shower. On my right arm, there is a sort of scar. It's very faint, barely visible as if I suffered an injury a long time ago that has healed practically completely by now. The thing is, I've never suffered an injury on my right arm. Yet this scar-like thing is there.

When I run the fingers of my left hand along the scar, I feel absolutely nothing. Although it doesn't bother me at all, I made a mental note of checking on it the next few days. If it disappears as mysteriously as it has come, I will be relieved. And if not, I will keep an eye on its progress and take any measures deemed appropriate.

I didn't mention the problem—as it can hardly be called a problem, to begin with—to my wife, or to my colleagues at the office.

As a matter of fact, I forgot all about it as soon as I got dressed and started the day's regular activities.

*** *MISSION CONTROL HAS RECEIVED an error message. A standard check will be run. It may be a simple glitch in the system without any real significance, but no risks will be taken. Too much is at stake in this phase of the Project.* ***

2

A FEW DAYS HAVE gone by. Each morning as I rise, I check my right arm. The scar is still there. It doesn't go away but doesn't seem to get worse either. My wife asked me what I was looking at and I showed her the scar. She said that if I felt no pain, it was probably nothing to worry about. No doubt it will fade away.

Yet I'm not so sure that everything is all right. Am I imagining things, or is the scar becoming more clearly visible? Is my mind playing tricks on me, perhaps because I'm studying my arm so attentively every day, or is the problem indeed getting worse?

Just to be sure, I made a picture of the scar and decided to make one every morning. That will allow me to check its progress. Or its decline. At least I will have some hard data to compare it with.

*** THE STANDARD CHECK DID not yield any results. No trace of an anomaly could be found. A glitch in the system would have been the logical conclusion if it hadn't been for a second error message confirming the original one. The Project Manager decided a full-scale check was advisable. ***

3

MORE THAN A WEEK has gone by.

I showed my right arm to my wife and asked her to compare it to the series of pictures I have taken. I simply needed a second opinion, as I no longer believed my own eyes.

"Does it hurt?" she said. I replied that it didn't.

She went back to the very first picture I took and held the camera next to my arm. "I think you're right," she finally said after a close study. "This thing is getting worse. Very slowly. It's clear when you compare it with what it looked like a week ago, not yesterday."

"So what do I do?" I asked.

"Keep an eye on it," she said. "Make a picture every day. If it gets really worse, you go see a doctor."

"That seems reasonable," I said.

*** IT HAS NOW BECOME clear that the error message was not a glitch or a random incident unconnected with the Project but in all probability an anomaly. As its true nature and the exact location remain unknown, a thorough investigation was ordered that ought to shed light on the situation. The Project Manager is adamant about avoiding any anomalies that may jeopardize the Project. ***

4

A WEEK LATER I discussed the situation again with my wife.

"Look," I said, "the skin around the scar is changing color. It's a bit darker now."

"A touch of red," she added, nodding in agreement while she studied my arm.

"There's also this nagging pain," I continued. "It's nothing serious, it's in the background. I can easily ignore it, but this thing seems to be going in the wrong direction."

"Try applying disinfectant," she suggested. "Or some skin care product. Why don't you ask your pharmacist? She usually gives you sound advice."

"Excellent idea," I said. Later that day I went to the pharmacy, explained what was wrong and showed my arm.

"It's probably nothing serious," she said, "but I'll give you something. An ointment that might help. Still, if the skin gets darker, if the pain persists or grows worse, you should see a doctor."

"Fine," I said, hoping that the problem would be solved very soon.

*** THE FINDINGS HAVE BEEN checked and double-checked. The error messages were indeed referring to an anomaly connected with the Project. This is very bad news indeed. The investigation should supply full information on the anomaly. It is hoped that the problem will be dealt with before any major damage is caused to the Project or even to the location itself. ***

5

THE OINTMENT HAS NO effect. The skin around the scar keeps changing color, a deepening shade of red, and the pain grows gradually worse.

My wife and I compared my arm and pictures of it again, and we reached the same conclusion: I should see my doctor. Even if the problem doesn't cause any major discomfort, it's clear something strange is going on.

The doctor examined my arm and said: "This looks like a scar that's still healing, which explains the light pain. Still, it should get better, not worse. What you're telling me doesn't make any sense. I must admit I have trouble believing your story, even with the pictures you showed me. Maybe you should simply give it more time. Keep using that skin care product you mentioned, and take painkillers if the pain gets really worse, but that would surprise me. And if it goes completely the wrong way, I'd like to see it again, although frankly, I can't see that happening."

I'm not too happy with the doctor's refusal to believe my—admittedly—preposterous story, but there is little I can do about it. So, I keep using the ointment and take pictures every day.

*** THE MOST IMPORTANT THING *now is to locate the anomaly, determine its nature and find a way to control it. Unless quick and drastic action is taken, there may be severe repercussions and damage beyond repair. The Project has gone to red alert. The Manager is overseeing every action personally and conscientiously. An incident that may lead to the Project backfiring cannot be tolerated. However, it may be too late already.* ***

6

More than a week has gone by.

I stopped using the ointment. It's clearly pointless.

The scar is now a dark red, and the pain is growing more persistent. Not to the point that I need to take painkillers, but I'm seriously worried by now. It's obvious something mysterious and ominous is happening to me, and I don't have a clue what it could be—nor how or when it will end.

One afternoon at the office, I experienced for the first time, difficulties when working on my computer. The muscles in my arm contracted, and I felt pangs of pain in the part of my arm where the scar is.

Now, this is bad news indeed. If this grows worse, it may cause serious problems. What if I become unable to work at my normal level of performance? What if I have to call in sick because the arm no longer co-operates? Apart from the medical and professional consequences, there would be financial troubles. I shudder at the very idea.

I hoped the problems at the office would not return.

But they did. And as I had feared deep down, they were growing worse.

*** WE ARE FINALLY GETTING *clearer readings. The anomaly which occurred as a by-product of the experiment has now been* *located. This unforeseen and unforeseeable incident should never have happened. The Project Teams are now working on a way to reach the location and control the situation. The experiment is likely to be cut short. The Project Manager insists on preventing the anomaly from spinning out of control. ****

7

A FEW WEEKS HAVE passed. I reached the point where I am no longer able to function at work. The scar has turned a bright red, and I'm in constant pain. The muscles in my arm contract with the slightest movement I make. I can no longer use my right arm in a normal way. Typing on a keyboard is a nightmare. Even simply picking up a pen or a coffee mug is a major challenge.

My boss was compassionate, I have to give him that. "Do whatever it takes to solve this," he said. "Go to a hospital, if your doctor can't help you. You can't go on like this."

He was right of course, and my wife basically said the same thing. So, I took sick leave and went to the doctor again. The man said he failed to understand what was going on with me, had never read about any similar case in medical literature, and arranged for my admission to a local hospital. "But frankly," he added, "I have no idea what they're going to do about it, apart from running tests."

I have high hopes. In the hospital, they should be able to treat me. If not, where can they? Failure is not an option. This will just have to work.

*** CONSIDERABLE PROGRESS HAS BEEN made, and a solution is being worked out. The anomaly will have to be taken care of at its location, whatever the cost. Collateral damage will be unavoidable and will in its turn have to be dealt with, as no traces of our intervention may be left— or must be limited to a bare minimum. Practical details will be given at the intervention team's briefing—unfortunately, there will be no time for a test run. ***

8

I'VE BEEN ADMITTED TO a hospital. They ran a whole series of tests on me. The verdict is quite clear: I have a scar, the result of an injury I must have suffered. Only I didn't. They didn't buy the story I told them, despite the pictures I showed them. Of course, I know very well pictures may be fake. Only they're not.

They said they would keep me here for a few days, and check my progress. I told them there would be no progress, quite the opposite, but they waved away my remark. I suppose they'll see for themselves.

In the meantime, they're treating the scar with a product that smells terribly but doesn't really help, and they give me painkillers, which make the problem more bearable but don't solve it. Painkillers never do.

A few days later I was told the scar showed no signs of healing, on the contrary. I replied that this regression had been going on for weeks now, and they finally started believing me, although it was against all logic—as if I didn't know that.

They said they would do everything in their power to deal with the problem. They sounded pretty convincing, which restored my hope a bit.

*** *THE INTERVENTION TEAM HAS been briefed. Several options were considered, as the team members may have to improvise based on the situation in the field. Our analysis has shown that the anomaly has collided with an as yet unidentified person. The exact location in space and time has been determined. There are high hopes that the anomaly will be neutralized, with minimal collateral damage. However, the future of the Project remains unclear. Anomalies of the kind we have witnessed extend the margin of error beyond control and may jeopardize every Project activity.* ***

9

A WEEK HAS GONE by. I'm on a steady diet of painkillers now—without them, it would be hell. "The scar is no longer a simple scar," so I was told. "It's become an open wound. We have no idea how this happened, and we don't know how it will evolve from this point onwards."

My arm is fully bandaged now, and I can no longer use it. I sleep for hours on end, no doubt because of the sedatives I'm given. Just like the medical staff, I wonder what will happen next. What could the logical outcome be? I prefer not to think about it. I realize a scientific paper on my case may be published in a medical journal, but that brings little solace.

The last thing I heard was that my situation is deteriorating rapidly and I will be transferred to the Intensive Care Unit. That isn't exactly good news, but it was to be expected.

But what will happen at the ICU? And what will come after that? The mystery just keeps getting bigger. Will I live to see it unraveled at some point?

10 (Epilog—excerpt from a press conference)

YESTERDAY NIGHT THERE WAS a breach of security at the hospital. Some intruders managed to gain access to the building and to the ICU without triggering any alarms or without being seen. As confirmed by surveillance video footage, they clearly knew what they were looking for. No medical equipment was damaged or stolen. For reasons that remain unclear, they came to retrieve patient X (we cannot divulge his real name for privacy reasons) who was in the ICU. Patient X, who had already lost consciousness, was suffering from a sort of regressive injury unknown to medical science and his situation was deteriorating fast. It has been suggested that this condition may be the reason why he was abducted. It is feared that patient X's removal from the ICU may prove extremely harmful or even fatal for him. His current whereabouts are unknown. The police are investigating the matter.

*** *(PROJECT MANAGER'S LOG ENTRY)*

The Project will be terminated. The last experiment was a disaster, aggravated by collateral damage deemed excessive and unjustifiable. The anomaly that occurred in the course of our time travel experiment tore a hole in space-time and collided with a person who should have remained uninvolved. The bullet-like impact caused a major injury requiring a long period of healing. In this particular case, however, an additional problem arose because the wound was inflicted by an anomaly hurtling back in time. To the victim and his contemporaries, this was bound to be inexplicable, and it might cause ripples in the fabric of time with far-reaching consequences. To avoid major temporal disturbances, it was decided to send a team of special agents to neutralize the anomaly and to retrieve the victim, even if this intervention would in its turn cause additional ripples and disturbances. Without this second intervention, however, the victim would not have been transported to the scene of the accident (i.e., the collision) at the proper moment, resulting in massive disruptions and perhaps even a paradox, leaving the Project Team with irreparable damage to deal with. As soon as the victim was hit by the anomaly, the injury that had been healing in reverse (or "unhealing") disappeared. The victim was then removed from his time, where his presence had become a liability, and placed in temporal quarantine. In his own time, he will be considered missing, and his case will never be solved. This is a very awkward situation, but still the best option available for the Projects sake.

There will be no more experiments. All further Project activities are canceled until further notice. The anomaly has been successfully neutralized. The Project's Board of Directors will decide the victims fate. We all know what that means. ***

THE END

FRANK ROGER was born in 1957 in Ghent, Belgium. His first story appeared in 1975. Today he has a few hundred short stories to his credit, published in about 40 languages. A story collection in English, The Burning Woman and Other Stories, was published by Evertype in 2012. Apart from fiction, he also produces collages and graphic work in a surrealist and satirical tradition. Find out more about his work at www.frankroger.be.

STOPPER

David Christenson

THE HISSING OF THE garden hose stopped, and the science fiction writer turned away from the mad scientist's door to see a pudgy neighbor in shorts and T-shirt who had paused from watering his window box flowers, with a stone-faced stare, nozzle still dripping. Was it a stare of curiosity? Anger? God forbid, lust? The writer decided it didn't matter, gave the neighbor the quickest of smiles, and turned to ring the mad scientist's doorbell, pausing to appreciate the front of his little bungalow: it could fit the category of "cute," if not haunted by the chronically prickly demeanor of its inhabitant.

After a few moments, the scientist admitted the science fiction writer. Standard greetings were offered, drinks poured, and seating was arranged face-to-face on plush beige furnishings, in a strikingly plain living room that was mostly as beige as the easy chair in which the writer settled. On the floor between the writer and the scientist was a machine, of which the details mostly defied description, save for a notable four: a braid of wires and cables sprouting from the back (or perhaps the front, or side) of the machine and snaking through a doorway into an adjoining room; an outsized chrome toggle switch atop, within reach of the scientist; a monitor, currently blank; and the machine's voice, a constant low meditative hum.

The writer produced a stenographic notebook and a ballpoint pen. "When you invited me to your home, I wasn't sure what to expect," the writer said, and suddenly self-conscious, crossed her legs and cleared her throat.

Just then the doorbell rang—the scientist excused himself—and it was the pudgy neighbor. "Hey, Benzoni, sorry to bother you," he said, with a knowing glance at the writer, "but we've been having some problems, and I wonder if you've been doing some kind of electrical thing here. Our wi-fi won't work at all. The TV keeps switching over to some kind of reality show about these red monsters, we can't even look at them. Oh, and last night the vacuum cleaner started up by itself without even being plugged in, and it wandered into the front bedroom and scared the bejeebers out of the kids."

Benzoni mollified the neighbor with a promise to add a layer of shielding to his walls, watched as the pudgy man retreated, then slammed the door. "Philistine," he muttered.

The writer cleared her throat again. "As I was saying, I didn't know what to expect when I came here. I didn't anticipate that you'd move your latest experiment to your own house."

"I should have informed you, Ms. Wetherell. The Dean opposed my continuing this experiment at the university," replied Benzoni, with a fleeting disinterested glance at Wetherell's knees. It was clearly a mistake to wear a skirt and this tight-fitting blouse to this meeting; what was she thinking? But Benzoni was apparently too preoccupied to notice her body.

"Fortunately," Benzoni continued, "students are always available to move heavier items, for the price of pizza and beer."

"What was the Dean's problem?"

Benzoni rubbed at his beard, agitated by the memory. "The Dean seemed taken aback when I described the level of electrical power required. Also, he claimed this equipment was taking up too much room in the lab—a sorry excuse to shut down an experiment of this importance, but an accurate criticism, I have to admit."

Given her own experience with Benzoni, Wetherell had doubts, unvoiced, that electricity and architectural space were the only problems the university had with this man. He had always been polite to her, of course—his "chronicler," or his "Dr. Watson," as he called her—but she remembered the glowering scrutiny of passing students and faculty distinctly as she would enter or leave his campus office. In fact, the first time she called upon him, she had to ask a department secretary for directions to his office, and the secretary's initial response was, "Are you sure?"

Benzoni continued, "Here, even though I've miniaturized it somewhat, the equipment fills the whole den, wall to wall, so I've extended the main switch mechanism to the living room here, where we can be comfortable as I initiate the final process

"So, electricity isn't an issue in your house?"

"Normally, it would pose the same problems here. But some help from the more creative students with engineering know-how, I've taken measures to bypass the usual safeguards, linking the laboratory equipment directly into the main grid, and I wouldn't be surprised if we black out the neighborhood when the switch is pulled. Maybe the whole city." Benzoni smiled at this prospect. The switch mechanism stopped humming for a moment to emit a high-pitched beep, then resumed its hum.

They each took a sip of a drink, and Wetherell contemplated the switch thing. It combined aspects of a spaghetti-stuffed toaster-oven with features of a manual typewriter and pieces of what looked like a bicycle helmet, but it also reminded her, in ways she could not define, of a small mammal, perhaps a muskrat. Or perhaps a huge grapefruit.

"Unfortunately, since this is now an unauthorized and, dare I say it, a rogue experiment, you and I will be the only witnesses," continued Benzoni. "I trust since we've previously discussed this in my office, you will be able to write a proper account of it. Don't worry, you won't be expected to collect data; I have numerous recording devices in the next room for that. I'm hoping you will record personal impressions of the experience. And you do have a talent for explaining difficult concepts."

"Thank you. I know I can't hope to educate the public about something this advanced, but I hope I can convey something of the magnitude of this experiment." This little flattery had its desired effect, as Benzoni smiled and lifted his chin ever so slightly. "To sum up our previous conversations," Wetherell said, "this is a time-control experiment." Benzoni nodded, and she continued, "Your plan is to twist time to make it run backward."

"In essence, yes. We will focus the power to create a tiny and short-lived field that will envelop a few random subatomic particles. In effect, these particles will travel a short way into the future—a few nanoseconds—within a field, or bubble, in which the flow of time is reversed."

Wetherell tried to bring to mind some of the physics she had briefly studied a few years prior for a novel involving interstellar travel. She ventured, "Is it a sort of warp bubble? Based on the Morell bubble, or Fong's bubble?"

"No! My bubble! My bubble! Don't associate me with those charlatans! Weak thinkers infesting the inferior colleges! I owe nothing to them!"

"Sorry! Please, I'm just trying to understand what you're doing—I admit that my knowledge is limited here."

Benzoni took a deep breath and a sip of his drink and seemed to calm down. "I believe you understand the experiment sufficiently. I don't expect you or your readers to grasp the physics of it, and it would take years of education for someone like you to engage with even the easiest concepts behind this experiment. After all, my colleagues certainly didn't appreciate my advancement on their little theories."

A sound like a groan came from the den, rising within a few seconds in pitch and volume until it mimicked the scream of a screech owl. It then ended in a thunderous crash that shook the house, overturned their drink glasses, and caused Wetherell to drop her notebook and pen and grip the arms of the easy chair. The crash was followed by a sickening sensation of vertigo; there was an aroma of lilacs, followed by the smell of wet dog; a couple of floor-to-ceiling cracks appeared in the plaster walls, and a hanging light fixture overhead began to swing like a pendulum.

"You will please excuse me a moment," said Benzoni, and rose to saunter into a bright green light now flooding through the den door.

The feeling of dizziness ceased, but Wetherell could still hear Benzoni tinkering and banging about in the den. At her feet, the switching mechanism was vibrating and making a quiet hooting sound. Did it look as though the mechanism had moved closer to her? She drew her feet back. She had a nagging notion that the mechanism would leap up and start humping her leg.

Benzoni returned and sat down with a sigh. "Just a little glitch back there. I worked it out, and I believe we can proceed." Benzoni reached toward the chrome switch, and the mechanism seemed to rise up a bit, like a dog about to be petted.

"Before we start," said Wetherell quickly, nervously, and Benzoni sat back, folded his arms and listened with feigned patience. Wetherell continued, "Have you seen the most recent story on my website?"

"Hmm. I'm not sure. Since you gave me a passcode I've been trying to follow your work, time permitting, but the most recent one I recall involved space aliens probing our bowels and stealing our gut flora to supplement their digestion of earth food. Frankly, that was an interesting idea but disgusting in its execution." He sniffed.

The switching mechanism made a crackling sound, in seeming agreement.

"No, not that story. I've published another story about a week ago that was inspired by this experiment. It's about probability. The idea is, in terms of probability, the universe is shaped like a funnel, with the wide end toward the distant future where probability widens to the infinite, and with the narrow end at the present moment. There probability shrinks to nothing and becomes reality, then extends into the past in a straight line we call history."

"Now I remember. The story about the piano player and the divorce and the—what was it—a teddy bear?"

"That was just my way of personalizing the idea for the reader," said Wetherell. "The point is, I'm a little concerned about the effect of your experiment on the space-time continuum." Benzoni winced at that phrase, but Wetherell hurriedly pressed on. "For example, what if the effect expands beyond the field you create? What if there's a sort of domino effect on all matter?"

"Impossible. As I said, it will take a huge amount of power to affect only a few particles, and the power at hand is finite, self-limiting. It's all in the math, but I'm afraid the math is beyond your comprehension. Now, if you will observe," and he reached for the switch again.

"Wait," said Wetherell. Again, Benzoni drew back, this time with a scowl. "I'm sorry to be a bother," Wetherell said, "but are you familiar with the idea of the stopper knot? Like, on a hoodie or sweatpants?" She glanced at Benzoni's pressed slacks, starched white lab coat, and bow tie. "Or, you know, any piece of clothing with a drawstring. A knot in a string, like an overhand knot, that stops the string from passing through a smaller opening."

"I'm familiar with knots in string. As you may notice, I did tie my shoes today, all by myself. Are you suggesting I'm creating a knot of some kind?"

"Okay, I admit I don't understand your experiment totally but suppose instead of just reversing time in a small field, this creates a sort of fold or stopper knot, in the space-time continuum." (Benzoni winced again) "And, I don't know, maybe this knot won't pass through the narrow end of the probability funnel, the present moment?"

"My dear," Benzoni said, "First, please stop saying 'space-time.' 'Space' is an antiquated notion promoted by inferior intellects, who are incapable of transcending the boundaries of human perception."

Wetherell wondered what kind of perception Benzoni had, if not human. At that moment the doorbell rang; Benzoni groaned: "It's my neighbor again. Pay no attention.

"As I was about to say, again, this is a self-limiting experiment on an infinitesimal scale. And your ideas about probability are amusing, but I must inform you that probability is not a force in physics; it's a mathematical notion, not even properly called a theory, in my opinion."

The ringing of the doorbell gave way to an insistent knocking; Benzoni ignored the noise. "And again, the consequences of this experiment are utterly clear in the calculations, to which I have applied extensive scrutiny based on three decades of experience in the field. Now, if we may proceed, without further interruption," and he reached forward again to the chrome toggle, "all I have to do is throw this little swi—"

The knocking at the door stopped. Unfortunately, so did the rest of the universe.

THE END

DAVID CHRISTENSON is a writer working in Minneapolis, Minnesota. He has been a cattle farmer, antique picker, beekeeper, crime reporter, daily newspaper editor, photographer, medical fact-checker, poet, advertising salesman, welder, graphic designer, and rare-book dealer.

TIMELESS IN CHRONOVILLE

John A. Frochio

1. wherein a boy walks a girl home from school

ON A DAY NOT much like any other day in a small town not much like any other small town, a boy walked a girl home from school. It was the day before the boy's fifteenth birthday, and he was talking incessantly and excitedly, which was not like him at all. The boy's name was Jon Beau, and the girl was named Danica.

Jon Beau was tall and slim, fair-haired, fair-complexioned, and his eyes were that deep blue that signified a thinker of deep thoughts, or at least a pretender of such a person. Danica was dark-haired, dark-complexioned and petite, with dark eyes that evoked a combination of mystery and passion, which was too soon an evocation at her young age.

His discourse was all over time and space. He told her how he had passed his father several times coming and going in and out of existence earlier that morning and how he had tried to talk to his father about his goals and dreams, but his father was always too busy or just not there. Really not there. He could be anywhere. And who knew where his mother was or if he would even see her before he turned fifteen? Danica listened intently to his goals and dreams because she too had goals and dreams and she would be turning fifteen soon as well.

He said, "I'm just overflowing with ideas about where I'll take my first-time walk. Where should I go? Should it be someplace safe and sensible, yet not too tedious? Or someplace much more exciting, with a hint of danger?"

"When I'm of age, I want to go to Victorian England," she said, "when women were prim and proper and pampered, and they dressed up in beautiful, elaborate gowns of silk and lace, and they had fancy hair-dos, and the men were either gentlemen or rogues."

"Which type of man would you prefer?"

She blushed. "A little bit of both, I expect."

He laughed.

"Well, I want to go to a place where men were masters of their destiny. The Roman Empire. The age of Vikings. A time when men fought hard and bravely for a great cause."

"Those sound like dangerous places to me. I think you have to be a more experienced walker before they allow you to go to those kinds of places."

"Well, maybe a time and place of great historical significance. The discovery of fire. The Mayflower's landing. The Lewis and Clark expedition. The signing of the Declaration of Independence. The Sinking of the Titanic. The Deconstruction of America. The Death of Money."

"Those could be pretty exciting walks."

"Or pretty boring. Do you know what I really want to see someday? I've thought about this a long time, but I never told anybody. I..." He hesitated. "I want to see the end of time."

She stopped and stared at him. "Are you crazy? I thought I knew you better than this. You know all the stories they tell about the ones who walked to the end of time. They either never came back, or they came back mentally deranged."

"I know, I know. Maybe I'll just go see the dinosaurs. Hey, by the way, don't forget my birthday party's tomorrow."

She grinned broadly. "Of course not. I always have time for a party."

2. wherein the boy manages to get his parents together in the same room at the same time

AFTER DINNER ON THE evening before his fifteenth birthday, Jon Beau snagged his father and mother before they took off to who knew where. He cornered them in the room affectionately called the living room, even though no one lived there or spent much time there at all.

"Can I talk to you guys a minute before you go off walking somewhere?"

"Of course, son," said his mother, looking distracted in her sequined gown and enormous embellished hat. "Tomorrow is a big day for you. You must have a lot of questions."

"Well... Hey, wasn't that couch green yesterday?"

His father and mother stared at the brown couch and shrugged.

It wasn't strange for things to disappear and new things to appear from one day to the next. Though there were strict rules about changing the past, even small changes in the past could sometimes make noticeable changes in the present day. What was especially odd was that some people noticed these changes while others didn't. This effect, called Alternate Memory Retention, was still unexplained by science to this day. Even Stephen Hawking was consulted by an emboldened time walker and found no logical explanation for the phenomenon.

"Anyway," Jon Beau continued, "what I want to know is what each of your first-time walks was like."

"Let me think," she said. "I believe, I went to the era known as the Roaring Twenties. You know, flappers and big bands. I loved that time. So exciting. Since I was young, I couldn't really enjoy it like I wanted to. That came later."

"And you, Dad?"

"Dinosaurs," he said. He was fussing with the controls on his silver jumpsuit.

Jon Beau frowned.

His father went on, "That was my first walk. It was awesome. I went back there over and over again. Still, do even today on occasion. Later I liked to hang out with Kurt Cobain and try to cheer him up. Couldn't tell him anything, though. The mandates, you know. Now I mostly like walking in the future among the high tech wizards and sparkly nanodragons. That or dinosaurs."

His mother added, "Our now time is ordinary, plain, unadorned. We don't have many mysteries, except for a few oddities like the Old Man who lives at the Farthest Edge of Town. Nobody can explain him. We really need time walks to allow us to fulfill our dreams, to provide us our cup of mystery, our escape from the dull now."

In his room later that evening, Jon Beau mind-messaged Danica for a while until he was too tired to think anymore. He fell asleep counting all the ways the world might end.

3. wherein the boy has dreams about the end of time
SOME OF JON BEAU'S dreams that night:

1. Different colored couches and other furniture were floating in the air. Things began appearing and disappearing and reappearing faster and faster until everything was a blur until Jon Beau noticed his sweet Danica approaching him from out of the fog of blurred confusion. Then, just before she reached him, the world was swept away in a whisper.

2. Patches of darkness began to appear over here and over there, like stains and scars and blotches and stigmata, until everything finally became engulfed in darkness.

3. Danica was running toward him in a panic. A giant ball of all things stolen from time walks was rolling towards them. This one ended quickly, with a bang, not a whimper.

4. Then there was the one about the giant whirlpool in the sky sucking everything up into it.

5. A big, busty maid with dustpan and broom, humming to herself as she went about her work cleaning up the world.

And on and on...

Jon Beau lost count as the dreams blurred into each other.

4. wherein the boy awakens to a strangely tortured disharmony
THE NEXT DAY JON Beau awoke to a rousing chorus of "Happy Birthday" perpetrated by a strange and motley crew. He soon found out that several generations of his family had been gathered up throughout time by his parents just to sing to him on the morning of his special day.

Most of them looked wide-eyed and a bit perplexed, but they all put their best efforts into the task. Whether they knew the tune or not, it represented a common bond that tied them all together. Who knew what methods of persuasion his parents had utilized to solicit their agreement to this eccentric mission!

Not long after the surprise wake up call, pandemonium broke out as the warily wondering wanderers scattered in all directions. His parents spread out to corral his ancestors and return them one by one to their individual familiar times.

Bringing people back from other eras was strictly forbidden by the time walk mandates, but his parents had a bit of a rebel in their souls. They were, however, always careful to clean up as best as they could after their indiscretions.

Breakfast was a little less exciting, yet different nonetheless. His mother tried to use a futuristic device she had obtained somewhere (who knows where?) to produce a complete breakfast of eggs, hash browns, toast, bacon, orange juice, and coffee. What came out wasn't recognizable as real food, but at least tasted half decent. He forced himself not to laugh at his mother's sincere efforts to make it special for him.

His parents gave him a chameleon robe for a birthday gift. This was a fairly recent innovation in time walk apparel that was helpful when you wanted to blend in with the surroundings of a potentially hostile time period or when you didn't have access to appropriate clothing. All of the better cross-temporal clothing line shops were beginning to carry these now.

His time walk mentor was due to arrive at 1:00 PM. Mentors were mandatory for new time walkers. Twenty hours of mentoring was required, longer if the mentor so stipulated.

Jon Beau could hardly contain his anxiety and excitement.

5. wherein the boy meets his mentor

PRECISELY AT 1:00, THE time walk mentor arrived at Jon Beau's house. He was a gruff middle-aged man, all business, and terseness in a drab gray suit, with lightly graying hair poking out from under a dark gray fedora. Ironically, his name was Mr. Gray. Or perhaps intentionally? His attire stood out in an era where wildly individual styles ran rampant, where no set style was the norm, or more precisely, all styles from all eras was the norm. Because of this vast and colorful diversity, the rarest of styles was drab gray, which was the clear style of Mr. Gray. Jon Beau did not know if this was by design or simply poor taste. He knew enough, however, not to question his mentor about his personal taste in attire.

Mr. Gray went straight to the business at hand.

"The basics and the mandates. That's what you're going to learn today."

First, he reviewed the basics. After he had drilled these thoroughly into the boy's mind, he quizzed Jon Beau.

"What is the power behind the time walk?"

"Two things. The human mind and the enhancement implant which we usually receive before we are six months old."

"Correct. What powers the implant?"

"A nano-battery pack which is disabled until a state-licensed mentor activates it with a special high-frequency remote device."

"Can the implant be deactivated?"

"Yes, the implant can be deactivated by a strong electrical surge or by a mentor or time walk enforcer if you are caught breaking any of the mandates."

"Tell me how you actually time walk."

"It's a combined effort of using your brain with the enhancement implant. Uh, let's see: the implant taps into unmapped regions of the cerebellum where extrasensory senses are proposed to reside."

"How do you make it work?"

"First, you concentrate on the time period you want to visit. The more you fine-tune the time and place, the better since this narrows the target of your focus. When the enhancement kicks in, you'll see a distant spot of light. Focus on the light, and you're on your way."

"How do you get back?"

"You concentrate on your home and focus on the light. Then you're back to where you started. Conservation of time causes you to return to your now time by the exact amount of elapsed time you spent away. It's always easier coming back because it's like a ball that bounces up and comes back down. It takes more energy to get you up than it takes to bring you back down."

"Can you take anything with you when you time walk?"

"Yes. Anything you touch up to a maximum mass will join you in your time walk. For example, your clothing always goes with you, but the earth beneath your feet has too much mass to time walk with you."

"What if you run into yourself or other time walkers?"

"This is the strange part. There is no danger of overlapping visits. Any visit you make to the same time period automatically replaces a previous visit. Every visit is your first visit."

This last item was known as the Time Balancing Principle. Time continually tries to correct itself. This explained why time travelers weren't encountering each other and other time travelers over and over again. Once a time walker leaves a time period, time restores itself to its steady state as best as it can, so that the next visitor will find virtually no evidence of another's visit. The most popular explanation for this phenomenon was that time travelers were actually visiting "instances" of a time period generated specifically for that visitor and not the actual time period itself. This theory, however, did not explain the "perceived" changes that many encountered in their present time. Some theories concluded that memories were faulty and therefore could not be the true determinate of whether there were actual changes or not.

It was all very confusing, and most people simply chose not to think about it too much.

Once Jon Beau understood the basics, Mr. Gray immediately began describing the mandates. After an intense review, Mr. Gray asked him to recite each one, word for word.

"One: You cannot bring anyone back from another time.

"Two: You cannot leave anyone behind in another time if they have no other way of returning.

"Three: You cannot bring any object back from another time if it is 'owned' by someone else. Something is considered owned when it is important to someone in that time period.

"Four: You cannot transport weapons of any kind to or from another time.

"Five: You cannot leave objects of any kind in the past that may ultimately be the cause of a 'significant' historical change.

"Six: You cannot attempt in any way to be the cause of a 'significant' historical change.

"Seven: You cannot use any knowledge gained from the future to make any 'significant' change to the past or present.

"Eight: You cannot go to a time period where you already exist. The results of such an action would be unpredictable.

"Nine: Remember to dress appropriately for the era and climate.

"Ten: You may time walk to places that are known to be dangerous only at your own risk.

"Note: Examples of 'significant' changes can be found in Appendix A of the *Time Walk Mandates Handbook*."

Mr. Gray seemed pleased with Jon Beau's recitation, in that he was not scowling. "Very good. Now finally, what is the government's official position statement on time walking?"

"REMEMBER: Time walking is a privilege and is meant for recreational purposes only. Please do not misuse this privilege."

"Excellent! You've learned the mandates very well. Now you must remember to keep them." A brief burst of excitement followed by his usual gruffness.

Jon Beau was too exhausted to respond.

After a short break, Mr. Gray asked Jon Beau, "So where would you like to go for your first-time walk?"

Jon Beau's face lit up.

"Woodstock. The original, of course."

"An excellent choice. I see you've anticipated this and have already dressed appropriately."

Jon Beau wore a shirt of many colors and torn jeans, typical attire for that time period.

"You will feel a sharp stabbing sensation in your head when I activate the enhancement. When it passes, let me know."

He felt the stab and cringed involuntarily. When the feeling passed, Jon Beau noticed that Mr. Gray was now wearing a chameleon robe.

"Now, hold my hands and concentrate. Concentrate on the time and the place. Focus on that distant point of light. Do you see it? Focus."

6. wherein the boy takes his first walk in time

AND HE WAS AT Woodstock. 1969. Max Yasgur's farm. A sea of people as far as he could see. Sweet smells in the air. Mud under his feet. Lots and lots of mud!

Country Joe and the Fish were on stage. The crowd was swaying, and a deafening roar rose to the sky.

"Give me an F!"

"F!"

Jon Beau looked around and didn't see his mentor right away. Then he made out the gruff man's figure oddly blended into the background like a ripple in a pond.

Mr. Gray assured him that he would remain close. Jon Beau smiled and dove into the maddening crowd. He immediately became a part of the seminal celebration, swirling in its drug-laden maelstrom.

The music blended with the drugs and the flesh and the sweat and the rush. Jefferson Airplane was playing "White Rabbit." He moved with the music and felt the tangible purpose of the festival fill his spirit.

"Groovy," someone said.

Sharing a doobie, he agreed wholeheartedly.

7. wherein the boy returns to the here and now
"TIME TO GO BACK."

The voice came from somewhere to his left. He squinted and tried to find his mentor. He had lost track of time.

"Come with me. Your first walks should not be too long."

They held hands and returned. It was easy, just like the book said. It felt like a rubber band snapping back into its natural shape.

"You did very well for your first walk, Jon."

Mr. Gray handed him a slim booklet, a manual on Time Walk etiquette.

"These are not as important as the mandates. Those you must learn completely and never break. But these are simple 'common courtesies' that we highly recommend."

Jon Beau leafed through the booklet. *Never use time walking for gambling purposes.* (Gambling was pretty much non-existent nowadays. What would be the point?) *Never time walk to escape responsibilities.* (A gray area there.) *Never time walk in the middle of undesired conversations.* (Common courtesy.)

He chuckled.

Mr. Gray worked out a schedule of visits over the next couple weeks. Before he left, he deactivated Jon Beau's implant.

Mr. Gray explained, "Until I sign your certificate of graduation within two or three weeks, you will be activated only in my presence."

After Mr. Gray had departed, Jon Beau hurried to get ready for his party. All of his best friends and most of his relatives would be there. He couldn't wait to tell them about his adventure!

8. wherein the boy parties down
HE BEGAN WATCHING THE clock at 5:30. 5:31. 5:32... Damn! Why was time moving so slowly?

At 5:45, his friends and relatives began arriving. By 6:15 everyone except his Uncle Alec had arrived. Most people were very time conscious. Every minute counted. Except for a rare few like his Uncle Alec, who never cared much for time constraints which he frequently compared to straitjackets.

Uncle Alec showed up at 6:47.

Uncle Alec was an odd character. He had jaunted all over time in his youth, then suddenly stopped time walking altogether. Though he loved to ramble on about his past adventures, he would never tell anyone why he stopped time walking. Jon Beau resolved to find out someday.

Jon Beau noticed that Danica looked exceptionally nice this evening in 1950's Americana style sweater and skirt. He was happy that she spent the effort to look so stunning for his party.

First came the games. Then the party food. Finally the opening of the gifts. His gifts were more grown-up oriented gifts: clothing of various eras, hairpieces, a walking stick, a watch on a chain, makeup kits, all the necessities of a time walker. Danica got him a state-approved time walker's medical kit. All useful gifts.

Afterward, as was traditional, they all gathered in a circle to hear about Jon Beau's first-time walk. He didn't leave out a single moment, a single event, relating each and every step of his walk in fully embellished detail.

Uncle Alec always provided a running snide commentary to anyone's story. However, he was unusually quiet this evening as he listened to Jon Beau's overzealous words. Everyone noticed his odd behavior, but no one mentioned it.

9. wherein the boy engages in post-party contemplation

DANICA WAS THE LAST to leave. She cuddled with Jon Beau on their new magenta couch that he had never seen before this evening and watched an old black and white jungle adventure on a wall TV, a TV that seemed much bigger this evening than he remembered.

"So, you didn't go with dinosaurs after all?" she asked.

"No. I found out my Dad did dinosaurs."

"Didn't want to copy your Dad?"

"Your first walk has to be special. It has to mean something to you. I remembered a paper I did for school on the Hippie Culture a while ago. I remembered how fascinated I was with this rebellious generation that had a purpose, a clear purpose driven by love and peace."

"A lot of them were drugged-up whackos, though, weren't they?"

"Well, yeah, and a lot of them never grew out of that state of mind—if they even survived. But still, as a group, they had a common goal. Have you ever felt like our society was just floundering around with all of its freedoms and unlimited access to all time and space? It's like we live in a world with no purpose, a self-centered, timeless place, and the only places with purpose are those places we walk to when we want to get away from the so-called real world."

She nodded. "It does seem like going to school and getting a job are just things we do to kill time between time walks. Nobody has any great goals for their lives anymore."

"Because the great goals exist in other times, other places. Those far-away goals have become our goals. But they're only temporary."

"What can we do about it? It's our way of life."

"At least now I understand why people get hooked on time walking. They get to go to places that have real purposes to fulfill."

She nodded.

On the TV screen, a half-naked jungle man was saving a half-naked woman from an alligator. He had a goal to accomplish, and nothing was going to prevent him from completing it, even if it meant fighting the dangerous creature to the death.

They became absorbed in the story from a far-away time that played out before them.

After a while, he said, "Which is the cause and which is the effect? Did the advent of time walking make us this way or was time walking a way out of our purposeless lives?"

They cuddled closer against a sudden chill.

Later that night after Danica departed, Jon Beau wondered how he could bring purpose back into his world. He wondered how he could make Danica a part of his new purpose-driven life. He had a lot to think about, he realized, as he drifted off into sleep.

10. wherein the boy walks boldly into the future
THE NEXT FEW WEEKS flew by in a blur.

Jon Beau received his certificate, and the implant was permanently activated. He became very adept at adapting to other cultures and blending into the background as necessary. Hungry for adventure, he experienced many different cultures in many different parts of the world in many different time periods. He even visited the dinosaurs, once.

There were certain places he would walk to when he wanted to get away from the meaninglessness of his life. In fields or forests untouched by man, he would spend long hours in quiet contemplation, trying to make sense out of it all. He found and laid claim—if one could actually "lay claim" to places in space and time that were accessible by all—to several spots unmolested by human hands that overlooked beautiful rolling hills or scenic deep blue lakes.

By the time Danica celebrated her fifteenth birthday, Jon Beau was a relatively experienced time walker. After her mentoring was complete, they began taking time walks together. They soon accrued several favorite walking spots.

In unpopulated paradises, they discussed their future together. Time walks were a great way to escape their mad world and contemplate their future. They grew closer during these special moments. Their intimacy blossomed in faraway times and places.

Back in the real world, his father worked in sales, and his mother was a dance instructor. Her parents both worked in the health care field. But jobs seemed of little importance to their parents and most people in their world. People simply worked for the necessities of life. All jobs were of equal value, homogenized and socialized and sterilized. Everything else revolved around time walks.

They both wondered what they were going to do with their own lives. They did not want to live only for the time walk as others did. They wanted more for their lives. They wanted real purpose.

Those who just take and take from other times—what impact would that have without giving anything in return? And, Jon Beau wondered, what impact on the end of time?

One day Jon Beau told Danica that his Uncle Alec was visiting his family later that week.

He told her, "I'm finally going to ask him why he stopped time walking."

"You told me he wouldn't tell anyone why he stopped."

"I've become close with my uncle recently. I think maybe he'll tell me. Anyway, I figured it wouldn't hurt to try."

One evening, when Jon Beau was alone with his uncle in their family room, he asked his Uncle the question. Without hesitation, as though he had been waiting all this time for Jon Beau to ask him the question, his Uncle Alec told him his story. He spoke in emotionless tones, as though reading a long and tedious passage from a technical manual.

11. wherein the boy hears his uncle's story

"I used to be wild and carefree, like your father always says. Now I'm just carefree, which is still a good thing but safer. I did a lot of crazy and dangerous things growing up, mostly when I time walked. I loved to go to forbidden places. I always pushed myself to my limits and beyond. I was not a very smart kid.

"When I finished school, I got a job on a construction gang. We built bridges and tall buildings. A dangerous job, some would say, but that was how I liked it. After coming home from a day of hanging high above the earth, I would eat my supper and go out looking for more danger.

"I found purpose in my life in perilous situations. Past wars and catastrophes. Nations in revolution. Places in turmoil. Deadly environments, natural disasters. Horrors, terrors, evil times. I tried them all. I walked among dinosaurs and gangsters and the immoral and the heartless. I fought Jesse James and Blackbeard the Pirate. I tangled with Bigfoot. Needless to say, I barely survived so many close encounters that I could not count them all.

"Then one day I heard how very few of even the most experienced time walkers ever attempted to visit the end of time. Of those who attempted it, most never returned. Of those who returned, all of them went mad.

"Of course, this intrigued me. When I did further research, I found that twelve of the known thirteen who did return were in insane asylums somewhere. No one knew where. The thirteenth survivor was the legendary Old Man who lived at the farthest edge of town. You've heard of him. The legend persists until today. It is said that he lives far past all signs of civilization, far past the last of the ethanol farms, well-kept fields, and decent roads, far beyond where anybody had any desire to travel.

"I was driven to find him. It took many months to track him down, but I was resolute. Some called me bull-headed. But I eventually found him. And I went to see him.

"The Old Man lived in a big old house, due West of town, far past where the roads ran out of places to go. The house was big and ugly and in severe disrepair. It appeared on the verge of collapsing under the weight of its own rotting wood.

"I cautiously looked around for him and finally found him in the back of the house, weeding a lush vegetable garden.

"He looked up at me as I approached him and said, 'Let me tell you about the end of time.'

"So, you know why I'm here?' I asked him.

"Yes," he said in a voice so quiet I could barely hear him. His eyes, though, held the intensity of a tyrant or a hungry beast.

"The Old Man began talking.

"First you have to dress right. You have to dress for the coldest of all coldest weather. Lots of layers. Cover your face.

"Use goggles, a breathing mask. I recommend those new self-cleaning, UV protection goggles. I think I have a coupon I can give you. Remind me before you leave.

"The wind is powerful. Be prepared to stand firm against the mightiest of all mighty winds. Wear heavy boots. Eat a light meal before you go there. Nothing heavy.

"Go with a spiritual mindset. It's best to take God with you. Whether you believe in God or not, take Him along. Don't argue this point. Just do it.

"What else? Ah, yes, there's the brightness and the darkness. That doesn't make sense, does it? Well, most of it was the darkest of all dark places. But some of it was the brightest of all bright places. With all that darkness and brightness going on, it was damn hard to make out anything. You know what I'm saying?

"So, at first, I wasn't too impressed. But when those blurry images began to take shape amid that brightness, I got scared real quick.

"What am I saying? I'm saying that what I was beginning to see there at the end of time made me scared as hell. That's what I'm saying.

"The bottom line: don't stay too long. It's hypnotic. It draws you in. It's hard to pull away. But if you don't pull away, you either get sucked in forever, or your brains get sucked out.

"So, when you're standing there, as soon as that thought occurs to you—the thought that I just planted in your brain, pull out immediately. Then you might survive—mostly intact—like me.

"I asked the Old Man what the images were that scared him so badly.

"I can't say."

"You won't tell me?"

"'I can't say because I can't remember. Maybe that's why I'm still sane. Mostly sane."

"The Old Man went back to his garden. I knew that was all I was going to get from him. As I walked away, I remembered the intensity of his eyes. It occurred to me that I recognized those eyes. Somehow, I recognized them.

"It wasn't until much later, when I was more than halfway home, that I suddenly realized that he had my eyes. I was looking at myself. There was an old version of me living in that decrepit house beyond the farthest edge of town. That was me after I had gone to see the end of time.

"I gave up time walking. I stopped living life dangerously. I'm a landscaper now. I'm good at what I do. I no longer desire to see the end of time. I have a purpose to my life now. I'm happy now."

He never explained to Jon Beau how he came to believe that the Old Man was actually himself after having gone to see the end of time, or why he thought that giving up time walking altogether would stop the cycle of events which would lead him to that fate. And he never acknowledged the paradox of meeting himself, which most scientists agreed would be deadly to the frail fabric that linked space and time, and therefore a chain reaction may already have been initiated that would bring about the end of time. He was, however, happy and content with his decision and his life. Perhaps that was enough to keep time and space from tearing apart.

12. wherein the boy has more dreams about the end of time

SOME OF JON BEAU'S dreams that night:

1. The images falling out of the brightness at the end of time gradually morphed from formless shapes into the faces of all the

people that he had ever known. They were all staring at him with deeply piercing eyes. The eyes were beckoning him to come join them in their great and timeless moment, hanging eternally in that last moment of existence. Here is the purpose of everything, they were telling him. This final moment of eternal satisfaction.

2. Variations of No. 1, with a little more or less pathos and a little more or less comic relief.

Etcetera.

13. wherein the boy revisits his Uncle's odd account

LONG AFTER HIS UNCLE Alec left, Jon Beau continued to consider the strange story his uncle told.

He certainly heard about the legend of the Old Man who lived at the farthest edge of town. There were countless stories and unsubstantiated rumors about him and how he came to be a recluse. Nobody really knew the truth.

Was his uncle's account the truth or just another in a long history of speculations? His uncle was a great story teller, and it was common knowledge that there was a lot of exaggeration and poetic license in his accounts.

Was Jon Beau really supposed to believe that this old man who lived in their time period was his own Uncle Alec who, at some point in their future, returned from a visit to the end of time to retire to a house in their present time? That clearly broke one of the mandates of time walking!

But suspending all disbelief and assuming that his uncle was telling the truth, he asked himself, "So what was the meaning of his strange encounter with his older self?"

Perhaps the Old Man was warning his younger self not to go to the end of time. Or was he just offering some helpful advice? Would his Uncle eventually avoid the classic time paradox?

A better explanation was that his uncle was simply deceiving himself about the true identity of the Old Man. Or the Old Man was truly mad. Either one made perfect sense.

At that moment, Jon Beau determined to visit the Old Man someday in order to get the answers himself.

14. wherein the boy careens into his destiny

TWO YEARS LATER JON Beau finally tracked down the location of the Old Man. By then he was out of school and working as an interior decorator. He was sharing an apartment with Danica who was taking an online study course in bio-pattern engineering. They continued to plan a purposeful future together in their own now time.

She accepted, though did not quite understand, the obsession with which he had for the Old Man and the end of time. She promised she would be waiting for him if he made it back alive and sane. After all, their lives by now had become permanently entwined.

Jon set the auto GPS coordinates in his green rover and kicked back and relaxed. It would be a long ride.

When the clarion announced their imminent arrival, he awoke and immediately noticed the Old Man's crumbling house. He keyed off the engine, stepped outside onto bare earth, took a deep breath and slowly scanned the scene of decay and disrepair.

It seemed much worse than his Uncle's description. However, time had passed.

He approached the house with cautious steps.

This was it, he thought. The moment of revelation or disappointment. He didn't know which to expect. What story would the Old Man spout today? Would it mean anything to him or to his future? Or would it be the same old bag of tricks and tips he heard from his uncle?

He found the Old Man in his backyard painting on an easel. A fine impressionistic interpretation of the distant hills graced his canvas. Paintbrush in hand, dripping sky blue, the Old Man turned to look at Jon Beau with deep blue piercing eyes.

Eyes so familiar, he thought.

He stared deeply into them. They were old and tired eyes, but not his Uncle's.

Yet so familiar.

At that moment, time appeared to open up to him like a bright flower blossoming in a desert, showing him the right path he should be taking through the purposeless void, even before the Old Man opened his mouth to speak.

The Old Man spoke. The advice the Old Man gave was different from the advice his uncle received so long ago. But on the other hand, it wasn't very much different.

He listened attentively.

***

15. wherein the boy finds a purpose

JON BEAU RETURNED TO his beloved Danica, and they lived a long and fruitful life together. Not quite happily ever after, but happy enough and full of many accomplishments in home decoration and in bio-engineering and in the natural creation of three smart and beautiful children, from now until the end of their very own now time.

THE END

JOHN FROCHIO grew up and still lives among the rolling hills of Western Pennsylvania. He is semi-retired, working part time supporting computer automation systems for steel mills. He has had stories published in *Interstellar Fiction, Beyond Science Fiction, Twilight Times, Aurora Wolf, Liquid Imagination, SciFan Magazine,* as well as anthologies *Triangulation (*2003), *Triangulation: Parch (2014), Time Travel Tales* (2016), *Visions VII: Universe (2017)*, and *2047: Short Stories From Our Common Future* (2017). He has also published general fiction novel *Roots of a Priest* (with Ken Bowers, 2007) and sf&f collection *Large and Small Wonders,* (2012). His wife Connie, a retired nurse, and his daughter Toni, a flight attendant, have bravely put up with his strange ways for many years. His author's webpage is www.johnafrochio.wordpress.com

THE WINDS OF TIME
Mike Adamson

I HAVE ALWAYS BEEN given to flights of fancy. Maybe it's why I followed a band with a name like *Dawn Wind*. The imagery the name conjured was enough to fire the imagination, and from there the haunting melodies and rhythms, the sparkling riffs and snappy drum-work made for an experience which came to shape my world.

Often, I was told I was a groupie and spent way too much time following a local mob from pub to pub, catching them at halls and markets, wherever they could get a gig. Over the years I became friends with the guys, helped them pack and lug their gear and clean up venues after a midnight finish more times than I could count. It's the natural role of one who loves the music.

But there are times when the unnatural comes calling, and an imaginative mind can sometimes not recognise it when it arrives, or indeed be too accepting of it if it does.

My friends said I would crawl through fire to a *Dawn Wind* gig, and they were probably right. Jacobsville was a one-horse town up the country, and how the band came to be booked to play the village hall I had no idea, but no sooner the notification on the band's email list than I was searching for transport options to get out there.

My old wreck had more or less reached the end of its days. I didn't fancy abandoning it beside a dusty highway and thumbing a lift home, so the country buses were the next best bet. The further out, the fewer services are available, and it turned out Jacobsville was served by two services each way, each day. The second north from the city would get into town in the late afternoon, a few hours before doors-open, and I could get the morning service back the next day.

An overnight in the sticks was in order. With a sleeping bag lashed to my pack, I was quite prepared to sleep rough—I certainly couldn't afford a room at the one and only hotel, though I looked on the bright side and imagined spending half the night with the band, passing a bottle.

The bus left from an inner-city stop around noon. It was a hot and unsettled sort of day, definitely bushfire weather, and I'd monitored the alerts all day on my phone. Nothing was burning out Jacobsville way—the gig was still on. I made it into town on an earlier service and waited in the shade of the tall city towers, my pack by my feet and a water bottle in my hand. A snack-bar lunch was fattening and unhealthy, but tasty.

My phone rang with its signatory *Dawn Wind* riff, and I pulled it out of my pack.

"Rory?"

"That's me, who've I got?"

"Deano. You headed for the show tonight?"

"Of course, I am. I'm halfway there already."

"Oh, right...."

"Why?" Something in his tone gave me an abrupt thrill of unease. "I mean, where else would I be? This is *Dawn Wind* we're talking about."

"I know, dude, I know... it's just...." It wasn't like Dean to be shy.

"Come on, out with it. Are the fire warnings up north now?"

"No. No, nothing like that. It's just my sister...."

"What about her? Is she okay?" I added the last hurriedly as the unease became full-blown. I liked Cheryl and always had, and Dean knew it.

"Yeah, yeah, she's fine. But she had a dream, dude."

"Your sister's always having dreams. What was it this time, end of the world as we know it again?" Abruptly I realised I was drawing odd looks from others waiting for the bus.

"It was about you. She said you headed off into the country... and you never came back."

"What?" My eyebrows had risen into my greasy crew cap. "Oh, come on, guy, you know she dreams about everything under the sun. Doesn't mean shit, and you know it." All the same, the unease settled like a ball of dough in my belly.

"She was real upset this morning. I got the story out of her and promised I'd call you." He sounded somewhere between embarrassed and concerned. "I know there's nothing to it, but it was pretty bloody real to her and... well, you know."

"I know," I returned quietly. "Look, I'll come see her when I get back tomorrow. That's a promise. Tell her I'll bring her a signed poster from the show."

"Okay, dude." He knew there was no way I was going to reconsider the trip, and I could tell he felt a fool for bringing it up, even implicitly. "Well, have a great time, say hi to everyone for us."

"I will," was all I could find to say as I spotted the bus approaching. "Gotta go. Bye."

I was soon in a seat up the back with my pack around my feet and watched the city flow by until the urban fringe replaced it. The yellow fields of summer gradually appeared, and I found myself looking at the grey, unsettled sky, feeling the wind buffeting the coach. And no matter how I closed my eyes and turned up the *Dawn Wind* tracks in my ears, I couldn't quite shake the sense that, just maybe, Cheryl knew something we didn't.

I found the motion of the coach, and the flow of traffic in the other lane a bit mesmeric and began to drift off. It was a long trip, and I knew the coach did a rest stop on the way, so I hunched into my light summer jacket and let the miles go by. An album's worth of tracks later I jolted awake when a major wind gust broadsided the coach and the driver corrected violently. A horn blared in the other lane and passengers looked up from their phones and books with a momentary start.

Bloody weather, I thought, and fiddled with my phone, checked messages and texts. I sent a text to Cheryl with lots of smiley faces, but as I did, I wondered if I was doing it to cheer up her or myself.

The day was a strange mix of yellow and grey, lowering clouds over the reaped fields, and I began to think *tornado*. They were unknown in this part of the world, but there was a first time for everything. Unable to rest, I checked the weather and fire warnings, but it seemed I was just jittery. No alerts were posted for the northern pastoral lands.

I sighed, swigged water from my bottle and resettled myself. Maybe twenty passengers were on board, each keeping to themselves. They looked like morning trippers on their way home. Country towns are the outer end of the transport system. Buses bring folks into town in the morning and take them back in the afternoon and evening, so trying to get home from an evening event in the country is far from easy.

I drowsed again for a while and might even have dropped off to sleep as, before I knew it, we were at the roadhouse rest stop. The bus pulled in, and we had fifteen minutes built into the schedule to stretch our legs, hit the bathrooms and go shopping. The stop woke me up well enough. I snapped a few pictures with my phone of the angry sky over the stark yellow fields, then gratefully found the bathrooms and put them to use. I wolfed a prepacked sandwich and soft drink and was crumpling the remains into a bin when the bus honked for passengers to reboard.

The afternoon was not getting any less miserable, and I had visions of storms tonight. Fewer passengers reboarded. Several had been collected here by friends or family and departed by car, so the bus was quieter, which somehow made things more dismal. Now we stopped more often, and passengers were leaving. I had a vision of being the last one aboard, heading on into the odd, unnaturally early twilight, and a shiver went up my spine.

As I said, I've always had an imaginative soul; but to find myself the last of a group of travellers at the farthest point from home whispered odd things to my subconscious.

The wind was shaking the bus again, and when I looked up from my phone, I saw dust-brown haze driven across the plains. They say winds charge the air with positive ions that make you feel strange, sometimes giddy, sometimes elated. But they never leave you untouched.

There are legends about the winds, things our ancestors lived with because the wind was their daily companion. We have so far misplaced our sense for the ways of the living world, we're lost outside our safe, artificial walls. Even if you've never heard of any such thing, you'll *remember*, because some things, the race can never forget.

Between the dust, the lowering light and the blows of the wind on the windows around me, I began to feel very low and tried to pull myself together. I put my ear-buds in again, pulled up another selection of tracks, closed my eyes and shut out the dire sights.

I'd be fine when I got to Jacobsville, found a cafe and sat over coffee until friends began to arrive for the concert. Then all would be normal, bright and cheerful, and the fun of the show would wipe away all these morbid impressions.

Yes—I'd be fine when I got there.

I STARTED AWAKE, MY heart thudding.

For a long and terrible moment, I couldn't remember where I was. Such feelings weren't new, but the moment went on far too long, and I was quite distressed by the time I remembered what I was doing. The driver yelled again from the front.

"Hey, buddy, end of the line. Wakey-wakey, or you'll be heading back to town with me."

I raised a hand in acknowledgement, cast around for my bits and pieces, hefted my pack and made my way to the doors with a nod of thanks. The bus stop was in the main street, and Jacobsville was part of the name of a few businesses.

As the bus pulled out, I thumped onto a bench seat and grabbed out my water bottle for a long drink. I felt I hadn't drunk in an age, and the roadhouse seemed a long time ago. I scrubbed my face with dry hands and breathed deeply, mastering myself. Why did I feel so unwell?

At last, I began to improve and looked up at the grey sky. The temperature seemed to have lowered a little with the weather front moving through, and there was a sense of rain later. I checked the time and shouldered my pack. From my pocket, I drew out a printout of the town map and headed through the dusty streets toward the hall.

Nowhere was far from anywhere here. When I sighted the hall, I had my bearings. I turned back and found a coffee shop on the main street. I needed a large straight white and something sugary, and soon I was sitting at a rickety old table by the window, a mug steaming before me with two doughnuts to soothe my nerves.

I looked out at the stormy afternoon for a long time, and something felt *different*. I couldn't put my finger on it for a long time, and let my mind drift... looking forward to the show, wondering who'd be there. But when I realised what was wrong it left me more perplexed than ever.

The light.

The light was subtly wrong. I'd started this trip in the early part of a hard, post-climate change summer, so why did it feel later in the day than the hour suggested? I had an hour to go before anyone else would be showing up, but I had the distinct impression the sun would be down before the hall opened for the event.

That's not right, I thought blankly. *At this time of year, it should be light until the set break.*

Puzzling for a while, I finished my coffee and ordered another. When the spotty-faced kid looking after the shop brought it over, I tried to engage him in conversation. It wasn't easy, but I got a few words out of him. He must have noticed the *Dawn Wind* flash on my pack.

"So, you're here for the show at the hall?"

"That's right," I said, suddenly glad somebody knew something that tallied with my expectations.

"I'm a big fan of *Slime Crawler.*"

Good for you, I felt like saying, but just smiled as I took a bite of doughnut.

"I have most of their albums. *Kraken of the Apocalypse* hasn't come out yet. Something about problems with the download agreements." He grinned and leaned against the next table. "You gotta love their top-end riffs!" He proceeded to mime air-guitar to a sound only he could hear, face contorted in apoplexy.

Why is this greasy sprog going on about Slime Crawler? I thought to myself. I was spared any more of his musical impersonations as the door chime rang and he turned to look after another customer. I sipped my coffee and grazed through the second doughnut, and the hands of the ancient clock behind the counter moved with leaden slowness.

The afternoon was grim, and to my jaundiced gaze, it seemed a lot was wrong with this world. The vehicles seemed not just old but worn out, dripping the same rust that had gnawed through the ancient corrugated metal sheeting you still found in these parts. Wood was sun-split and warped, paint peeling and faded, and dirt was omnipresent. Rank grass grew through broken concrete sidewalks, and the hum of insects was like a promise of the storm. The very smell of the ages was on the place: a mustiness as if this town clung to existence at the most tenuous outer edges of human reality.

One step further into the threatening evening, and it seemed I would pass beyond human ken altogether and enter some sphere I could not imagine.

No amount of music in my ears would pull me out of this mood. I needed to see a familiar face, to know things were as they should be. I checked coverage, but I was outside range on my service. Great, I thought blankly, stuffed my phone into an inside pocket and drained my cup. I had to move before this feeling of lethargy glued me down, and the shop was closing soon anyway.

I dragged on my pack and stepped out into the cooling, oddly dimming evening, looked each way along the street and wandered toward the yellow, dry-as-tinder grass of the municipal reserve. The flower beds were dead, the seats graffitied. It looked as if the place hadn't seen care in years. When I sat and turned my collar up, I felt I was bouncing from one bad place to another.

The wind worried at my hair, tugged my cap off—the same wind that seemed to have something against the human race today. I turned my face to it, and its intermittent gusty nature was like an impalpable slap to my cheeks.

Go away! it said.

You're stuck with me, I responded glumly, and shut out my feelings to let time go by.

But the wind was unrelenting, blowing my cap off twice, and the second time I picked it up I cursed and made my way to the information shelter where noticeboards told of the historic heritage of Jacobsville, and flyers fluttered on a pin-board. I passed a disinterested few minutes, letting my eyes scan the history of this pastoral village, then went on to the local ads. Not really seeing anything, just letting my eyes run along lines of text on colourful printed pages tacked up—a garage sale, a special offer coupon for the hairdresser, happy hour at the pub, a *Dawn Wind* concert—

My heart leapt as I saw the show flyer, and I grinned. It was their standard sheet, with the details for tonight's event added in, and I felt much better as I saw it. But only for a moment.

The flyer was held by only two of four pins, the others having pulled through the paper, which was crisp and yellowed, and the inks were faded. It was either an excellent aging job, or this flyer had been weathering for some time.

I blinked, put out a hand and steadied the fluttering paper, absently pulled a pin and refixed the loosest corner to gain it some life before the wind completed its destruction. And I stared hard at the sheet. Yes, it was my band; yes, it was today's date, December 5th.

Was it?

The notion struck me cold, and for a long moment, I couldn't react. Then I made myself take out my phone and see not just the time display but the date as well.

December 5th.

I heaved a silent sigh of relief and began to chide myself for an idiot until I remembered I was outside coverage. Therefore, my phone was running on previous settings. It wasn't in touch with the network timebase in order to update—if an update was required.

I hunched my shoulders and tried to make sense of it. The easiest thing was to tell myself I was being ridiculous and all would be well when the band's familiar vehicles rolled into town, any time now, to set up and do the sound checks. But when I looked at the poster, faded and tattered, I couldn't accept it. This was tangible proof: something was very wrong.

Still, the rational mind needs more, and I set off along the street from the park toward the hotel. I was sure to find a newspaper or something showing a date, and when I entered the hubbub of the front bar, it was before me. A big screen TV on which the local news was playing. The date and time were in the corner of the screen.

March 2nd.

I turned and stepped out into the windy early evening, squinted against a flurry of dust that skittered through the balcony area, then I settled at a vacant corner table, in a wrought iron chair that must have been a hundred years old.

Three months. How? Now the faded, frayed paper made sense. The kid talking about another band… Cheryl's dream. *You went out to the country and never came back.* The words took on a terrible meaning, and my own disbelief stung me with a scorn all its own.

I was alone, evening was approaching, I knew no one, I had limited cash in my pocket and no credit card. If there was an ATM in the hotel, maybe I could tap my account for enough to snag a room for the night, and pray the first bus in the morning was on time. Yes, this was probably the best thing to do. But three months—how to explain it? I couldn't explain what I did not understand.

A few vehicles went through, farm pickups and SUVs. Rough and ready types were coming into the bar. I tried to shrink inside myself and be inconspicuous, but it wasn't easy. A city geek with a *Dawn Wind* flash on his backpack was the opposite of inconspicuous in these parts, and I carefully turned my pack, so the flash was concealed from the casual glance. Maybe *Slime Crawler* was more their speed.

I thought I should buy a drink if I was going to spend any time here. A couple of other tables were now occupied, and farm types and local kids were laughing and smoking as if nothing was wrong. Perhaps to them, nothing was. I heard a few rumbles and thumps in the thickening air as a gold sunset flushed the clouds, and I tried to decide if it was oncoming thunder or just *Slime Crawler's* sound checks over at the hall. I'd certainly hear them from the main street. Maybe I should go to the show to kill the evening—screw in earplugs and stay at the back. It would get me off the street at least.

As I was thinking, the wind flurried, blew in my face like a slap, and I had the creeping impression fate was laughing at me. *Make all the plans you like, they'll come to nothing*, was the spiteful impression at the back of my head. I was wrestling with rejecting it as mere pessimism when a shadow moved in my peripheral vision, and a smell of old tobacco overlaid the omnipresent dust.

Two bottles thumped down on the table, uncapped and frosty, and a dark shape settled into the chair opposite. One hand thumbed a broad hat back over straggling silver hair, and a face like seamed walnut wood smiled at me.

"You look lost, kid. Wet your whistle. Being scared gives you the mother and father of dry mouths."

For a moment I was too stunned to speak, and the old man must have seen the gears of my mind spinning, trying to mesh. He smiled indulgently and let me find my words. "What—what makes you think I'm scared? Or lost?"

"The look on your face, for one thing. The fact you're sitting outside a bar on a stormy evening with a bedroll on your pack when other strangers your age are over in the hall waiting for the noisefest. The odds of you making a trip all this way up from the big smoke by accident are pretty remote, and you've not got your phone in your hand." He sat forward, face catching the glare of lights through the ancient leaded windows of the pub. "So unless I'm reading it all wrong, drink up and tell me about it. I'm the only ear you've got right now."

The beer tasted glorious, chilled from the bar fridge, and I realised he was right. My mouth was dry as the street. A great whirl of gold-orange cloud made the village seem a friendlier place for a moment, but the wind tugging the awnings was now cooling rapidly. I knew it would be one of those nights not easily forgotten, even if it was survived.

"You're right," was all I could grunt at first.

"What's your name, kid?"

"Matthews. Rory Matthews."

"Dan Netherby." A hard hand was thrust across the table, and I shook it, uncomfortable in the act. "You look like you have a story to tell but are afraid no one will believe it."

I grinned bitterly, but my mind was working again. "And you sound like you've heard a few things others might not believe, too."

"Well, now, you could say." He took a pull at his bottle and rested back in his seat.

He was dressed in jeans and shirt, and a stockman's coat made him seem twice the size. Hot for the afternoon, ideal for the night that was coming. Silver whiskers decorated his face but strongly created character, and I saw something trustworthy in his crinkly eyes.

"You hear all kinds of weird shit in these parts. Road stories. We have our share of murders that'd curl your hair. People who vanish right off the face of the Earth. And we won't even talk about the things that creep around this big sky after dark."

I glanced involuntarily at the fading twilight, aware we were seeing more by artificial light than sunlight now. The day disappearing into the west desperately held my attention, as if I needed to hold onto even the appearance of the same day I had left home.

"Which are you, Rory? The traveller? Sure. The kid stood up by his date? The runaway who needs to stay wide of his dad? The seeker, looking for he-knows-not-what? There's no guitar over your shoulder, so you're not the poetic one. Are you seeing the world, one flyspeck at a time? Meeting someone? Looking for a lift?" He paused, drank and looked me hard in the eye. "Or just plain… lost."

"I knew where I was going and what I was doing when I left home this morning," I whispered.

"And…?" The word was a rumble in his throat, a coaxing.

Making the words come took more guts than I knew I had. "I was on my way up for a concert at the hall." I nodded to the distant thumps and bangs in the night air. "But not this one. I went to sleep on the bus on the way up, and…" On an impulse, I took out my phone, brought up time and date, and turned the glowing screen to Netherby. He eyed it impassively and I waited for his outburst.

It never came. He snorted a deep breath through flared nostrils and took another swig. "And right now, you think you're either mad or stoned." He eyed me levelly, waiting for my input.

Desperation flared in me. "What do you want me to say? I have no explanation, I just know I've lost three months, and I'm stranded for the night in the middle of nowhere."

Netherby laughed richly. "Not quite, kid. The middle of nowhere starts a bit further on. But you do have a problem, don't you?" He hunched forward and lowered his voice. "You think you're the only one?"

"W-what?" was all I could blurt, covering my ineptitude with an intake of beer.

"It's one of those crazy tales of the road," Netherby went on softly, setting his bottle down. He visibly gathered his thoughts. "It doesn't happen often. Last time was, oh, a year or more back. These long roads between the towns out here can do strange things to your head. You see the mirages in the summer, lakes of water across the horizon, shining blue—normal enough. Then there's all the stuff you can't explain. One thing we know. It's always in weather like this." He inclined his head to the last of the twilight and the oppressive feel of the clouds up there. "Angry sort of days, days when the wind hates you."

A thrill went up my spine. The wind…

"And things happen. Locked doors are suddenly open. Livestock in one field are found in another. A flash flood down a creek when we know there was no rain yet, anywhere. Where did the water come from?" He shrugged widely and raised a finger.

"And sometimes people disappear. Or appear." He took a slow drink and looked around, speaking softly. "We don't tend to talk about it, but we all know it. This is a strange part of the world, and many would tell you it's haunted to hell and back. Be that as it may. One of the weird things it does is spit people and things around in time. If something goes missing, don't worry, it'll turn up one day—so we say around here. Sometimes things don't, but we keep on waiting. Who knows how far forward or back a fold in time goes?"

"Back?" My ears pricked at that. "You mean things appear from the future?"

"Seems that way. A friend of mine had a new blue wheelbarrow. Then one day he had two of them. Identical right down to the scratches. For a while he had two, then one of them disappeared again, being the first one that had reached the point in time where it did its backward movement. From then on he only had one again." The old man raised his beer in an ironic salute and drained it. "And, you're thinking what's good for a wheelbarrow might be good for a man. Right?"

"I'd be slow on the uptake if I didn't."

"It's the winds," Netherby said, almost tangentially. "They blow one way, you get sucked into the future, we reckon. If they blow the other, you get spat into the past. Maybe there's something special about what's been through time… it's like the winds can smell it on you, and pluck you back again. Or forward further. How are we to know?" He belched softly and rose. "Don't go away."

He disappeared into the bar for a while and I sat with my heart racing as the night thickened about me. I knew it was still early. Many shops on the main street still showed lights, but one by one they were going out as doors were locked. Soon there would be cheerful neon only at the convenience store and the fast food takeaway. My heart was thumping for a whole new reason now, though.

Could I get back? Could I hitch a ride on a wind going the other way?

Netherby returned with two more beers. I couldn't fault his generosity, and was more than a little thankful for this Samaritan, even if the rational part of me still couldn't accept what I heard as more than country hearsay. Timeslips? People disappearing? Haunted? Things in the night sky?

Oh please, I might have an imaginative soul, but I'm not stupid....

But you are three months out of your time, so listen to the man.

I drained the first bottle and nodded my thanks as he passed me the second. "Cheers. I wish I could pay you back."

"My pleasure. Now, you were contemplating the chance of recovering your lost time."

It struck me then: he spoke in an educated way, giving the lie to his rough and ready appearance. He had plenty of native wisdom, but the way he put words together told me he was either educated or...even older than he looked. It's a long time since people grew up speaking that way. As the thought ran through my head I must have stared a little, for he snorted a laugh and raised his bottle in salute.

"I was wondering how long it would take you to realise it. This is why I can recognise those the winds have touched." His deep, measured way of speaking had the air of another time about it, and now it made sense.

"How long?" I asked softly.

"For me, sixty years." He looked around the street. "No, I didn't try to get back. I actually like the future. It's not as bad a place as you people seem to think. It's cruel and corrupt, and the music's appalling, but it has its forgiving points too. And I had no one to go back to, anyway. Been here ten years."

"And you look out for others the winds blow in."

"Call it a vocation." He reached over, and we chinked bottles. "Travellers in time, son; brothers." We drank silently, then he turned and put his elbows on the table. "It's only three months for you. The world hasn't changed a damn. Is there anyone who'll have missed you if you walk in on today's date? Family?"

"My friends. My parents will be out of their minds with worry."

"Unless you succeed in getting back. There's a good way to test it."

"What's that?"

"You on Facebook?"

"Isn't everyone?"

"Log on and look for your recent activity. If you've been posting any time since December 5th, son, you made it."

I raised my eyebrows at that. "Great idea. Unfortunately, I'm out of cover on my phone."

"There's pay terminals in the back room of the bar, five bucks for half an hour."

I nodded and breathed a gusty sigh. "Damn. What if… what if there's nothing?"

"Then you didn't make it back." The statement was flat and frank. There was no other way it could be. "Your choice is to try anyway, or forget it and make your excuses any way you need to for being a missing persons case all this time. Just don't tell them the truth or they'll have you off to the shrinks faster than you can spit."

"There's another possibility. I tried, and the winds took me way off target. There's no guarantee, is there, that they'll take you back where you belong?"

"Guarantee? No. But things have a way of snapping back into position. Like the wheelbarrow. The winds can nudge you out of place but never cut your connection completely." He frowned and shrugged. "Even now, I travel carefully and never in this weather. I don't want to be pulled back. I get a sixth sense, an itch I can't scratch, when the gate is trying to open. I just stay put and hope like hell." He drank a gulp. "And stay awake."

"Sleep is the key?"

"It might be. It sure makes it easier. If you get on the bus in the morning, son, and the winds are still angry, do your best to sleep. And if you know how to pray—do."

We drank in silence, and I heard the beat from the hall, a deep, droning, pounding rhythm, the stomping hell-metal of the new generation. I tried to imagine how it had been for Dan Netherby, adapting to our world after his own; and then imagined how it would be for me if the winds took me sixty years on. It would be late-century, and the thought of the world I could wake into was enough to chill me to the bone.

Coastal inundation, fifty-plus degree summers, enforcer robots and famine riots. We'd been in the era of the Resource Wars since long before I was born, and they were only going to get worse. I shuddered faintly and put a hand in my pocket to check my cash. "I better go log on," I said softly.

***

I PAID AT THE bar and received a Wifi password to set in motion a half-hour session. Three battered old terminals were wired up on a bench in an alcove, and I logged on with a cold knot in my stomach. Waiting for the connection was agony, but when I was on, I traded a tight smile with the old man who leaned against the corner of the bar, casually sipping his brew.

I pulled up Facebook, entered username and password and held my breath.

My page was active. I could have jumped for joy, but contained myself and scrolled down, seeing posts from friends, my own posts—pictures from concerts dated January and February, conversations with friends... none of the details was important. The mere fact I'd been there to post them told me I had an adventure to complete.

I was about to log out and relax when I scrolled back to the top and saw my most recent post. It was short and sweet:

Thanking myself for the great tips! [Wink! Wink!] You know what I mean! Come on!

I blinked. Tips? What was I talking about? I let the stool rotate to glance back into the bar, looked at Netherby in some confusion until my eyes went up over him to one of the big screen TVs, now locked to a sports channel. I looked back at the post: the timestamp was *earlier today.*

My smile spread slowly. I pulled out a notepad and pen from my pack, opened a new tab and pulled up Google. I searched on the results of all the international sporting fixtures over the summer.

"You got the idea now, kid," Netherby said softly as he strode over. "Three months of records for every sport in the world that takes a wager. What've you got to lose?"

"Nothing, I guess," I whispered as I scanned the results of matches great and small. Cricket, rugby, soccer, tennis, gridiron, golf, basketball—it made no difference. Horse racing and motor sport—definitely. I worked with a will, and when my half hour was up, I bought another, and then another.

Dan Netherby sat quietly drinking, and when he brought another over for me, I found it was black coffee. I needed a clear head, and the two I'd had already were fuzzing me in an unwelcome way. I went to the bathroom, splashed my face with cold water. When I came back, I bought potato chips, anything to put a layer of grease on top of the alcohol vapours. I needed my brain functioning properly.

Two hours later I was getting low on cash but had filled pages, recording the winners, by how much, on what odds, of every match and race I could access, locally and around the world. I could have gone on to look at stock market and currency exchange fluctuations, but they were beyond my mental capacity. Betting I could understand, and I knew I'd have to wager carefully, not winning so often as to arouse suspicion. Open an online account and deliberately wager to lose small amounts but win big ones, was my strategy. Odds—I had a lot to learn in a crash course, the day I got back.

If I got back. My insides were still a knot of apprehension about it; at least the hard effort of gathering the means to turn poverty into wherewithal was a distraction.

Eventually I realised the pub was getting quiet, and the thumps from the hall were no more. A few concert goers arrived for last drinks before closing time and looked in no condition to drive. Many would be camping or sleeping in their cars, and the cafes would provide breakfast trade to hung-over metalheads. When I saw we had limited time before the bar closed its doors I made a few last checks and logged out. I stuffed the precious notebook into my pack.

I looked at my Samaritan and raised my eyebrows.

"Good luck, kid," he said and stuck out a tough hand, which I shook with genuine pleasure this time. When he drew it back, there was a slip of paper in my palm. "That's my home number. If you make it through, wait till the afternoon of March 3rd, then call me. It'll be good to share the secret at last." He gestured at the sky with a nod of his head. Lightning flickered beyond the leaded windows of the front bar.

"I think I can afford a room for the night," I said softly. "If this works, I won't be scrimping."

"The bus goes through Main Street at 7.50. If the wind's still blowing, be on it. If not…wait for the wind to blow. *I mean it.*" He turned up his coat collar and tugged his hat down. "I won't be sleeping tonight. Not when the thunder's around. I need to keep my grip on the world."

I wondered if I should have gone with him, but I was dead tired and wanted to close my eyes. I had to sleep sometime, and if sheer weariness got me away from the gnawing anxiety, it would be something. I nodded my thanks and watched the man from the past step out into the cool night air. He stood in the wash of light from the front doors of the bar, momentarily silhouetted in blue glare as the sky did its thing.

Be lucky, I wished him silently. *And I'll be lucky for both of us.*

I hit the ATM in the hall for a hundred dollars and talked to the barkeeper. He sent me to an office where I hired one of the upstairs rooms for the night, and they told me breakfast was at 7am for those leaving town early.

The room was spartan but comfortable in an old-fashioned way. The bathroom was down the hall, and I washed up before I turned the key in my door and lay down between cool sheets.

In lamplight, I looked again at the ATM docket and smiled because the balance was in four figures, much more than it had been when I left home this morning—three months ago. I set the phone alarm for 6.30, tried to settle and watched the window flare to the storm which grumbled over the long-reaped lands.

Maybe this was the summer breaking. The first rains would bring back the green. I tried to think of it in those terms—a beginning and a gift, for in every adversity is also opportunity if one is both brave enough and quick enough to see it.

I WOKE IN A grey first light that was late coming and beat my alarm by ten minutes. Too much was boiling in my heart and mind for me to sleep comfortably. I'd tossed and turned half the night, at last catching a few hours of mercifully dreamless sleep. Before I opened my eyes, though, I smiled. The wind was shaking the trees outside, and the window rattled faintly in its frame. *Good.*

I rested, fretted, turned over a few times, but soon got up, dressed and used the bathroom. I stuffed my things into my pack and went down to the dining room by seven. The hotel offered a decent breakfast as part of the price, and I wolfed cereal, fruit juice, bacon and eggs, toast and conserves, and a pot of tea. In fact, I hadn't eaten so well in ages. I had time to relax, listen to the country radio station playing the morning news and trade sleepy greetings with the couple of other residents who had stayed over.

At 7.35 I went up, retrieved my pack—made sure the crucial notebook was where it should be. I used the bathroom one last time, turned in my key and walked out into the cool, blustery morning.

The road was wet and the air muggy, an uncomfortable start to the day. The storm had abated, but the wind still fretted at the awnings of shops and swirled dust and leaves along porches and boardwalks. Was it enough? I might never know, but I had my opportunity. If I missed it, then I got back "today" and all my work last night was for nothing.

But if the winds could pluck a stray back as casually as they had flicked him into the void, all my tomorrows were mine for the making.

I was at the stop two minutes later and found several people joining me, day-trippers heading for Saturday shopping in town. I kept to myself, barely daring to breathe as I hoped against hope that the wind wouldn't drop. *Keep blowing*, I thought, as desperately as a sailor in the horse latitudes. Playful gusts lashed the trees, litter went skittering down the street, and people spoke of the wild weather in hushed tones.

Maybe they were thinking the same as me—the wind might have some tricks to serve up. The difference was, I *wanted* it to happen. I prayed as I'd never known I could that when I hit coverage range the date would not be March 3rd.

When the bus arrived, I went through the ritual of tickets with my heart in my mouth, feeling light-headed, giddy and unwell. I was lost in a dream, it seemed, and I had to undream it. The slip with Netherby's phone number was in my pocket, and as the bus pulled out to begin the run, I opened my pack and checked the notebook for the tenth time. Yes, all the records were there. I knew all the details of over a hundred sporting events, and if I used the information carefully… ah….

The wind rocked the bus as it headed out through the yellow land. Dead eucalypts writhed in tangles of silver-white limbs against the racing greyness, and farmhouses were lonely spots of colour in the wide, flat country. Traffic was sparse. I settled into my seat, collar up and cap tugged down, to listen to my *Dawn Wind* albums and try not to let anxiety eat me up.

Stress, combined with only a few hours of poor rest, finally took its toll. I drifted off to sleep, my pack between my feet. I knew as I slept, it was the best thing to do. Part of me was feeling for the jolting of the wind, yet even now another part did not believe any of this. I dreamed I was still on my way to Jacobsville, and the events of the last day were no more than a figment of my imagination.

Honestly, I would've liked to wake pulling into the place and find it was the day I left.

I woke with a jolt as the bus climbed through a major pot hole at the entry to the roadhouse, and my heart raced—halfway there already. I slipped a hand into my pocket—Netherby's number was still there. No dreaming.

Dare I check coverage at this point? I was probably in range now, but couldn't make myself do it. My head was fuzzy as if I'd been too deeply asleep, and I rubbed my eyes, made myself look hard. Were these the same passengers I'd got on with? Not all of them, but there had been stops here and there since I went to sleep. The simplest answer is usually the right one, after all.

I took a walk with the other passengers, bought candy and ate as if my life depended on it. I stood in the car park, felt the endless wind across the grain lands striking blows at my face. So long as it was the same angry, quarrelsome, swirling gale, I thought I had a chance. The more I heard it rush in the tops of trees, which shed leaves into drifting waves across the road, the more I felt I was still inside the event, whatever it really was.

When the bus pulled out again, I tried to rest. My insides were trembling with the fear I would never get those three months back. Suddenly they were very precious, not least because I hadn't yet come up with a reasonable excuse for my disappearance.

And what had happened to family and friends in the same time? I remembered my Facebook posts from the period and wondered—did they guarantee I was moving backward in time, or was this merely one possible cycle of events?

If it was true that time was an infinite cycle of eddies, and all possibilities were real, then the course we chart through them, determined by random chance from moment to moment, could take unexpected turns if ever preconceptions were involved.

My experiences on the strange, windy evening in Jacobsville constituted a preconception on a grand scale; but—imaginative soul or no—part of me wondered if any such person as Dan Netherby actually existed. Would I find him if I searched the online phone book?

When I'm back, I told myself. *I'll do nothing until I'm back.*

THE BUS WHEEZED INTO town on time, depositing shoppers in the CBD for a few hours' spending before the last connection went back up the country. When I stepped down, I realised I didn't recognise any of the passengers from the roadhouse stopover. Surely there should have been the same few who got on with me in Jacobsville? I'd lost track of them somewhere along the line, and the mystery deepened.

For better or worse, I was back. The digital time and temperature clock outside the markets told me I was on schedule, but the city seemed especially busy for a Saturday. I found a seat at the busy bus stops, and finally pulled up time and, all importantly, *date,* on my phone. The answer rocked me back, and I drew a deep breath, squinted and looked again.

December 4th.

Those mischievous winds had one last trick to play. They had deposited me a day early. This was a Thursday, and just as Dan Netherby's friend had enjoyed the benefits of two identical wheelbarrows, for the following 48 hours there would be two of me in the world. "Temporal duplication" was the term I recalled from science fiction reading. I didn't remember bumping into myself and agreed with myself that staying clear was the best course of action.

Two days to kill—I couldn't simply go home. I knew a backpackers' hostel where I could get a cheap bunk for two nights, use shower and razor, but be responsible for feeding myself. I was abruptly glad of the hotel breakfast: this could be a hungry two days.

But, first things first. I had enough cash left from the ATM I'd used three months in the future to buy myself an afternoon online at an internet cafe, and I had a lot of studying to do. With a reserved smile, I researched the theory of gambling odds and opened myself an online betting account. My history of sporting results did not begin until tomorrow night, and I meant to be ready.

It's strange, when you think of it, the way fate can bless or curse people. It cursed me to be swept into an impossible situation that could have turned out very badly indeed, then blessed me with both an almost-accurate return ticket and the foresight to bring something back which was to my benefit. Dimensionality is about perspective—or should that be the other way around? I had obtained the perspective of hindsight on the future. When Friday rolled around I was in a coffee shop across the road from the bus stops… watched myself appear, take a seat and wait for my trip up-country to the concert I'd never catch. I saw me take out my phone to answer the call from Deano and remembered I'd promised Cheryl a signed band poster. Well, maybe I could offer her something a lot better, given time.

Time. I smiled and made a note in my now-well-used notebook. The afternoon of March 3rd was when Dan Netherby expected me to give him a call, and I'd do so with pleasure. I transferred his number to the book alongside the reminder. I also noted down, as nearly as I could remember it, my Facebook post for early on March 2nd next year.

I saw the bus arrive, and when it pulled out my other self was on his way to meet his fate. I relaxed, sipped coffee and checked the cash in my pocket. I would empty my account if necessary, sure the situation was only temporary.

I had an afternoon to spend on a computer. After all, I already knew who'd win this evening's cricket match, by how many runs, in which over, who was Man of the Match, who was the top scorer, *and* the bowling figures. Six factors, all of which were bettable. I should win three large wagers and lose three small ones to allay suspicion.

In the future, they'd call me Rory the Lucky, and tell tales of my summer of unparalleled good fortune.

THE END

MIKE ADAMSON holds a PhD in Archaeology from Flinders University of South Australia. After early aspirations in art and writing, Mike returned to study and secured degrees in both Marine Biology and Archaeology. Mike currently lectures in Anthropology, is a passionate photographer, a master-level hobbyist and journalist for international magazines. Recent sales include the anthologies *Mind Candy Vol, I, Endless Apocalypse* and *Visions VII: Universe*, and the magazines *Daily SF* and *Compelling Science Fiction*. Mike has garnered an Honourable Mention in the Writers of the Future contest on four occasions, and has placed a total of over fifty stories to date.

THE WISHING PLACE

Aaron Moskalik

TOM STEWART HATED DREAMING. Even his daydreams were haunted. He should've known better than to schedule study hall. Unfocused, his eyes rested on a doodle-filled sheet of paper as the end of day announcements buzzed in the background.

"… I hope to see everyone at tonight's football game. Allenville takes on the Middleton Minions. Go, Sawyers." Assistant Principal Stevens' lackluster attempt at school spirit elicited snickers from around the room. The bell sounded.

A head leaned over Tom's shoulder, peering at his paper. "Who's the girl?"

"Hey, Finnagan. What girl?"

"The one you drew over and over for the last hour." Buck Finnagan leapt over the row of auditorium seats and settled in next to Tom. "She's cute enough."

"No idea." The sketches on Tom's paper were all of the same girl at different ages. He had a notebook full of her at home too. *Who was she?* He'd grown tired of that question years ago. He crumpled the paper and stuffed it in his backpack. "Come on, let's get out of here."

Tom's legs crumpled under him as he tried to stand. *Now, this too?* He hadn't had an episode since grade school. The doctor said it was psychosomatic. Dad said it was a goddamned waste of *his* time.

"You okay?" Buck's shocked concern drew looks from the other students filing out.

"I'm fine." Tom swatted the offered hand away and pulled himself up. "Foot fell asleep is all."

Buck didn't look convinced, but he kept his voice down this time. "You gonna be able to play tonight?"

Tom levelled a look at him. "I said, I'm fine."

They left the auditorium and headed toward their lockers. A knot of boys stood around a focal point in the atrium. Buck gave Tom a smirk and a nudge as they walked past.

The crowd parted, and Rose Blain emerged, dragging all eyes in her wake. "Well, well, if it isn't Tom the Sawyer and Buck Finn." Her eyes flicked past Buck and fixed on Tom.

"Ha, like we never heard that one before." Tom's heart worked a little harder to push a stew of hormones to the furthest reaches of his anatomy.

Rose pouted and continued her advance until she stood where Tom's throbbing heart threatened to betray his cool. "You never heard that before from *me*." Rose smoothed down Tom's collar and allowed her hand to linger for one immortal moment on his chest. She looked up into his eyes. "I just wanted to wish you good luck against the Minions."

Tom put on his most confident grin. "I won't need luck, but you can wish me a happy birthday."

Rose's lips crinkled at the corners. "Happy birthday then." She turned and looked back over her shoulder. "See you at the game."

Tom remained rooted until Rose disappeared into the crowd.

Buck gave a low whistle. "Dude."

"Yeah." Tom shook his head to clear it. His legs felt weak for a whole different reason.

"I have a twist of Hawaiian if you need to mellow out," Buck offered.

Tom stabbed a finger into his friend's chest. "You better stay crystal clear blocking for me tonight. Coach warned us about the all-state linebacker the Minions have. Besides, I gotta get home. My dad has a surprise waiting for me."

"What do you think it is?"

Tom sighed. "Something over the top."

TOM ENTERED THE RENTAL. His dad had managed to stay current on it for over a year now. *I'm home.* He categorized the changes since that morning. His bedroom door was still closed, the pizza boxes and other assorted clutter were gone, and Pine-sol permeated the air: good. The smell of cheap cologne, stale tobacco, and whiskey: bad. The sound of clanking plates and humming coming from the kitchen: to be determined. "Hey, Dad. It's been a while."

"Happy Birthday, Tom. Come on in,"

In the kitchen, Edward Stewart was washing the stack of dishes that had accumulated over the past week. He wore a rumpled and stained dress shirt rolled up to his elbows, only half tucked in. His graying hair had picked up an oily slept-in sheen. A finger of whiskey stood at the ready in a tumbler on the counter top.

"How was the *business* trip?" Tom asked, grimacing at his inflected sarcasm.

Ed turned. His eyes shone with a forced brightness. "Great. We took more than we gave. How's school?"

"Same as always. Big game tonight, so I can't stay long."

"Sure. Let's get to it then. Cake or gift first?"

"Cake, please."

"Ah, you're in luck." Ed slid a small sheet cake off the top of the fridge and onto the kitchen table. He rummaged in the junk drawer until he produced a book of matches and a box of half used candles. "How many we up to?"

"Fifteen, Dad." Tom failed to hide his exasperation.

"I know. Just testing if *you* knew." Ed counted out fifteen of the longer candles and placed them on the cake in no apparent pattern. His hand shaking, he used most of a book of matches lighting them. "Okay, make a wish."

Wish. The scent of mothballs and potpourri wafted across his consciousness. A woman ruffled his hair. *Hey, kiddo.* Longing blossomed in his chest. *Mother, I wish I'd known you.* He blew out the candles.

They each ate a piece of cake in silence. Hope, fear, shame, disappointment, even love. Over the years, Tom had felt them all sitting here with his old man. Comfortable would've been nice for once. He should've wished for that.

Ed broke the silence. "I have a surprise for you." He stood and opened the door to the garage. When Tom approached, he flipped on the light.

Tom expelled the breath he'd been holding. "It's a car." The statement came out flatter than intended.

"A 1982 Pontiac Grand Am to be exact, but don't contain your excitement on my account."

"No, it's awesome, but you realize I'm fifteen, right? I won't get my license for another year. And, just an observation, the car's older than I am."

"It would be, wouldn't it? It belonged to your mother. I put it in storage when she died. Don't worry, it's got new tires, belts, and it's all tuned up. It'll give you something to practice with." Ed dangled a set of keys from a finger. "Give your old man a ride to the game?"

Tom moved his gaze from the keys back to the car with its square headlights, beefy grill, and oversized tires. Something about it just fit. "You're on!"

"Oh, I almost forgot. You got a package." Ed pulled a manila envelope from the mail slot by the door and handed it to Tom. *Happy Birthday* was written in large flowing script above the address.

"This is addressed to a 'Jimmy'. You sure it's for me?"

Ed shrugged. "The address's right, and you're the only birthday boy here."

Tom opened it and pulled out a children's book and a blank card. He flipped the card open and read: *Be careful what you wish for, love Mary.* "Who's Mary?"

Ed took the card from his unresisting fingers. As he read, a faint glimmer of recognition crossed his face. He handed the card back. "No idea. Probably someone's idea of a joke."

Tom narrowed his eyes. "You know something. What's this about?"

Ed held up his hands. "I don't, honest. I just remembered something is all. When your mother was pregnant, we chose the name James for a boy and Mary for a girl. A coincidence, I'm sure."

"If that's true, then why's my name Tom?" A worm of queasiness wriggled up from his gut.

A series of emotions flickered across Ed's face like a slot machine's tumblers. They finished on drunk, angry, and who gives a crap. "Tom's plenty good for you." He slammed the kitchen door behind him.

***

TOM BOUNCED BACK TO his feet, slower this time. Ninety-Five had been pounding him into the turf all game. The Minions' star player had a hundred pounds on him, every ounce of it muscle.

Tom pulled Buck's face mask close and glared into his bloodshot eyes. He reeked of weed. "At least *try* to slow that beast down next time!"

The quarterback, Jack Sweney, dragged Tom back. "Cool it, kids. Huddle up!"

In the huddle, Jack continued, "We're gonna try something different. Play action. Make sure you sell it, Stewart. Suarez, run a post."

They broke, and Tom took his place a yard behind Jack. His legs threatened to buckle beneath him. He snarled and stamped in defiance. *Not now!*

Ninety-Five crouched behind the Minions' line, exuding a lethal combination of speed and agility. Tom could almost make out the face in the shadow of the helmet; his dad's bloodshot eyes glared at him, dismissing Tom as an annoying inconvenience in a wasted life.

Tom growled and clenched his fists. Only half aware of the snap, he sprang forward, ignoring Jack and the ball as he accelerated toward the gap with every ounce of anger he possessed.

The twenty other players receded from the field leaving just Tom and his target. He was a bull charging a matador. He lowered his head, aiming his horns at the red numerals nine and five. His helmet exploded in a flash of white. The world went black.

THE TRACKS DISAPPEARED INTO the dusty gloom of the covered bridge. Jimmy leaned on his braces as he considered all one hundred eighty-nine ties between him and the far side. He turned back towards Pottersville.

His sigh was a white cloud in the crisp air. The footbridge lay past the store and several ramshackle homes, one-half mile there and another half mile back on the far side of the ravine.

The package on his arm had grown heavy, a snotsicle dangled from his nose, and his braces bit into raw, blistered skin. The railroad bridge was the quickest way home, and he'd been over it countless times. Still, he wavered.

The whistle sounded at the Glassworks. Jimmy had forgotten his mother's shift ended early on Christmas Eve. *She'll be angry I made this trip alone.* He dragged himself, painful step following painful step, into the tunnel, careful to plant his braces in the center of each tie before dragging his useless feet forward. Seven, eight, nine, ten. He counted the ties as he always did. By fifteen, the tunnel was dark.

In Jimmy's dreams, one brace always lodged under the rails. He would struggle to get free, then a train appeared, whisper quiet, bearing down on him faster than he could scream.

No trains would visit the faltering sawmill, not on Christmas Eve. *Right?* His body shuddered.

Thirty-five, thirty-six. Shafts of weak December sun slipped through the graying boards and striped the gloom like golden prison bars. Fifty-two, fifty-three. A light breeze moaned through the ageing structure as it vibrated beneath him. Seventy, seventy-one. The wind blew harder and whistled as it ripped at the boards and shook the bridge. He quickened his pace.

Ninety-four, ninety-five. The bridge rumbled, and Jimmy found it hard to keep his balance. He paused, slumped over his braces, ninety-four ties before and behind him. A spot of pale light marked both ends of the tunnel. The light behind him went out. The air in the tunnel rushed forward, stifling his scream as a train exploded upon him. The world went black.

JIMMY DRAGGED HIMSELF UP the steps. *I'm home.* Mother flung open the door and crushed him in a hug. His package fell forgotten in the snow.

"Jimmy! I was worried sick. How many times did I tell you not to go out alone? What if your braces break or God knows what?" Mother glared into his eyes, and her hands shook.

"Sorry, Mom, I just wanted to get you and Mary something for Christmas." Jimmy left it at that. He'd already asked himself the same questions on the long trek to the footbridge on the edge of town and back.

Mother pulled Jimmy close again. He rested his head against her wire thin body. In the kitchen, Mary peered at him, her large brown eyes twin pools of fear and relief.

Mother nudged him toward the door. "Go in and get cleaned up. I'll see what I can fix for dinner."

Jimmy only had the energy to nod at Mary as he passed her on the way to the washroom, shedding outerwear as he went. He leaned on the sink and stared at his pale face in the battered mirror on the medicine cabinet. As Mother had explained, his head was misshapen due to forceps in the hands of an inexperienced doctor. One eye drooped as if half asleep and his thin lips hung to one side like a torn pocket.

Mary appeared behind him. She held up the package he had dropped in the snow. "What did you get me?"

"If you help me wrap, I'll let you see."

Mary's eyes widened.

"Get wrapping paper, tape, and a pair of scissors. I'll meet you in my room."

Mary scampered out, and Jimmy washed his hands and face. Warmth had restored some of his strength. He pulled himself into his room and slumped back onto his bed. Mary came in moments later carrying the supplies and the package.

Her eyes remained focused on the package as Jimmy cut the twine and unfolded the brown paper. Inside, the colorful scarf he bought for Mother wrapped around Mary's gift. He smiled as Mary leaned in for a closer look. "Roll out some paper so we can wrap Mom's present."

Mary yelped in protest but did as asked. She riveted her attention on the scarf as Jimmy unwound it to reveal a paperback. "*Charlotte's Web*! Will you read it to me?"

"Tomorrow. Let's wrap it first."

As they wrapped her present, Mary grew quiet, her face shrouded by her hair as she toyed with the tape.

"What's wrong?" Jimmy asked.

"I wished for you." Mary's voice was a whisper.

A chill settled over Jimmy. "In the Wishing Place?" He glanced toward his closet. "We promised each other we would never do that again. It always takes more than it gives."

Tears brimmed in Mary's eyes. "You died. I didn't know what to do."

The chill crystallized along Jimmy's spine. "When?"

"Later tonight." Mary mouthed the words in a barely audible squeak. "The policeman said you were hit by a train."

Jimmy's mind swirled. At one time, they'd used the Wishing Place for every whim. They would sit between the old wardrobe and the toy chest in his closet and make a wish, maybe for candy, a new pair of shoes, or that Buck would stop bullying him at school.

The Wishing Place always delivered, but for every wish, there was a greater misfortune. Toys disappeared; Mother's car broke down; Jimmy was placed in the remedial class. Their lives were a Goosebumps story.

The last time they used the Wishing Place, things got serious. Mary won a contest at school and received a white rose as a prize. On the walk home, the rose lost half its petals before she could put it in water. Upset, she wished it was like new again.

The day started over. This time Jimmy walked home with her and suggested they take the train bridge to save time. Mother worked for the sawmill at that time and had decent medical insurance, so he had custom fit braces that made walking easier. Halfway into the tunnel, one of his new braces got stuck under a rail, and he broke it getting free, but as wished for, Mary got home before her rose wilted.

Mother couldn't afford to repair the brace. Jimmy wished it hadn't been broken.

They went back months this time. The sawmill laid off workers, including Mother. Her insurance went away, and Jimmy didn't get his custom braces. She took a job at the Glassworks, but they paid less, and she worked overtime most nights. She couldn't help Mary with her homework. Mary never won that rose.

Those wishes were small potatoes compared to cheating death.

Dinner was subdued. Mother had prepared soup.

"Did they hand out Christmas turkeys at work this year?" Jimmy stirred his soup. Its thinness magnified his hunger.

Mother shook her head. "The only thing they passed out today was pink slips."

"What's a pink slip, Mommy?" Mary asked. "Can I see it? Is it pretty?"

Mother smiled, but her eyes remained grim. "No, not pretty. A pink slip means I have to find another job."

A warm ember of hope sparked to life in Jimmy's belly. Maybe this was all the Wishing Place would take. Mother's face, deeply lined and thinner than the soup, said this was already too much. Shame washed over Jimmy. "Mom, I'm sorry I worried you today. I thought I could make it back before you got home."

Mother's eyes grew stern, and Jimmy braced himself for the tongue-lashing he deserved. Instead, her head slumped into her hands. "I'm so tired. I can't do this alone." Her words floated there, a truth she could no longer hide, followed by tears she could no longer hold.

Harsh words would've stung less. They would've said everything's going to be all right. Jimmy sat stunned.

Mary jumped into Mother's lap and hugged her. "Don't cry. We're all here. Together."

Jimmy joined the hug, feeling even more ashamed. "I love you. I'll do better, I promise."

Mother smiled, and it reached her eyes this time. "I wouldn't be able to make it another day without either of you. Now, finish your soup. I have a surprise for dessert."

After dinner, they all turned in early.

Jimmy couldn't sleep. After hours of trying, he left the warmth of his bed and crawled to the living room. A small Christmas tree occupied one corner of the room. Under it, his gifts sat beside those from Mother.

Jimmy passed by and headed for the cigar box hidden under some papers on the mantle. He pulled himself up and returned cradling the box in his lap. It released the strong, masculine smell of tobacco when he opened it.

A pipe and a harmonica rested inside. Jimmy picked up the pipe and imagined Father sitting in the La-Z-Boy, his feet up, blowing smoke rings like Gandalf the Gray. Jimmy set it back and picked up the harmonica, running his finger over the engraved name, Edward Stewart.

A displaced envelope fell from the mantle. It was addressed to Mother, but the return address grabbed his attention: E. Stewart. With trembling fingers, he took out the letter and read.

Jimmy heard a cough behind him. "What're you doing up, kiddo?"

"Couldn't sleep." He slid the letter under the box.

Mother sat next to him radiating dry warmth. "Me neither." She dangled the pipe between two fingers, scrunching up her nose.

"Mom, why did Dad leave?"

For the first time, she didn't evade the question. "Your father isn't like you. He's weak and can't handle responsibility."

"But what if he wants to now? What if he wants to come back?"

Mother's face became grim. "I won't let him. Not now. Not ever. I know you won't believe me, but he would just break your heart when he left again."

Mother tried to put her arms around him, but he pushed her away. He brought out the letter. "He says he wants to come back. He made a mistake and is sorry. He can help us, Mom. He has a good job and a nice house."

Mother shook her head. Her eyes were hidden by the darkened skin around them. "Let's talk about it in the morning. Okay? Now we could both use some sleep."

TOM REGAINED CONSCIOUSNESS. PRESSURE filled the eggshell of his head and light stabbed through his eyelids. He groaned.

"Tom, you awake?"

"Who's Tom?" he tried to say. All that came out was another groan.

"Easy. You had a concussion. None of this would've happened if I hadn't been high."

Tom recognised the voice but couldn't place it. He had just been talking with Mother. But his mother had died when he was born, right? And his name was Tom. Why did he think it was Jimmy?

"Your dad was here earlier. He seemed pretty upset—and drunk. Even Rose came by. I think she likes you, dude."

Tom cracked one eye. The room was awash in white, and he was lying in a bed. He turned toward the voice. His head threatened to roll off his shoulders and burst like an overripe watermelon against the floor. A figure sat in a chair and wavered in and out of focus. Buck.

"Hey, you are awake. I'll call a nurse. Maybe they'll give you something to dull the pain." Buck left the room, and a muttered conversation took place somewhere nearby. The sound faded and the world went black again.

After a struggle, Tom reopened his eyes. The room was dark, and the only sound was a soft chuffing of machines. "Buck?"

No answer. He turned his head; the pain was buried beneath the cotton that shrouded his mind. The chair beside his bed was empty.

Tom sat up, cautious of the IV line in his arm. Lights of varied color and size glowed from instruments scattered around the room, casting strange shadows. He switched on the bedside lamp, revealing his backpack on the floor.

Tom heaved the pack onto the bed. Deep in the cotton of his head, a red throbbing raised a muffled alarm. He took a few slow breaths and then unzipped the pack. A ball of paper rolled out. Study Hall. He smoothed it out and sucked in his breath. He knew who these sketches were. Mary, Jimmy's sister. My sister?

Tom took the manila envelope from his pack and poured out its contents. Goosebumps prickled his skin. It was a well-worn paperback copy of Charlotte's Web.

He picked up the envelope. The return address read: M. Stewart, 320 Sycamore, Pottersville, NY.

THE RENTAL WAS EMPTY. IT had been for days and would remain so long after he left. Tom didn't know how he knew this, but it filled him with both relief and sadness. He had nothing to say to his old man, and there was nothing he needed to hear from him. Yet, a younger boy still needed to press his head to his dad's chest and breathe in that pungent mixture of old spice and tobacco one last time.

There wouldn't be another time. Tom ignored the note on the counter. He already knew what it said. What it always says. He picked up the car keys that lay on top of it.

It was Thursday. Tom had spent the better part of a week in the hospital waiting for the doctors to clear him. Various people stopped by to wish him well: Buck, Coach, Jack, even number Ninety-Five from the Minions, Billy Hawthorn. His dad was a no-show, however, as was Rose, much to his disappointment.

Mostly though, Tom had lain there alone with his thoughts. He thought about Jimmy—and Mary. She was out there somewhere. How, he wasn't sure, but she had sent him the book, right? And he'd been drawing her all his life. The only thing that was clear to him was he would never know peace until he found her.

He grabbed an old county map from the desk drawer and stuffed it in his pack. He paused a moment in the doorway to the garage, taking in Mother's Grand Am.

Minutes later, Tom guided the car down the main street out of town. He checked his watch. Three-thirty. School just let out. He cut over a few blocks and drove past the High School.

Jackpot. Rose was walking home. Alone. His pulse quickened. He caught up to her and rolled down his window. "Hey, Rose. Need a lift?"

A brief smile betrayed Rose's hauteur as she identified her accoster. "Well, if it isn't Tom Sawyer. Good to see you're feeling better. Where'd you steal the wheels?"

Tom rolled alongside Rose as she walked. "It's a gift from my mother."

Rose stopped. "I thought you lost your mother when you were born."

"You seem to know a lot about me."

Rose shrugged. "Just what the kids say. I could use that ride if you think you can handle this thing."

"Hop in." Tom waited for Rose to settle in. "Which way?"

"Three blocks up on the right. Do you have any Halloween plans tomorrow?"

"Halloween? No, I'm headed out of town."

"You realize you don't have a driver's license, right? Where out of town?"

"Pottersville. I have some family there."

Rose didn't reply for a few beats. "Now you're starting to worry me. You sure they cleared you to leave the hospital?" Genuine concern showed on Rose's face.

"What? Why?"

"They say Pottersville is haunted. It's been deserted for years, so I'm pretty sure you don't have any family there." Rose pointed. "Here's my house."

Tom stopped the car, and Rose got out. She came around to the driver's side. "You sure you're okay? You could come in for a few minutes."

Tom shook his head. "Thanks, but I'm fine, really. There's something I need to do, and it won't make sense if I try to explain."

"You could try anyway." Her unflinching eyes, heartbeat by heartbeat, drained his ability to resist.

Tom broke eye contact. "Maybe when I get back." He waved and stepped on the gas harder than intended. After a narrow miss with a parked car, he continued on his way.

Rose was right; Pottersville was deserted. Tom rolled to a stop, gravel popping under his tires. He was at the end of what was little more than a two-track. A railroad gate blocked further progress.

In the thirty minute drive here, Tom had crossed into another world. The remaining industrial age buildings of the village were in a post-apocalyptic state of decay.

Tom had spent an hour exploring. Three bridges had spanned the deep ravine. The bridge for car traffic was washed away, and the decrepit footbridge was structurally unsound. That left only the covered rail bridge before him.

Tom got out of the car and slipped on his backpack. The sun had set behind the mountains, and the crisp autumn air nipped through his flannel shirt.

Like Jimmy, Tom wavered before the entrance of the bridge. No train would ever traverse this tunnel again, of that he was sure, but in his heart, he knew he would never return once he entered. The white paper of a posting caught his attention: DANGER – demolition of all structures within the Pottersville village limits scheduled to start 10/31/1997.

Time was short. If he wanted to find 320 Sycamore, he had to get there today. Tom took a deep breath and plunged forward. As if by habit, he counted the ties as he walked. He reached one hundred eighty-nine.

Tom emerged from the far side to discover an armada of black clouds had sailed over the mountains, hastening nightfall and bringing an icy wind. He ran, exulting in this simple pleasure as if it were his first time. His route felt familiar, and he let his feet guide him.

He stopped before a small house, its windows broken and roof sagging. Faded wooden numbers above the door read 320.

Rain sluiced from the sky, soaking him in an instant. He bolted through the unsecured front door. The empty window casings of the main room provided no protection as the wind and rain continued their attack. He retreated deeper into the house, stumbling down a short hall and into a small room. Two small windows allowed the elements to harass him further. He found his final refuge in a small closet and slid the door closed behind him.

Calming warmth and the smell of potpourri and mothballs wrapped around Tom as he settled between an old wardrobe and a chest. His head ached, and his eyes were heavy. The doctors had warned him to take it easy. He released a breath he hadn't known he'd been holding. I'll just rest a few minutes until the storm blows over. His eyes closed.

JIMMY AWOKE ON CHRISTMAS morning heavy with dread. Silence smothered the house until the faint slaps of bare feet on the cold wood floor preceded Mary into his room.

"Jimmy? Something's wrong with mommy." Panic left Mary's words bruised and breathless.

Jimmy threw off his blankets, and cold air ripped away any remaining sense of security. Mary led him into mother's room. She lay in her bed, unmoving.

When Jimmy reached her side, mother's eyes opened. She attempted to smile. "Hi, kiddos. Merry Christmas." Coughs wracked her body, and her eyes closed again. He touched her forehead and jerked his hand away from the unexpected heat.

"She's very sick."

"What do we do?" Mary asked. Tears brimmed in her eyes.

"I'll call for help. You get a glass of water."

In the main room, Jimmy picked up the handset to the rotary phone and dialled 911. Nothing. Not even a dial tone. He hurled the phone away and cast about the room. Father's letter lay on the floor where he had left it the night before. This all began when Father left. Mother's words came back to him. He's not like you. He's weak. What if he wasn't? What if he had stayed?

Jimmy returned to his room passing Mary on the way. "Where you going? Did you call for help?"

"No, but I'm gonna fix this right now."

Mary looked confused, then her eyes widened. "No Jimmy. Wait!"

He ignored her and settled into the closet, pulling the door closed. "I wish Dad never left."

TOM WOKE, HIS HEART pounding. A rumble vibrated through the floorboards. Judging from his full bladder and ravenous hunger, he'd been asleep for hours. Sunlight seeped under the crack of the closet door.

He recognized his surroundings. A visceral dread discharged from the hair on Tom's neck—The Wishing Place. What had been Jimmy's final wish?

He wished Dad never left.

Realization seized every cell of his being. I am Jimmy! That wish had changed everything. The forceps responsible for his cerebral palsy had been replaced by the cesarean that killed Mother. Father had stuck around to care for him, but Mary had never been born. He pawed through his backpack and produced the copy of Charlotte's Web.

Then where did this come from?

The rumbling outside grew louder accompanied by crunching and a metallic jingle. Bulldozers. The demolition had started, and he didn't have much time. He was in the right place, at least, but Mary's note was right, he needed to be careful what he wished for. This was his one and only chance to make it all right.

He considered his current life. I can't complain. He was popular, healthy, and the hottest girl in school liked him. A loud thud shook the house followed by the splintering of lumber. It would all end if he didn't get out now.

He weighed the book in his hand. Mary needs me. She didn't deserve to be forgotten; she deserved to be born and to know her mother—even her father.

The whole house started to lift off its foundations. Dust rained down, choking him. He had seconds. Unbidden, his dad's words came back to him. Tom's plenty good for you.

Love you too, even if you completely bailed on Jimmy and resented me my whole life. Large chunks of plaster fell around him, and the back wall of the closet started to collapse. Time was up.

Third time's the charm, Dad. Don't mess it up this time. "I wish I'd never been born."

"HEY, MARY, MIND IF I walk you home?"

Mary turned. "Hi, Buck. Sure."

A soft snow fell. A few flakes frosted Buck's unkempt hair. He had a backpack slung over one shoulder of his Pottersville

Pioneers letterman's jacket. With hands jammed into his pants pockets, he took on a sheepish air.

"So," he started as they turned away from the school, "do you know what you're getting for Christmas?"

Mary laughed. "I never know. My dad goes all out and spoils me rotten."

"Nothing could spoil you." Buck scuffed his feet.

Mary's cheeks warmed. "Thanks, that's sweet. What about you?"

"Me? I'm already rotten. No need for anyone to spoil me."

Mary punched him in the arm. "No, silly. What're you getting for Christmas?"

"The usual, I guess." Buck paused. "Hey, I did get you something." He unzipped the top of his backpack and took out a small gift-wrapped package. "Merry Christmas."

"You shouldn't have." Mary accepted the package and unwrapped it slowly. I hope it's not expensive. Inside was a paperback.

"The Adventures of Tom Sawyer," Mary said, not sure what else to add.

"I know you like books, and this is my all-time favorite." Buck lowered his voice to a mumble. "Actually, it's the only book I've read."

"Thanks. That's sweet. Well, here's my house. Merry Christmas."

Mary hurried to the door and waved. Buck stood there, watching her, a half smile on his face. She closed the door.

From the kitchen came the sounds and smells of cooking. She poked her head around the corner. "Hi Mom, I'm home. What's for dinner?"

Mother glanced up and smiled. "Hey, kiddo. We're having your father's favorite."

Mary crinkled her nose. "Not tuna casserole again." She continued down the hall and into her room.

Mary put the new book down on her bed. She had read Tom Sawyer, of course. It was an entertaining read, but not half as good as Huckleberry Finn. Something about how Huck overcame his rude upbringing by an alcoholic and abusive father touched her. She'd be lost without the strong guidance of her own father. By comparison, Tom Sawyer seemed just a foppish boy with little sense.

Mary had consumed hundreds of books, but the first book she'd read by herself, Charlotte's Web, was by far her favorite. She got it for Christmas eight years ago, although she couldn't remember who gave it to her. She took a month to read it that first time. Her five-year-old mind struggled to understand some of the finer points, but when she finished, she flipped to the first page and started all over again.

Since then, Mary had read it once every month. After the first dozen times, she could skim through it in hours. The part that drew her back was when Charlotte died after saving Wilbur one last time, leaving Wilbur to wonder how he deserved such a friend.

Mary read it for the ninety-fifth time in October, and then the book vanished. She had searched everywhere, but it might as well have never existed. Father had bought a new hardcover edition to replace it. She picked up the copy of Tom Sawyer and placed it next to her 'It's the thought that counts' shelf.

"Hey, Princess, what're you up to?"

"Daddy! You're home early."

"It's Christmas Eve, so I decided to knock off." Mary's father nodded toward the Tom Sawyer. "You have a new book?"

"Yeah, Buck Finnagan gave it to me." Mary's cheeks warmed again.

"Buck, huh? You like him now? I thought you said he was just a dumb jock."

Mary feigned shock. "I would never!" She lowered her eyes. "He's nice, and he likes me. The other girls say he's cute."

"Not your type?" Father asked. Mary shrugged. "Don't give him another thought then. Come, Mother says dinner's ready. It's your favorite, tuna casserole!"

"I thought that was your favorite."

Father made a face, and they laughed.

After dinner, Father turned on *It's a Wonderful Life*. Mary took her customary spot on the rug. As always, she identified with the young Mary Hatch and wondered where her George Bailey was. Maybe he had never been born, and she was destined to be a dried up spinster librarian.

The movie finished. Father's eyes were fixed on a point far beyond the here and now. "I wish I was half the man George Bailey was."

"Eddy Stewart!" Mother looked shocked. "You're the closest thing to George Bailey the real world has seen. This town would've dried up years ago if it weren't for you."

"Maybe, but there're plenty of businessmen around, and I'm just another. I mean I don't have George's generous spirit. If I do something for someone else, it's out of obligation or guilt. Besides if it weren't for you, I'd still be drinking and no good to anyone."

Mother took a softer tone. "I think if you ask Mary, she'll say you're plenty generous. And George Bailey wouldn't have amounted to much without his Mary Hatch, now would he?" She snuggled up close, and Ed put his arm around her, pulling her in for a kiss.

A spike of jealousy stabbed Mary. They had it all figured out, but with all the questions spiraling around her head, she doubted she ever would. She slipped off to bed before her mood could darken further.

Mary awakened early from a strange dream. She was in a tunnel with a boy, familiar but unknown to her. She pleaded with him to get off the tracks, only to see him swept away by a train. The boy came back, older, and assured her everything would be all right before disappearing again.

The alarm clock informed Mary it was five AM. She slipped on a housecoat and peeked out her door. The house was quiet. The moon, shining through the main room windows, provided enough light to see the door to the spare room across the hall, half open. Strange. That door is always closed.

Mary seldom went in the spare room. Whenever she did, an ill-defined uneasiness afflicted her, as if some missing part of her was trying to claw its way back in. She could usually ignore it, but sometimes it would stay with her for days.

She had last been in the room two months ago. The unease had overwhelmed her. Her memory of the next hour was fragmented and feverish: the closet, an envelope with Happy Birthday written on it, someone named Jimmy.

Mary shivered as she returned to the present. She eyed the spare room. Perhaps Father had hidden her gift in there last night. She couldn't imagine what it might be. She crept closer and peered through the opening. The room was dark, its windows shaded. A faint glow issued from under the closet door. Mary jerked back, her heart performing an impromptu drum solo. She chided herself. Father hid something was all, something with an electronic display.

Mary pushed the door open and stepped into the room. Her eyes adjusted to the gloom, revealing the outlines of the bed and boxes stacked in haphazard piles. She inched her way toward the closet.

Just as she placed her hand on the door, the glow went dark. Mary stopped, her heart doing an encore performance. The gift explanation no longer fit, nor any other she could think of.

She could open the door now or stand here tormenting herself. She slid the door back in a decisive gesture.

Nothing. The closet smelled of potpourri and mothballs. An old wardrobe sat to one side and a chest on the other. Something small lay on the floor between them. She bent down and picked it up. Weight and feel were enough to confirm it was her Charlotte's Web.

How had it gotten here?

Holding the book again calmed her, and she sat down, cradling it in her lap. She flipped it open. In the darkness, the words were hidden from her sight but not her mind. Her friends Wilbur, Charlotte, Templeton, and Fern came to life. How she had missed them!

She let her mind wander. Wilbur had Charlotte. Mary Hatch had George Bailey. All her favorite stories had hard-won love or friendship at their core. Am I that lonely? Why? That familiar unease returned and bloomed into an exquisite longing. The air thrummed with haunting energies.

"Someone is missing. I wish…" Mary held the moment of fraught potential. "I wish he were here."

THE END

AARON MOSKALIK starts his day writing speculative fiction in Oak Park, Michigan before dropping his daughter at school and earning a paycheck as a Software Architect. He has published stories in *Nature* and *Perihelion Science Fiction*, among others. To view all his published works, visit aaronmoskalik.com.

113 FEET

Josh Roseman

"THIS IS A REALLY bad idea, Elle," Barry says.

"You didn't have to come."

"Don't be stupid," he snaps. "Phil would kill me if I didn't come with you."

Barry is fiftyish, portly and gray-haired. Seeing him take off his shirt is an experience I wish I'd never had.

"I have friends with certifications," I say. "It's not like I couldn't have asked one of them."

"How many of them have actually been down there?" It's almost a growl, and I'm actually cowed a little. "That's what I thought."

I sit on the hard bench, wood planks covered in thin, all-weather carpet, and fiddle with my regulator.

"How far away do you think we are?" he asks.

"Don't know. Ask the captain."

Barry looks up at the bridge, where Al the captain stands driving the boat. Al is even older than Barry, narrow, hard and tanned almost leathery with decades of exposure to the sun. Instead of going up to talk to him, though, Barry goes around the cabin to stand by the bow, leaving me bouncing up and down on the bench as the boat zips across the water. The light chop makes the horizon rise and fall faster than is comfortable. I can take it, though, and if I get sick enough to throw up, at least I know enough to do it over the side.

My guess is that we're ten minutes from the dive site. Maybe fifteen.

After waiting seven years to get my answers, fifteen minutes isn't much of a wait at all.

I WAS SEVEN WHEN I first realized my dad was doing more than just studying the life cycle of coral reefs. I'd been in the ocean with Grandpa; I knew what they looked like. I knew there were natural ones and artificial ones; I knew that if you touched a reef, part of it could die and that if you touched fire coral, you'd burn.

The big tank at Dad's office had plenty of coral inside. I separated myself from him—it was easy; he was so focused on his work that when I said I had to go to the bathroom, he didn't even notice—and went off on my own.

No one watched me climb up on a chair. No one noticed my nose was so close to the water that all I could smell was salt. No one saw me reach in and brush the back of my hand on the bright-orange coral flower.

The scream made Dad come running. He picked me up as I cried and shouted, carried me to a chair, and told me to hold out my arm. Then he poured clear liquid over my skin: vinegar, like what Mom used to clean the floor. It didn't make the burn stop hurting, but it helped, and after a few minutes I started to calm down.

"What happened?"

When I looked at Dad, it was through a blur of tears. "I reached in the tank," I said. "I touched the coral."

"Oh, come on!" Dad said—almost yelled. "I've told you before: This isn't a game! It's not a place to play! This is my job, and if you can't behave, you can stay home with your brother next time. You got that?"

I stared at him for a second, then burst into fresh tears. Dad shook his head and crouched in front of me. "I'm sorry, Eleanora. I didn't mean to shout. You just... worried me. And you know you shouldn't have touched something that was going to hurt you, right?"

"I..." A hiccup. "I'm... I'm sorry, Daddy..."

He leaned forward and hugged me, rubbing my back. "Come on. I'll get my things, and we can go home."

"Kay."

He asked me to sit in his desk chair and wait while he called Mom. He'd left his computer turned on, and I read some of what was on the screen. I didn't understand all the big words, but I was pretty sure it didn't have anything to do with coral reefs.

I COME OUT OF the cabin after exchanging my t-shirt and shorts for a wetsuit. Barry's on the bench, buckling his vest. Al is by the ladder to the bridge. "How long will we be out here?"

"We brought enough air for two dives," I tell him, checking my watch. "Figure a couple of hours."

"It's more than 100 feet down," Barry says. "Be real, Elle. How long do you think we'll be able to stay?"

I glare at him. "You can stay up here. I'll dive alone if I have to."

He mouths something nasty before going to work on his fins; I sit across from him and do the same. I'm faster than him, though; before he's even finished buckling on his vest, I'm already on my feet, hanging onto the railing at the stern. I hold my mask to my face and, as the boat rises on a small wave, I step off and into the water.

I WAS TEN THE first time I got into Dad's files. He got fired the summer after second grade; we had to move, and I had to change schools. But Dad got a new job, and Mom did too, and we were doing okay. I was aware, I suppose, that our circumstances had changed, that we didn't have enough money to live like we used to, but I was a kid. I didn't really care about it the way an adult might.

Jason noticed. He was fifteen, moody and broody. My parents yelled at him a lot, and he yelled back. I tried to stay out of the way.

I also tried to stay out of sight when Mom and Dad went out, and Jason had someone over. It wasn't hard; they'd sit in the living room and watch one of my parents' R-rated tapes, and I hid in my bedroom from the explosions and the adult stuff.

Dad usually locked his office door, but he must have forgotten this time. I always tried the door, just in case, just out of curiosity, and when it opened, I couldn't help but go inside. Jason and I were never allowed in there when he wasn't around.

I clicked on the lamp and sat in Dad's big leather chair. The desk was very neat, very organized, and I made sure to put his folders back when I finished reading them. Or, I should say, skimming them: I might have been good in school, but there were some big words like "transdimensionality" that I didn't understand. I stuck to sentences that said things like "portal," "rift," "xoordinates," and so on.

Dad had been doing this research for a long time; there were notes dated before I was born. I remembered times when he'd been away for a week or longer, times he'd come home from those long trips with his arm in a sling, or limping, or bruised. How dangerous was this stuff?

The noises from the living room stopped after an hour, and I quickly cleaned up and ducked out, locking the door behind me and stealing off to my room to try and make sense of what I'd read. From what I could understand, Dad believed there were portals somewhere in the ocean. One was close to where we lived. He used to work for the government. He had a hypothesis—I knew that word, thanks to Science Fair—that the portals were "beyond our current level of technology." Dad's notes had wondered who made the portals. And, over and over, he'd written: "Where do they go?"

That had given me chills, enough that I'd tucked myself into bed and tried not to think about it.

Mom and Dad got home around midnight, and when Mom came to check on me, her touch on my shoulder was so reassuring that I "woke up" so I could get a hug.

Whatever it was Dad thought was at 113 feet, it gave me the creeps.

BARRY LEADS THE WAY, one hand around the line, a spiral of blue and white stripes. I follow his bubbles. The water grows cool at 30 feet, then colder at 60 and 90. I wish I'd gone with the dry suit, but they always make me feel clumsy. The wetsuit is thin and black and easy to move in, and I can handle the chill.

It's dimmer when we get to the bottom, the line attached to the wreck by a heavy metal ring. The tips of my fins touch the boat, and I float there, taking a moment to turn on my mask-mounted light and another, brighter one in my vest pocket. Barry fiddles with his own light, looking at me.

I check my computer, then hold it up. We're only at 93 feet, and I've got plenty of air. Mark always said I seem to come up with more air than I bring down with me, and if I'm going to do this right, I'm going to need to regulate my breathing more strictly than ever.

Barry, on the other hand, has used a surprising amount of his supply. I want to pull out my slate and berate him, but that'll just waste time. Besides, he's already looking around, getting his bearings. He turns back to me, and motions that I should follow. He's been down here before; he's the expert.

I WAS TWELVE WHEN I got my dive license. Dad had been away more and more through third and fourth grade, long weekends and unexplained trips, and I guess when he saw how much I liked snorkeling during a family trip to the Keys, he tried to buy my forgiveness.

It worked, too. When I opened the long white envelope, I nearly hugged him to death.

The classes were held at a dive shop half an hour from home. After dinner, Mom drove me and I did boring school homework in the backseat. Naturally, I already would've finished my dive class homework the day it was assigned. I spent a month learning the rules, the equipment, how to clear my mask, how to put together and break down and clean a dive kit, buddy breathing, sign language, and moving while carrying a third of my weight in equipment.

My first dive wasn't much; we went down about 30 feet, knelt in a circle on the sand, and covered the basics. But it got better, and soon I had my PADI Open Water certification. The real problem was finding someone who would dive with me; I wanted to go every weekend, but Mom worked Saturdays and Dad wasn't home half the time. After months of just showing up and hoping there would be someone who needed a buddy, jumping into the water while Dad sat on the boat, reading or doing research or whatever, I finally found a good partner. Mark was a year older than me but shy as a first-grader. Most divers weren't as young as us, and that didn't help him either.

Still, even though we didn't talk much about anything except diving, it was nice to have a friend my age on the boat. We dove together dozens of times, and though we didn't go to the same school, in ninth grade I asked him to Homecoming. He blushed and stammered and accepted. Of course, we spent most of the night just sitting at a table and talking about getting my advanced certification so I could join him on deeper dives. It beat the heck out of pretending I could dance.

THE WRECK IS NOTHING like I've ever been in before. The boat looks like it was 300 feet long before it sank. Most of it is down another 60 feet or so, on its side, but there's a good 50 feet standing vertically, the bow just below a sandy shelf.

Barry has his slate out. He's written something. *10 mins left. Hurry up.* I nod; he jams the slate back into his pocket and steps over the edge. I follow him down.

There's a hole at 125 feet; Barry catches the edge of it and shines his light in, then swims through. I'm close behind.

I've never been inside a wreck like this. It's a constant effort to stay vertical without getting confused. Barry's looking back at me, waiting to catch my eye; when he does, he waves his light upward at a doorway. I have to turn my body sideways and roll up through it, but Barry stays outside, shaking his head and pointing to his stomach.

I probably don't have much more time than he does, not at this depth, but I spend a few precious seconds writing him a message. *Which way?*

He points his light toward an even-narrower opening at the far end of the compartment. I clip my big light to my wrist; I'll need both hands to navigate. I take a deep breath, blow it out, and, regulator clenched tight in my teeth, I make for the doorway.

I WAS A WEEK away from my fifteenth birthday when I ran into Dad on a dive boat. Mark had driven me to the dock—he was going to do a wreck dive, then I would do a deep reef, then we'd all do a shallow reef. When we left my house, I'd noticed Dad's car already gone, but that was nothing new, and anyway, I didn't care. One more week and I could dive wrecks with Mark—who I'd come to realize was actually pretty attractive. Those two things crowded Dad out of my mind.

Three years of lugging a dive kit had made me stronger than most girls my age; I rarely had to put my stuff down between the car and the boat. But everyone within fifty feet heard my scuffed red tanks clang on the pavement.

"Dad?"

My father was on the boat, talking animatedly to a short, fat man about his own age. But when he looked my way, he merely gave me a half-wave, suddenly all serious, before going back to his conversation.

He was wearing a wetsuit.

"Your dad dives?"

I dropped my bag and went after my tanks. "He never told me."

Mark shrugged and followed me onto the dock; we handed our equipment over the side and, as another diver stowed it, we crossed the threshold. I dropped one of my tanks into the storage area in the middle of the deck, then bungeed the other along the side. My bag went under the bench for now; I'd put my equipment together once we were out on the water.

Mark had gone up to the dive shop, probably to go to the bathroom—he had a thing about going in the ocean—and I went up to the bow.

"Dad, what are you doing here?"

"Diving," he said, his voice flat. "This is Barry Katz," he added. "Barry and I have been working together since... well, for a long time."

I remembered Barry's name from Dad's ever-more-detailed notes—Mom had a spare key to his office, and it'd been easy to borrow it and make a copy. I held out my hand, and he shook it. "Hello, Barry."

"Hello." His voice was mild, not as deep as Dad's.

There was a heavy silence. Dad turned to me. "We have some things to discuss."

"You bet we do," I said. "When did you—?"

He cut me off. "I meant with Barry. I'll talk to you later, if you want."

I didn't stomp off in a huff. I definitely wanted to, but stomping was immature, and Mark would be on his way back to the boat soon. I didn't want him to see that.

Twenty minutes later, we left the dock. Mark and I stood on the port side, watching the other boats as we passed them. Eventually, we made it out to the open water; the boat sped up, bouncing only slightly on the clear, smooth ocean. I separated from Mark and tried to eavesdrop on Dad, but every time I got close, he frowned at me and moved away. I could tell he was trying to hide his excitement, but he only let his guard down with Barry, and that more than anything else pissed me off.

I did manage to grab his arm just before he began his dive. "Later, Eleanora," he said, smiling, and then was in and under and gone.

Mark gave me an apologetic look as he joined up with a couple of guys and followed Dad and Barry into the water.

I'd never been on a three-dive trip and was unprepared for the sheer boredom of waiting for the advanced divers to get back. I put together my dive kit. Tested my air. Pored over my log book. Did calculations in my head to figure out when the others would get back. I even talked to one of the other divers still aboard until I realized all he was interested in was staring at my chest.

Clouds started gathering about ten minutes before the first of the advanced divers was set to surface. I climbed up to the bridge.

"What's going on, Elle?"

Steve owned the boat; he and I didn't talk much anymore now that Mark was around, but I'd been diving from this boat for years, and we were friendly enough. "This weather," I said. "Did they get the forecast wrong?"

"Not that I know of." Steve flipped on the little radio mounted behind the throttle levers. Nothing on the news station about severe storms. Still, the wind was whipping up, and the boat was starting to rock, not so much that we were in any danger, but it was a little worrying nonetheless.

I rechecked my watch. Eight minutes left in the advanced dive.

Lightning flashed out of a sky that was suddenly dark; it hit close enough to the boat that I heard the snap of electricity.

"Shit!" Steve shouted, the word half-covered by a blast of thunder. "Get down!" he ordered. "Help anyone who comes up. They'll need it."

The boat was rocking more as I dropped down to the main deck, and I almost rolled my ankle trying to keep my feet. But I held onto the tanks, secured in place until I was at the stern. I grabbed a rope out of one of the buckets on the deck, tied it to the railing, then tied it around my waist. I didn't plan to fall in, but better safe.

Rain began to fall, lightly at first but soon enough pouring onto the boat, the decking slippery under my sandals, clothes plastered to my body, hair in my eyes.

The next flash cut through the storm. I saw two heads bobbing in the choppy water, two hands waving.

It wasn't the okay sign.

It was the trouble sign.

One of the other junior divers, Shawn, joined me on the other ladder, mask around his neck, rope around his arm. "What the hell is going on?"

"No idea!" I pointed out over the water, yelling over the roaring of the storm. "Do we go help them?"

"I'll go! You stay here, hang onto the rope!" Shawn pulled up his mask and dove in, snorkel barely visible after only a few seconds. I braced my feet and fed rough plastic rope out through my hands. More heads broke the surface; I called Shawn's name, but he couldn't hear me.

A few seconds later Shawn waved to me; I began hauling in the rope, helping the divers make their way back to the boat. "What's going on?" I asked, still yelling, but a snap of lightning and another rolling boom smashed down the words. I shook my head to clear it and reached out, grabbing the first diver by the wrist and pulling him onto the rocking, bouncing deck. "Are you okay?"

He spat out his regulator. "I'm fine! But someone's missing!"

I nearly dropped the next diver, but recovered and pulled him onto the deck. "Who's missing?" I asked him, gasping.

The boat bounced up, then slapped down; I looked out, saw Shawn swimming toward a trio—thank God, Mark was okay, I could breathe again. "Who's missing?" I shouted.

The diver wasn't listening. He and his partner were crawling along the deck, trying to get to a bench.

Mark and his partners were close enough now that I could help them aboard. More divers were with me now, working together to get everyone onto the boat.

Mark flopped onto the deck. I pushed him past, but not before I heard him try to tell me something.

"What?"

He yanked his mask down and heaved up onto a bench; one of the divers lunged across and bungeed Mark's tank in place. "Your dad!" Mark shouted over the wind. "That Barry guy, he can't find your dad!"

I dropped to my knees, nauseous. Barry was at the end of the ladder, and he was alone.

"Where's my dad?" I screamed in his face. "Where's my dad!"

Barry clung to the ladder; it rose in the water, smacking him in the face, knocking out his regulator. Two of us grabbed his arms and hauled; Barry's bulk splatted to the deck between us. "Where's my dad? Where's Phil Raymond?"

Barry couldn't catch his breath, but he could point, eyes wide behind the thick glass of his mask.

He was pointing at the water.

THE DOORWAY IS TOO narrow even for me, and I only weigh 125 pounds. I try a few angles, but time and air are bubbling away, and I have to make a decision.

I unbuckle my vest, fully aware that it's a stupid thing to do, but I get through the opening, pulling the gear in behind me. I hold up the big light in my hand and look around: down, left, right, straight ahead, but I see nothing.

Then I look up.

At first, I think it's just an air pocket. I've seen them on wreck dives: air collects in hollows and sealed places. But I notice after a few seconds that my air bubbles aren't collecting.

They're disappearing.

I check my gauge. 116 feet.

All of Dad's notes say that, whatever these portals are, they're all at exactly 113 feet. Three feet above me.

I take a deep breath, then give a gentle kick and float toward the silver surface. But a loud clanging makes me snap my head around.

Barry's banging his knife on his tank. He has his hand around his neck.

He's running out of air.

I check my computer, cursing. I could probably stay another five or six minutes before I'm in trouble, but Barry is already there.

I have no choice. I pull back and make my way through the narrow doorway, spitting out my regulator so I can swim into my vest. I shove the regulator back into my mouth and purge it, teeth digging into the rubber grips, glaring at Barry as I move past him.

I feel him behind me as we head to the line. The current is picking up, and I snag Barry as he's nearly pulled away. I clip both of us together, then to the line; we empty our vests and begin swimming upward.

The trip takes longer in this direction; we have to stop twice to decompress. The line is jolting around during the second stop, and Barry's dark eyes are ringed with white. I pull out my slate. *Whats wrong?*

He takes it out of my hand, holding the pencil the way a two-year-old might hold a crayon. *Storm. Like B4.*

I've dived in bad weather before—rain and wind just means a little adventure getting back on the boat. But I look up and realize with a jolt that the sun isn't out anymore.

I take the pencil. *Let go b4 surface. Come up away.*
Current?
I can handle it.

My computer ticks down the seconds then beeps when it's safe to continue. I unhook from the line and begin kicking, the muscles in my legs fighting the weight of my equipment. I glance back; Barry is behind me, but his kicks aren't going to be strong enough. I grab him by the tank valve and estimate the distance to the surface.

Ten feet.

I mumble another curse around my regulator and inflate my vest halfway, feeling it pull us upward. I know it's a risk, but I can't carry both of us.

We break the surface and inflate the rest of the way. A wave slaps me in the face, separating me from Barry; I turn and kick back toward him, legs burning. I get a hold of his vest, pull him close, and shout "swim!" around my regulator.

The next wave knocks his mask askew and, with a hand, I can see shaking even as we're tossed around, he pushes it back in place.

It takes everything I have left to make it to the boat. Al's thrown out a life preserver; I make sure Barry's holding it before grabbing the ladder and dragging myself up onto the deck.

Al helps me up onto a bench, stringy muscular arms keeping me from crashing across the deck and into the cabin wall. I get myself bungeed and undo my fins, shoving them into an empty tank holder before unbuckling the vest and lurching to my feet. Together we pull Barry up onto the deck; he coughs and sputters and spits out his regulator, but he's able to let us help him to a bench. We get him secured, and he yanks his mask down.

"It's happening again! Just like last time!"

"What happened last time?" Al says, his voice sharp through the wind.

"Seven years ago," Barry says, a little stronger, "we were here! Her dad... we were on that wreck... we found... and her dad..."

"Shut up, Barry!" I yell. "He's not dead!"

"Goddammit, Eleanora!" He's hanging onto bungees on either side, and I'm clutching the bridge ladder, but Al somehow is still on his feet, eyes narrowed. "Phil's dead! Phil's dead, and this is insane! What the hell are you trying to prove?"

"He's not dead!" It's a scream to the sky, to the storm, to the rain and wind and lightning and thunder. They rip the words away, but I just keep screaming it. "He's not dead! He's not dead!"

I WAS ALMOST SIXTEEN when they told me Dad was dead. Steve got us away from the storm, and the Coast Guard came, but I only remembered it in flashes. Mom met me at the dock, eyes red and puffy, and I threw myself into her arms, crying along with her. "They'll find him," I forced out between sobs. "They'll find him."

Mark drove us home. Mom and I huddled on the couch, watching the phone, waiting.

The call never came.

Mom and I kept checking with the Coast Guard, but they kept saying they hadn't found him. Mark stopped returning my calls; he'd had enough of me begging him to dive that wreck with me. But I never gave up, not even when a Coast Guard lieutenant came to our house, sat down in our living room, and told Mom and Jason and me that they'd officially declared my father dead.

Mom lost it, but I didn't react.

My father wasn't dead. Until I had proof, he wasn't dead.

RAIN POURS DOWN. I loop my arm through a bungee and start changing my vest to my second tank.

"What the hell are you doing?" Al glares at me, holding the cabin doorway.

"I'm going back down there!" I get the vest off the first tank, then scoot down to the second. It nearly crashes to the deck when I unhook it, but I yank the vest onto it and bungee it back in place.

"No way!" Barry yells. "No way am I going down there again!" He points to Al. "Get us out of here!"

"No!" It's a scream, enough to make Al stop, halfway up the ladder. "I paid you," I snarl. "I paid you, and this is my boat for the day. We're not leaving!"

"She's crazy!" The boat rocks, slams Barry against his empty tank, and he clutches his shoulder. It's a mistake; the boat skews back in the other direction and pitches him to the deck. "Elle, this is nuts!"

"He's not dead!" I screw my regulator onto the tank. "One hour! Then we're going again!"

Barry shakes his head, face white with pain, barely holding onto the railing in the middle of the deck. "I can't do it again, Elle," he says. I barely hear him over the storm. "I can't do it."

"Then I'll go alone."

I WAS SEVENTEEN WHEN I stole Grandpa's boat and took it out to the wreck where I'd last seen my father. The radio squawked at me the whole way: Grandpa yelling at me to come back, to bring the boat back so we could talk about this.

I stayed there for hours, snorkeling along the smooth surface of the water, staring into the depths, trying to make out the wreck that I knew was down there. Dad's notes, his log book, everything in his computer said there was something down there. Barry Katz wouldn't talk about it no matter how hard I pushed him.

I would've gone down to the wreck, but there'd been no way for me to sneak my dive stuff onto the boat. I tried, though, swimming as far down as I could, until my lungs burned and my eyes were blurry with tears and fatigue.

There was no way I could get there. Not without air. Not without equipment.

Grandpa's voice on the radio kept yelling at me as I leaned over the side, the sun low on the horizon. "I love you, Dad," I whispered. "I'm not giving up."

That night I came up with a plan.

BARRY IS GREENISH-PALE AFTER twenty minutes in the wildly-rocking boat. Al's on the upper deck, strapped in, waiting. I manage to get to my cooler, stowed in the cabin, and down a bottle of water and a bag of mini-muffins.

Instantly I realize my mistake. Fortunately, there's Dramamine in the cooler, as well as ginger ale. I dry-swallow the pills and bring the soda out to the deck, looping my arm through the ladder to stay upright. Barry's still on the bench, good arm threaded through a bungee. He hasn't moved since Al and I put him back up there. The sound of the storm is just background noise now, and though Barry keeps getting bumped against the empty tank holders, his voice is calm through the cacophony.

"I hate this."

I drink more of my soda, then lunge to where he's sitting and press the can into his hand.

He shakes his head. "I'm gonna lose it," he says.

"If you barf, you barf."

"Not that." He looks down.

I nod. "Want some privacy?"

He doesn't answer, just turns away. I get back to the ladder, then move to the side of the boat, facing the bow, letting Barry pee himself in relative peace. At least the rain, still coming down in sheets, will wash it away.

My watch eventually beeps. Only ten minutes until I can go back. The adrenaline suddenly gives out; I lean over the side and throw up. The current carries it away. and waves wash the side of the boat as if it never happened.

I stare at the sky, breathing slow and deep. "I'm not leaving," I say quietly, ignoring the salt spray that makes my eyes burn and itch. "I'm going back, and I'm going to find my father."

I stay starboard until my watch beeps again, then work my way to the rear deck and struggle into my gear.

"I'm not going," Barry says. "I can't go back again."

I shrug as best I can with the vest tightened across my shoulders. "Then I'm going alone." I stare across the middle of the deck at Barry. "If..." I swallow hard. "If something happens..."

Barry sees that I can't finish. "You're crazy, Elle," he says. "Please don't do this."

I reach back and undo the bungee. The boat rocks; I plant my fins and slide to the end of the bench. "I have to, Barry. I have to know."

I look up to the bridge, see Al leaning over the railing. "Don't do it, girl," he calls.

I shake my head, then pull my regulator into my mouth. Normally I'd take a giant stride into the water, but in this weather, I just hold my mask and regulator to my face, twist around, and fall backward with a splash that I'm sure neither Al nor Barry can hear over the storm.

Ten feet down the line, the silence is louder than the noise on the surface. I block it out and, hand over hand, pull myself toward the ocean floor.

I WAS EIGHTEEN WHEN I gave up on my plans to become a marine biologist—like Dad. For two years I was a lackluster community college student, but I didn't care. I worked in a dive shop and as a lifeguard, saving money. I'd need the best equipment—and I'd have to buy it myself—and I'd also need to charter a boat.

Right after I turned twenty, I ran into Mark at the dive shop and convinced him to have dinner with me. But when I told him what I was planning, he shut down.

"I don't dive anymore," he said.

"You're crazy," I told him. "You love diving."

"I loved it." Past tense.

"It was a one-in-a-million accident!" I snapped. "Come on, Mark. We used to... I mean..."

He shook his head. "I just... I can't. I'm sorry, Elle."

I slept with him that night, hoping it would change his mind, but even after that he still said no.

I left the next morning and didn't look back. Soon after, I got my two-year degree, then gave up on school and threw myself into my work and my plan. Mom and Jason confronted me, said I was obsessed, and I moved out. I spent more hours at the dive shop and on the beach. I even started teaching swim classes. Guys hit on me, and I turned them down. Girls tried to befriend me, but I played the bitch card. Parents hired me to babysit or give private lessons, and I did it for the money, but I detached myself from the people.

I had one purpose: find out what happened to my dad. Nothing was going to get in my way.

I STOP AT THE end of the line and check my computer, noting the maximum safe depth and time—depressingly short on the latter, depressingly shallow on the former—and set my watch. I won't give up until I know the truth, but I don't want to die down here either.

I drop over the side of the wreck and swim into the dark opening. This time, without Barry to slow me down, I'm out of my vest and inches from 113 feet in no time.

I pull out my knife. The tip grazes the silvery surface.

A blinding flash knocks me back. My regulator falls out of my mouth, and I grope for it blindly, holding my breath, my eyes a wall of blue afterimages. I finally shove it in my mouth and blow, purging the seawater. My second exhalation clears it completely, and I dig my teeth into the grips. My jaw is tired, lips stretched and sore, but I'm not stopping.

I take a minute to think—and to let my heart rate slow to normal—then lock the knife back in its holster. No metal: seems simple enough.

I pull open the Velcro that holds my left glove closed and tug it off. My skin is very white in the glow of the lamp. I reach for the silvery surface and, in a quick motion, push through.

There's air on the other side. Cold, dry air. My hand starts to shake, and I pull it back.

My skin looks okay. I check the sleeve of my wetsuit: no damage there. Whatever it is, it's safe to pass through.

I close my eyes tightly, looking away as I do, and extend my entire arm through the portal.

Nothing happens. Nothing bad, anyway.

I open my eyes, then check my air and my watch. Seven minutes to the point of no return, until I have no choice but to ascend.

But I have no choice in what I'm about to do now, either.

As quickly as I can, I strip off my dive equipment. I stick my watch into a vest pocket, hook my fins to the shoulder straps, then unzip my boots and tuck them into the fins' foot holes.

Zippers. I consider for a couple of seconds, then open my wetsuit. I have to release the regulator to wiggle completely out of it. If the air I touched is any indication, I'm going to freeze my ass off on the other side—my one-piece isn't made for warmth—but I don't care. Besides, the coldness of the water is already numbing my fingers. It can't get much worse.

One more look at the computer. Five minutes. 113 feet. I'll never get all this stuff back on in time; I'll be lucky to get into my fins and drag my air supply back to the line. There's coral everywhere, and I know it'll to rip me to pieces when I get out of here.

But I'll live.

A final check: no metal anywhere. I point myself toward the silver surface of the portal and pull my mask off, pushing it into a pocket in my vest. Seawater and particles tear at my eyes.

I take five deep breaths and, on the last one, release the regulator and kick forward, through the portal, and toward my father.

I WAS TWENTY-TWO WHEN I found my father. He was declared dead by the Coast Guard when I was fifteen, but I never believed it. They never found a body. I spent seven years trying to get back to where he was lost, seven years trying to find him.

And fewer than seven minutes on the other side.

I found out what happened at 113 feet the moment I swam through that silver surface and landed hard on a metal platform, shivering in icy, dry air.

"Doctor Raymond! Doctor Raymond, you'd better get out here!"

I blinked hard and tried to stand, but I was so cold that I couldn't do more than wrap my arms around my chest.

I heard clanging, felt the metal vibrate, and then the lights above me were blocked off. Someone draped a light sheet of cloth over my body, and I was instantly so warm that I almost passed out. Someone else pulled me to my feet.

"Doc..." I cleared my throat and spat out a gob of saltwater-tinged phlegm. "Doctor... Raymond?" I blinked a couple more times, but I wasn't hallucinating.

"Hello, Eleanora."

"Dad?" He wasn't dead. I was staring right at him. "Dad!"

I was on him in an instant, arms around him, and he was hugging me back. But tentatively, almost as if he was afraid of me. "I missed you, Eleanora."

I looked up at him. He seemed older than he should have been as if more than seven years had passed. "What happened, Dad?"

Instead of answering, he looked over my head. "How long?" he called.

The answer came through a P.A. System. "Four minutes, Doctor."

Dad nodded, then guided me to a bench. "Here. Sit."

I did as he said, wrapping the sheet around my body. My ears and toes were freezing, but I didn't care. He was alive. My father was alive.

"I only have a little time to explain," he said, his arm around me.

"Explain what? Aren't you coming back?"

He laughed. Not angry, not exasperated, just amused. "I've been here almost forty years. Why leave now? Besides, how would I come back?" He raised an eyebrow. "Do you have enough air in your tank to get me to the surface? I haven't been diving in..." His voice faltered, and he smiled. "Well, it's been a while."

"Don't they have tanks here?" I looked around but didn't recognize anything except the silver oval of the portal. "Where the hell are we, Dad?"

"Actually, Elle, the right question is 'when are we'."

"Damn it, Dad, stop wasting time!" I pushed his arm off and glared at him. "If I only have a few minutes, then tell me what happened!" My throat went tight, but I wouldn't cry. There wasn't time to cry. "Dad, please!"

He sighed. "The short version is this: about 150 years in your future, scientists discovered a way to go back in time. The system is overpowered in case something goes wrong, and that energy has to go somewhere."

"The storms."

"Yes. The storms. At least, over the ocean, fewer people are at risk." A young woman in a blue jumpsuit gave Dad a handheld computer. He scanned it, nodded, and handed it back. "Time's running out. Come on." We went back to the portal, standing in front of it. "It takes about an hour for the storms to clear when someone goes through. They tried it closer to sea level, but the storms were so strong that the man they sent through was ripped apart."

"But how come they started when I got close? I didn't touch the... portal?" He nodded, and I continued. "I didn't come through."

Dad gave me a look I remembered perfectly, a look that said I should've figured it out for myself. "How do you think we knew you were coming?"

I had no response to that, and even if I had, Dad was already watching a technician aim something at the portal. "Anyone there?"

"No, Doctor." Like everyone else except Dad, the technician was wearing a blue jumpsuit. Dad looked normal: slacks and a burgundy sweater. "Mr. Katz will arrive in 81 seconds."

Dad nodded. "Come on, Eleanora. It's almost time." I slung the cloth to the floor. Somehow, I was dry, and though it was still chilly in the lab or hangar or whatever this place was, I could handle it for another minute. Besides, I didn't care. I had to ask before it was too late.

"Why didn't you come back, Dad?"

He didn't answer; he just pulled me into a hug.

"Sixty seconds." It was the person on the P.A.

"Dad, please! Why didn't you come back?"

He was smiling again. I wanted to wipe it off his face, but I couldn't. Not when I saw tears in his eyes. "I'm a scientist, Elle. How could I turn down an opportunity like this?"

My fists balled, and I wrenched away. I wanted to hit him. Hard. "How dare you! How dare you leave us for that?"

"Forty-five seconds."

"How could I not? It was the chance of a lifetime! The chance to study history by actually being there. Things you only know in books... I've seen them!" His bright blue eyes were wide.

"Then let me stay with you," I pleaded. "I've got nothing back home! Please, Dad, let me stay!"

But he shook his head. "I can't, Elle. Things have changed these past few years. We have to be careful, or..." He cleared his throat. "I'm breaking all kinds of rules by even talking to you, and when you get there, you can't tell anyone."

"Twenty seconds."

I stared at him. "You've got to be kidding. I'm not keeping this a secret."

"Fifteen seconds." Red lights began to glow around the portal.

"Come on, Elle." He reached out as if to hug me again, but I moved closer to the portal. "Promise me!"

"Ten seconds."

I shook my head. The technicians were already well back. Dad took a couple of steps away, his eyes sad. I could barely bear to look at him.

"Five seconds."

"Good-bye Eleanora. I love you."

"Fuck you, Dad."

A sharp beep. I took a deep breath and jumped through the portal.

I'M WARM. I'M WARM, and I'm on my back.

I'm warm, and I'm on my back, and I'm laying on something hard.

I open my eyes, blinking against the harsh brightness of the sun.

"You made it."

Barry's voice.

I wheeze, then start coughing. He cradles my head in his arm, brings a bottle of water to my lips. I sip some of it. "Barry?"

My vision starts to clear. His hair is as wild as mine is after a dive. He smiles. "Glad you're back."

"Wh..."

"Couple of minutes after you left, Al helped me get my stuff on. I followed you."

"Why?"

The smile goes away. "I couldn't leave you alone down there. Not after... not after Phil..."

I feel my eyes well up with tears, but I fight them down. I have to know. "How long until the storm ended?"

"About an hour after I got to you. Why?"

"No reason."

A CATEGORY-ONE HURRICANE blew through two weeks later. I spent the day at Mom's. When I got back to my apartment

197

that night, I found an envelope on my pillow. My name was on it. The handwriting was my father's.

I threw it away unopened.

MARK'S LIVING IN VIRGINIA now. It takes me almost a whole day to drive to his house.

"Hi, Elle."

I slide past him, into the living room, and drop onto the couch. He sits in a chair beside me.

"I'm not diving. Ever again."

He leans forward, touches my knee. I cover his hand with mine. I know my face is blank.

"I found him."

Mark blinks. "You..."

I nod. "I found my father." A pause. "He's not dead."

"Wh... what?"

I meet Mark's eyes. "He left me. Me, and Jason, and Mom. I'm done with him."

"But, where is he?"

I shake my head. "It doesn't matter. And I don't care."

Mark pushes me for more, but I don't tell him. To the rest of the world, my father's been dead for seven years.

Time for me to join the rest of the world.

THE END

JOSH ROSEMAN (not the trombonist; the other one) lives in Georgia and engages in pogonotrophy on a regular basis, as well as occasionally suffering from sphenopalatine ganglioneuralgia. He has been published by—among others—Asimov's and Escape Pod, and his latest novel, *AFTER THE APOCALYPSE*, is out now from amazon. When not writing, he mostly complains that he's not writing. Find him online at roseplusman.com, read his weekly column at thenerderypublic.com, or follow him on Twitter @listener42.

AFTERWORD

WE WOULD LIKE TO personally thank you for buying and reading this book. Producing this anthology has been, and continues to be, quite fulfilling for us and we hope that it is enjoyable for you as well.

Please consider taking a little extra time to help others find this book by leaving feedback where you purchased it. Your opinion about this book truly matters, both to our authors who have contributed to the anthology and to other readers.

If you have any questions, comments, suggestions, or just want to say hello, please visit our publisher's website on Indie Authors Press, www.salgado-reyes.com, and follow our publisher's Twitter: @Indie__Authors

Indie Authors Press

www.ingramcontent.com/pod-product-compliance
Lightning Source LLC
Chambersburg PA
CBHW061154170626
46809CB00003B/1089